THE TWO LOVERS
The Goodly History of Lady Lucrece and her Lover Eurialus

Publications of the Barnabe Riche Society

Volume 11

Aeneas Silvius Piccolomini
(Pope Pius II)

THE TWO LOVERS:
The Goodly History of Lady Lucrece
and her Lover Eurialus

Edited with

Introduction and Notes

by

Emily O'Brien and Kenneth R. Bartlett

Dovehouse Editions, Inc.
Ottawa, Canada
1999

This book has been published with the help of a grant from the Humanities and Social Sciences Federation of Canada, using funds provided by the Social Sciences and Humanities Research Council of Canada.

Canadian Cataloguing in Publication Data
Pius II, Pope, 1405–1464
(De duobus amantibus. English)
    The two lovers : the goodly history of Lady Lucrece and her lover Eurialus

(Publications of the Barnabe Riche Society ; 11)
Translation of: De duobus amantibus, first published ca. 1551.
Includes bibliographical references

ISBN 1-895537-36-3 (bound)
ISBN 1-895537-54-1 (pbk.)

I. Bartlett, Kenneth R., 1948–   II. O'Brien, Emily   III. Title.   IV. Title: De duobus amantibus. English   V. Series.

PA8556.D4E5 1999   873'.04   C98-901184-4

For information on the series:

The Editors of the Barnabe Riche Series
c/o The Dept. of English
Carleton University
1125 Colonel By Drive
Ottawa, Canada K1S 5B6

For orders:

Dovehouse Editions Inc.
1890 Fairmeadow Cres.
Ottawa, Canada, K1H 7B9

Typesetting: Carleton Production Centre.
Printed and bound in Canada.

Table of Contents

Preface

The publication series of The Barnabe Riche Society has been established to provide scholarly, modern-spelling editions of works of imaginative literature in prose written in English between 1485 and 1660, with special emphasis on Elizabethan prose fiction. The program allows for works ranging from late medieval fabliaux and Tudor translations of Spanish picaresque tales or ancient Greek romances to seventeenth-century prose pastorals. But the principal goal is to supply much-needed editions of many of the most critically acclaimed works of the period by such authors as Lodge, Greene, Chettle, Riche, and Dekker, and to make them available in formats suitable to libraries, scholars, and students. Editorial policy for the series calls for texts carefully researched in terms of variant sources, and presented in conservatively modernized and repunctuated form in order make these texts as widely accessible as possible, while respecting the substantive integrity of the originals. Each edition will provide the editor with an opportunity to write a full essay dealing with the author and the historical circumstances surrounding the creation of the work, as well as with its style, themes, conventions, and critical challenges. Each text will also be accompanied by annotations.

The Barnabe Riche Society is based in the English Department of Carleton University in Ottawa, and forms a component of the Carleton Centre for Renaissance Studies and Research. Its activities include colloquia, the awarding of an annual prize for the best new book-length study dealing with English Renaissance prose fiction, and the editorial management of the series, backed by an eleven-member international editorial board. The society invites the informal association of all scholars interested in its goals and activities.

Acknowledgments

This project resulted from a discussion held in a small automobile in Sicily during an academic conference. Don Beecher, General Editor of the Barnabe Riche Society Series and Director of Dovehouse Press, proposed an edition of the first English translations of Aeneas Silvius Piccolomini's *De duobus amantibus historia* as a text for the Barnabe Riche Society. Before the journey ended I had agreed to undertake the work. By good fortune I learned that a gifted former student, then at Brown University, was writing a doctoral thesis on Aeneas Silvius (Pius II) and approached her with an offer of collaboration. Emily O'Brien agreed with enthusiasm, and it was thus that the project took shape.

The text, introduction and notes owe a great deal to Emily's wide knowledge of Aeneas Silvius and his world. The actual transcription, edition and collation of the text was checked, improved and debated by Don Beecher and Douglas Campbell: it is stronger as a result. My former graduate students, Margaret McGlynn and Chris Nighman, helped greatly in preparing the text and keying it into the computer in a standard format. Also, the librarians at the E.J. Pratt Library, Victoria College, provided their customary excellent assistance, as did those at the Robarts Library and Thomas Fisher Rare Book Library of the University of Toronto. Victoria College generously provided research funds that made the project possible.

The two anonymous readers chosen by the Humanities and Social Science Federation of Canada Aid to Scholarly Publications Programme made extremely useful, insightful and sensitive suggestions which have made both the edition and introduction much stronger. To them and to the Federation's ASPP we owe a great debt of gratitude.

Finally, I wish to recognize the constant support, advice and editorial commentary of my wife, Gillian, on whom I rely in all things.

Kenneth R. Bartlett
Victoria College
University of Toronto
April 1999

Acknowledgments

When Anthony Molho and Riccardo Fubini first suggested that I work on Aeneas Silvius Piccolomini's *The History of the Two Lovers* in the spring of 1992, it was not clear where the project would lead. What was clear, though, and from the very first time I read Aeneas' love story, was that they had introduced me to one of the richest and most intellectually exciting texts I had ever read. In the early stages of working through my ideas, I discovered that I was not alone in feeling this way. By coincidence, my former teacher and mentor, Kenneth Bartlett, was also working on the text, and when he suggested that we write an edition of it together, I jumped at the opportunity. In a sense, though, this project was a joint one from its very inception and it continued to be so in various ways until it was completed. Many people have contributed to this work, and to all of them I owe a great debt of gratitude.

First and foremost, I thank my advisor, Anthony Molho, who has patiently read and reread this work in its innumerable incarnations. His constant guidance and support throughout this project have been invaluable, and more than I ever could have asked for. To Riccardo Fubini I owe a similar debt of gratitude. His enthusiasm for the project and his expertise in the field gave me the inspiration, direction and courage I needed to pursue my ideas. I cannot thank him enough for his support and generosity. Finally, I want to thank my co-author, Kenneth Bartlett. It has been both rewarding and exciting to work with one of the people who originally inspired me to pursue a career in Italian history. I am deeply grateful for his helpful advice at various stages of this project, and for the opportunity to work on it together.

I was fortunate to be able to present my ideas on *The History of the Two Lovers* to the Brown University Italian Studies group. I am grateful for the helpful questions, criticisms and suggestions offered there by my colleagues, as well as for the chance to share my ideas about Aeneas' text. For their more informal advice and support, I would like to thank Joanna Drell, Ilaria Brancoli-Busdraghi, Ray Marks, Amy Remensny-der, Frances Gage, Susanne Saygin, Susannah Ottaway, Ingrid Tague, Saundra Weddle, Lorenzo Fabbri, Irene Herlihy and Antonio Nesti. I doubt they realize what important roles they have all played in the development and completion of this work.

The research for this project was done in many different libraries in Italy, the United States and Canada, and with the aid of many friendly and helpful librarians. In particular, I would like to thank the Biblioteca Nazionale in Florence, the Biblioteca della Facoltà di Lettre at the University of Florence, the Biblioteca Riccardiana, the Biblioteca Apostolica Vaticana, the Rockefeller Library at Brown University, the Centre for Reformation and Renaissance Studies and the Robarts Library at the University of Toronto. I am grateful for the support I received from Brown University, the Mellon and Fulbright Fellowships, and the Social Sciences and Humanities Research Council of Canada in the years I worked on this book.

My dedication to this project was sustained in large part by my deep love of Latin literature. For this, I owe my deepest gratitude to my teachers Elizabeth McLeod, Owen Lee, Joseph Pucci, Reginald Foster and Richard Toporoski. It is because of them that I have learned to see and appreciate the beauty, depth and music of this wonderful language.

To my family I owe my greatest debt of all. Without their love and encouragement, their wisdom and their unshakable belief in the value of my work, this project could never have been completed.

Emily O'Brien
Brown University
Providence, RI
April 1999

Introduction

The Life of Aeneas Silvius Piccolomini
(Pius II)

KENNETH R. BARTLETT

Aeneas Silvius was born in Corsignano in 1405 to a poor branch of
the noble Sienese family of Piccolomini. Intellectually gifted and
ambitious, he was sent to study law in Siena, where he studied
with Mariano Sozzini (1397–1467). His own interests, however,
focussed much more on the humanistic study of Latin letters
in which he excelled. All of his leisure time was spent reading, memorizing and applying the heritage of ancient learning.
He cultivated learned men throughout Italy, including Leonardo
Bruni, Guarino of Verona, and Francesco Filelfo with whom he
studied Greek in Florence.

Also, in his youth Aeneas indulged in a great many amorous
liaisons throughout Europe, some of which he recorded in his
letters and literary works. He fathered at least two illegitimate
children; one died young, the other was raised by his family.

In 1431 the young scholar entered the service of Domenico
Capranica, bishop of Fermo, and travelled with him to the Council of Basle. At the Council, Aeneas' genius shone. He transferred
his services first to the Visconti bishop of Novara and then to
Cardinal Niccolo Albergati, who was the legate charged in 1435

with helping negotiate an end to the Hundred Years War. Another visit to the north of Europe followed, which included a
secret mission to the king of Scotland.

In 1436 Piccolomini was again at the Council of Basle. His
great skill at Latin style, his eloquence and his ambition soon
raised him to be the spokesman for those conciliarist prelates at
Basel who were opposed the rule of Pope Eugenius IV.

Aeneas was sent by the Council to the Imperial Diet of Frank-
furt. There he impressed the Emperor Frederick III who crowned
him poet laureate in 1442 and appointed him an imperial secretary. It was at this time that he became the close friend of
the imperial Chancellor, Kaspar Schlick, by tradition the model
for Eurialus. In the summer of 1444 Aeneas wrote *De duobus
amantibus historia* (*The History of the Two Lovers*), which he set in
his native Siena during the winter of 1432–33 when the Emperor
Sigismund was there en route to his coronation by Eugenius IV
in Rome.

Soon after completing *The History of the Two Lovers*, however,
Aeneas rejected his youthful lustfulness and the literary works
it produced. He had decided to dedicate himself to God and the
Church. Sent to Rome by the emperor early in 1445, Aeneas made
his peace with Pope Eugenius, and back in Vienna in March of
1446 he took holy orders.

Eugenius IV died in early 1447. His successor was Aeneas'
friend, the Tuscan humanist, Tommaso Parentucelli, who took
the name of Nicholas V. Aeneas was ordained a priest and soon
after given the see of Trieste. In 1450 he was translated to the
see of his native city, Siena. Nicholas V's death did not mean
the end of Aeneas' career, as it did for other humanist associates
of that learned pope. His successor, the Spaniard Calixtus III
(Borgia), respected Aeneas' experience as a diplomat, his deep
knowledge of imperial politics and his friendly relations with
Naples. Consequently, in December of 1456 Aeneas Silvius was
raised to the sacred college as a cardinal. Then, in the conclave
of 1458, a moment Aeneas himself so powerfully describes in his
Commentaries, the bishop of Siena emerged as pope, taking the
title Pius II, a play on the *pius Aeneas* of Vergil's *Aeneid*.

As pope, Pius was guilty of the usual papal nepotism and
aggrandization of his family, making one nephew a cardinal and

marrying another into the royal house of Naples. Even the family town of Corsignano was rebuilt into an ideal Renaissance city and renamed Pienza in his own honour. It was also Pius who canonized St Catherine of Siena (1461).

In addition, the claims of papal monarchy were restated, despite Pius' early anti-curial position against Eugenius IV at Basel. He spoke powerfully against any argument in favour of conciliarism and he worked to reduce the independence of national churches, especially in France where royal influence over the French Church granted by the Pragmatic Sanction of Bourges (1438) was redefined.

Humanism was again favoured during Pius' short papacy. He supported some important scholars, such as Flavio Biondo, and he himself continued to write, despite the demands upon his time. In particular, he completed his *Commentaries*, which represents one of the great contributions to Renaissance autobiography, and the unique example of the genre by a Renaissance pope.

The great, defining issue of his papacy was, however, his calling for a new crusade to liberate Constantinople from the Turks who had conquered the city in 1453. Most of Pius' energy was directed to this end. He manoeuvered tirelessly, despite his age and physical weakness, to rally the support of all Christian rulers to his cause. Although the princes of Europe were not enthusiastic in their response, he did receive some promises of help. Having travelled to Ancona to await the fleet sent to war against the Turks, Pius took ill and died before the ships arrived.

As a humanist scholar and author, Aeneas Silvius was more than a splendid Latin stylist. He was a charming and revealing author of human nature, reflected not only in his huge correspondence but also in his literary works, such as his *Commentaries* and *The History of the Two Lovers*. In addition, his historical and geographical works—such as his *Account of Bohemia*, *On Asia*, and his *History of the Council of Basle*—make him one of the most influential of the humanist observers of fifteenth-century topography and politics. He penned biographical works, a book on education, and even tracts intended to convert the Sultan to Christianity, which were very popular and widely respected throughout Europe. His life, moreover, has been recorded for us pictorially by Pinturicchio in the Piccolomini Library in the cathedral of Aeneas' beloved Siena. This fresco cycle, commissioned by his nephew and successor as pope (as Pius III), represents the great moments in Aeneas' rich life of learning and service. Although *The History of the Two Lovers* constitutes only a minor work in the context of a life full of great achievements, it illustrates the essential character of the man for whom *nihil humanum alienum erat*.

The History of the Two Lovers
EMILY O'BRIEN

> When I recall that as a young man, both in age and emotion, I once wrote a tract on love, ... unrestrained repentance, shame and sorrow torment me greatly, since I know and have made it explicitly known that in that little book there are two things, namely an obvious but, alas, excessively lascivious and prurient tale of love, and an edifying moral lesson that follows it. Of these two, I see very many foolish people wrongly paying attention to the first, and hardly anyone (alas, what pain!) to the other. Thus is the unhappy race of man blinded and depraved.[1]

These remarks are from a letter which Aeneas Silvius Piccolomini wrote to a friend sometime after he became Pope Pius II.[2] The "tract on love" to which he refers is *The History of the Two Lovers, Eurialus and Lucrece*, a work which he had completed years earlier while serving as imperial secretary at the

---

[1] Aeneas Silvius Piccolomini, *Aeneae Sylvii Piccolominiei Pii Pontificis Maximi* II *Opera quae extant omnia* (Basel, 1551), Ep. 395, pp. 869–72:

> Tractatum de amore olim sensu pariterque aetate iuvenes cum nos scripsisse recolimus . . . poenitentia immodica pudorque ac moeror animum nostrum vehementer excruciant, quippe qui sciamus quique protestati expresse fuimus, duo contineri in eo libello, apertam videlicet, sed heu lasciviam nimis prurientemque amoris historiam, et morale quod eam consequitur, aedificans dogma. Quorum primum fatuos atque errantes video sectari quamplurimos. Alterum, heu dolor, pene nullos. Ita impravatum est atque obfuscatum infelix mortalium genus."

[2] The letter as it appears in this collection has neither official address nor date, but it is clear from internal evidence that it was written sometime after Aeneas was elected pope. The recipient can also be deduced from the letter. It is a certain "Carolus" referred to further on in the letter

court of Frederick III. The letter is the kind of document which scholars of intellectual history long to find. Not only does it give some sense of the author's attitude toward his own work, but it also sheds light on its reception by Aeneas' fifteenth-century audience. Most important of all, however, is the guidance it provides for understanding the text. From Aeneas' comments it is clear that there are two levels of meaning in the tale of Lucrece and Eurialus: on the one hand it is a story of romance and desire; on the other, it is a lesson in ethics which teaches a specific moral message.

For some time now, scholarship on *The History of the Two Lovers* has been following the directions which Aeneas maps out in this letter. The tale has been explored in considerable detail on the level of narrative, with close analysis of its theme, plot, character and compositional techniques. And while scholars have paid somewhat less attention to its moral dimension, they have, nevertheless, made important steps in uncovering its very complex message, and have thus moved far beyond the alleged position of Aeneas' contemporaries. In the course of these investigations, scholars have continued to identify many of the intellectual threads woven into the fabric of the text. What they have not yet demonstrated, however, is the story's precise position in its broader intellectual context. From the standpoint of narrative culture, its traditional classification seems somewhat problematic. Aeneas' story is described as a *novella*, a brief entertaining tale which also typically includes a moral lesson — a seemingly perfect match for the author's own description of his work. But while there are many aspects of the tale of Lucrece and Eurialus which fit the usual pattern of the *novella*, there are also many others which do not, and their significance to the story seems to demand a reconsideration of this classification. The tale's position in relation to moral discourse is similarly unclear. Scholars have now more or less agreed on the lesson which the story conveys, but they are still debating the very important issue of its relationship to traditional methods of ethical instruction

---

as "cypriaci gloria magna soli," but who has not been identified (Adrianus Van Heck, *Enee Silvii Piccolominei postea Pii PP. II Carmina* [Citta' del Vaticano: Biblioteca Apostolica Vaticana, 1994], p. 189, n. 42).

and moral culture more generally. Until these questions are answered, we cannot say that we have fully understood the story's
message.

The pages that follow will attempt to come to terms with these
issues, considering the story first as a narrative, and then as a lesson in ethics. In so doing, they offer a new interpretation of the
position which Aeneas' tale occupies in the intellectual culture
of both fifteenth-century Italy and sixteenth-century England,
and one which reveals its particular significance to the history
of ethics. Aeneas' work is much more than the classification of
novella suggests: rather than a love story which includes an edifying message, *The History of the Two Lovers* represents a treatise
of moral philosophy which is presented in the form of romantic
fiction. Its message consists not simply of a warning against the
sufferings of love: it is also a powerful statement of the realities
of human moral behaviour and a criticism of traditional ethical
culture which, both in its tools of instruction and its idealistic
goals, fails to take such realities into account.

*   *   *

The History of the Two Lovers tells the tale of an adulterous romance between Lucrece, the beautiful and virtuous young wife
of an Italian nobleman, and Eurialus, a handsome, high-ranking
imperial soldier and favourite of the Holy Roman Emperor, Sigismund. The story opens with a description of the lovers' first
encounter at the festivities held in honour of Sigismund's arrival
in Lucrece's hometown of Siena. The narrator recounts with
amazement how no sooner had Eurialus laid eyes on Lucrece,
and Lucrece on Eurialus, than the two fell deeply in love. The
romance that develops between them unfolds as a series of distinct stages. It begins with a long and penetrating psychological
portrait, first of Lucrece and then of Eurialus, as they struggle to
understand their feelings of love for one another and the moral
consequences of submitting to their desires. The hero and heroine paint their own portraits, exploring their feelings in a series
of monologues and dialogues, with only the occasional interruption of the author's commentary or description of events. In

the course of their struggles, passion eventually overcomes the concerns of conscience, and they both surrender to their desires.

The focus then shifts quickly to courtship: at the initiative of Eurialus, the lovers begin to communicate through letters in which they slowly and subtly reveal their feelings and intentions. The exchange serves to push forward the plot, but it also advances the study of romantic psychology which dominates the first part of the tale. Even more than before, the narrator steps back to let hero and heroine converse without interruption, inviting the reader to interpret the cryptic comments in what could almost be described as an exercise in romantic diplomacy. The exchange concludes once Lucrece and Eurialus have revealed their desires openly to one another, and have resolved all remaining doubts and concerns about proceeding with the affair.

At this point — now almost half way through the story — the pace quickens and the plot moves forward swiftly with an even balance between dialogue and narrative, and the occasional authorial intrusion. The action unfolds in a recurrent pattern: a scene establishing the strategy for a rendezvous, usually with the assistance of one or two loyal servants; an attempt at its execution, which either fails completely or, more often, is thwarted by the unexpected appearance of a third party; crisis, as the threat of discovery seems imminent; and resolution, in which the quick-thinking Lucrece successfully distracts the unwanted intruder and conceals her lover. Eurialus' response to these narrow escapes also develops in a consistent pattern: in the context of crisis, his passion fades quickly as he perceives the danger and recklessness of his actions; but as soon as the immediate threat is removed, he forgets these realizations and is soon overcome by powerful sexual desire. Cyclical though it may be, Lucrece and Eurialus' affair also has a forward motion. With each meeting, the lovers' passion grows more intense and insatiable, and the risks they take to satisfy their desires become increasingly dangerous, dishonourable and subject to suspicion. The turning point comes when the Emperor announces his return to Germany, thereby forcing the lovers to confront their future together. Another exchange of letters ensues and the issue is quietly resolved — or so it would seem: in the tale's dramatic conclusion,

passion takes its toll on both hero and heroine and the fleeting
joys of their love are replaced by long-suffering sadness and pain.

*   *   *

The History of the Two Lovers has traditionally been classified as a
novella, a narrative form which originated in Italy in the thirteenth
century, and which developed into one of the most popular in European literature from the Middle Ages through the early modern
period. In England, it enjoyed its greatest success from the middle to the end of the sixteenth century, precisely the period to
which the first English translations of Aeneas' text have been
dated. The *novella* evolved out of a myriad of different literary
traditions, including heroic *gestae* of ancient Greece and Rome;
collections of stories from the Far East (such as the *Panchatantra*
or *Five Heads*, and the *Seven Wise Masters*); French *fabliaux* — brief
and entertaining tales of trickery, quick wits and crude humour;
and perhaps most important of all, *exempla*, simple anecdotes
used to convey paradigms of ethical behaviour.[3] In the almost
two and a half centuries between its first appearance and the time
when Aeneas wrote the tale of Lucrece and Eurialus, the genre
evolved considerably, so much so, in fact, that it is impossible to
give it a single fully satisfactory definition. When used in a broad
sense, the term *novella* connotes a set of characteristics typical of
a large class of stories from this period (these characteristics will
be enumerated over the next few pages). It may also be used
more specifically, however, to refer to one phase or another in
the development of the genre.[4]

---

[3]Letterio Di Francia, *La novellistica dalle Origini al Bandello* (Milan:
Vallardi, 1924). See also Vittorio Rossi, *Il quattrocento* (Milan: Vallardi,
1933), 194–210; Goffredo Bellonci, ed., *Novelle italiane dalle origini al
'500* (1986); Gioacchino Chiarini, ed., *Novelle italiane: Il Quattrocento*
(Milan: Garzanti, 1982), 129–237. Each of these traditions continued to
develop independently alongside the *novella*. The role of the *exemplum*
in European ethical culture from the Middle Ages to early modern times
will be touched upon later in this chapter.

[4]The actual term *novella* was not always used in contemporary culture to describe works which have since earned this classification. Words

In many ways, classifying Aeneas' story as a *novella* seems to make good sense. Not only does the tale include many of the features implied in the broad sense of the word *novella*, but it also seems to resemble closely the stories of particular *novellisti* — those of Giovanni Boccaccio (1313–75) and of fifteenth-century humanists most notably. But in spite of these similarities, its classification as a *novella* is far from a perfect fit. In addition to the elements typical of the genre, the fabric of Aeneas' tale is woven of many other elements which diverge — sometimes significantly — from the *novella* tradition. A survey of these various elements leaves the very strong impression that the classification of *The History of the Two Lovers* is at the very least incomplete. It may even, in fact, be incorrect.

The features of Aeneas' story which seem to align it most clearly with the *novella* are its theme and plotline. Tales of love and sexual desire were the mainstay of the genre, and among these, adulterous affairs were by far the most common. The romance of Lucrece and Eurialus fits smoothly into this tradition, due to both the illicit nature of their relationship and the emphasis given to its sexual dimension.[5] Aeneas may have felt ashamed at having written a "lascivious and prurient" story, but in the context of the *novella* tradition his tale was really no more shocking than the next. The plotline of the romance also follows the typical pattern of the *novella*. Stories in this genre are usually tales of intrigue involving secrecy, deception and disguise. The mood is typically a mix of suspense and comic relief; the action centres on clever tricks, surprise and turns of fortune, and is interrupted occasionally with witty exchanges or obscene jokes. The romance of Lucrece and Eurialus unfolds along similar lines: the two lovers conduct their affair in secrecy (or at least so they believe); their rendezvous involve clever plotting,

---

like tales, fables, stories, were equally popular, and sometimes used interchangeably with that of *novella*. Boccaccio himself describes his *Decameron* as "tales or stories or *novelle*" (G.H. McWilliam, Foreword to *The Decameron* by Giovanni Boccaccio [London: Penguin Books, 1972], p. lxii).

[5]See, for example, the explicit physical descriptions of the heroine as well as the more subtle sexual imagery woven into the text. Love in the *novella* was traditionally more physical than spiritual in nature.

elaborate camouflage, and almost constant deception; and the feeling of tension, which mounts as the tale unfolds, is lightened by crude remarks and references. While to some extent this pattern describes the entire story of Lucrece and Eurialus' affair, it seems most evident in the second half of the tale. Here, where the romance is played out, the imprint of the *novella* tradition seems unmistakable.

Aeneas' story aligns with the genre more consistently in terms of its realism. *Novelle* were known in particular for their faithful and often detailed portrayals of contemporary society. Such realism is evident throughout *The History of the Two Lovers*, and at many levels. The tale is filled with images of daily life and references to domestic and civic customs, all of which are considered accurate reflections of fifteenth-century Sienese society.[6] In Eurialus' offer of bribery to Pandalus, in the strained relationship between Menelaus and his servants, and in the stark hypocrisy which colours the words and actions of so many of the story's characters, is seen reflected the moral corruption that existed at the imperial court in Vienna, where Aeneas had spent so much time.[7] What makes the story still more realistic is its link with historical fact: the tale of the lovers' romance unfolds against the background of a real historical event.[8] In 1432, Sigismund of Luxembourg travelled to Rome where he was to be crowned Holy Roman Emperor by Pope Eugenius IV. He made many stops along the way, including one of several months in the Tuscan hill-town of Siena. Here, in the context of this Sienese sojourn,

---

[6]Luigi Firpo, Foreword to *Storia di Due Amanti* (Torino: UTET, 1973), pp. 11–12; Achille Tartaro, *Letteratura Italiana*, vol. 3, *La forma del testo II. La prosa*, pp. 692–93. Aeneas had attended university here in the 1420's and was familiar with the city. See Eric J. Morrall, ed., *Aeneas Silvius Piccolomini (Pius II) and Nikolaus Von Wyle: The Tale of Two Lovers, Eurialus and Lucrece* (Amsterdam: Rodopi, 1988), p. 28; and Cecily Ady, *Pius II (Aeneas Silvius Piccolomini) the Humanist Pope* (London, 1913), pp. 15–17.

[7]Di Francia, p. 311; R.J. Mitchell, *The Laurels and the Tiara* (London: Hamill Press, 1962), p. 47.

[8]Although *novelle* sometimes had a basis in historical truth, what mattered most was plausibility, not historical authenticity. See Donald Beecher, ed., *Barnabe Riche: His Farewell to Military Profession* (Ottawa: Dovehouse Editions, 1992), p. 31.

Aeneas sets his tale of romance between Lucrece and Eurialus. Whether the love story itself has any basis in fact remains an issue of debate.[9] Since the end of the eighteenth century, the tale has been read as a *roman à clef* depicting the real romantic escapades of the imperial chancellor Kaspar Schlick, Aeneas' close friend and protector and a member of Sigismund's retinue during his travels through Italy. While this traditional interpretation still has the support of most scholars in the field, it has been challenged in recent years by arguments that reinterpret the old evidence in light of the rhetorical traditions of Aeneas' time, while at the same time offering new evidence from the text itself.[10] However one views its relation to historical truth,

---

[9]It should be noted that the word "history" is no indication of factual truth. The term was an ambiguous one, and could signify a real historical event or simply a narrative, or story.

[10]The argument for a historical reading of the story hinges primarily on two letters which Aeneas wrote in 1444, the same period in which he was writing *The History of the Two Lovers*. The first and perhaps more significant piece of evidence is his letter to Kaspar Schlick (Flora Grierson, tr., *The Tale of Two Lovers by Aeneas Sylvius Piccolomini (Pius II)* [London, 1929], pp. xv–xvi), in which he alludes to his friend's sexual exploits during his stay in Siena and makes an explicit connection between them and his story:

> and I have written the adventure of two lovers: nor have I invented it. For this thing took place in Siena, when the Emperor Sigismund was living there. You too were there and, if my ears have heard aright, made work for love. It is the city of Venus. And men who knew you tell how fiercely you burned, and that none was more passionate than you. As they think, no amatory adventure there befell, but you knew it.

The second is a letter addressed to Aeneas' friend and former teacher, Mariano Sozzini (c. 1397–1467), which, in the original version of *The History of the Two Lovers*, appears as the framework and introduction to the text. Here, Aeneas goes to great lengths to demonstrate to Sozzini the realism of his tale:

> But I'll not invent, as you insist, nor use the poet's reed, while I may tell what is true. For who is there so worthless as would lie, when he can shelter himself behind the truth? ... Nor shall I make use of old forgotten examples (*exemplis*), but I'll bring forth torches that burned in our own days. You will not hear the loves of Troy or Babylon but of our own city" (Grierson, pp. xviii–xx)

In 1724, S.F. Hahn was the first to use these two passages to put forward the argument that *The History of the Two Lovers* was a *roman à clef* recounting Schlick's adventures in Siena (*Collectio Monumentorum veterum et recentium* [Brunsvigae, 1724], vol. 1, pp. 406ff). Scholars have continued to reaffirm these conclusions with remarkable consistency: G. Zannoni, "Per la storia d'una storia d'amore" *Cultura* 9 (1890), pp. 85–92, goes one step further with his rather dubious identification of Lucrece as the wife of Mariano Sozzini; Arsenio Frugoni, "Enea Silvio Piccolomini e l'avventura senese di Gaspar Schlick," *Rinascita* 4 (1941), pp. 25–48, uses contemporary German chronicles to try to confirm the authenticity of specific details in Aeneas' tale; Rossi (p. 194) and Di Francia (pp. 309–11) both note how Schlick is "concealed" by the figure of Eurialus; Ady states that Eurialus is Schlick "beyond a doubt" (p. 16); William Boulting, *Aeneas Sylvius Piccolomini: Humanist, Statesman and Pope*, (London, 1908), believes that Aeneas intended to flatter the chancellor with his portrait (p. 138); Emilio Bigi, "La Historia de duobus amantibus," in *Pio II e la cultura del suo tempo*. Atti del I convegno internazionale 1989, ed. Luisa Rotondi Secchi Tarughi (Milano, 1991), concludes that Schlick is "very probably involved in the story, even if his role is not demonstrated explicitly" (p. 167); Morrall is more convinced, stating "there can be no doubt that Eurialus represents Schlick," and agreeing with Boulting that Aeneas could have written the story as a way of preserving his friend's honor (pp. 21–23). Morrall also points out that in several manuscripts of Niklaus Von Wyle's late fifteenth-century German translation of the story, the connection to Schlick is suggested in the title: "Explicit Historia ipsi Casparo Schlick eventa et ob sui honorem ac preces quamvis mutatis edicta nominibus" (pp. 40–41). See also his introductory comments to *Aeneas Silvius Piccolomini (Pius II), The Goodli History of the Ladye Lucres of Siena and of her Lover Eurialus* (Oxford, 1996), pp. xviii–xix.

The recent challenges offered to this interpretation have largely been based on close rhetorical readings of the text. Several scholars maintain that the passages in the letter to Sozzini which underline the realism of the tale are nothing more than a topos of humanist epistolography, and typical of a tradition which was "preoccupied with truth or at least the semblance of truth" (Maria Luisa Doglio, Introduction to *Storia di Due Amanti* [Torino: UTET, 1973], p. 34). Doglio's analysis of the structure, style and organization of the letter leads her to conclude that the story is meant "neither as a chronicle nor a transcription of fact, but rather as a literary fiction, still more delightful because it is disguised under 'the seal of truth' " (pp. 34–35). See also Paolo Viti, "La 'Historia de duobus

The History of the Two Lovers nevertheless remains a fundamentally realistic tale, and its connection with the *novella* tradition is thereby strengthened.[11]

Aeneas' story is also consistent with the genre in its misogynistic portrayal of women. There are essentially two female types in the *novella* tradition: the virgin or chaste wife, who defends her virtue against the menace of male lust; and the sensual and wanton seductress, whose allurements threaten to destroy the moral integrity or social position of the male hero. The seductress was the more popular of the two portraits, and her frequent appearance in the context of the *novella* has led many scholars to label the genre in general terms as "misogynistic."[12] In *The*

---

amantibus' de Piccolomini: fonte probabile della Mandragola," *A.A.V.V. Ecumenismo della cultura*, vol. 3, p. 251; and John Najemy, *Between Friends: Discourses of Power and Desire in the Machiavelli-Vettori Letters of 1513–1515* (Princeton, 1993), who notes the ambiguity between truth and fiction as a common feature of letter writing (pp. 35–37).

The case against a purely historical interpretation of the story is further supported by evidence from the text itself. The frequent and often direct parallels to characters and events in fictional tales would seem to call into question the story's claim to be a factual account ("[Aeneas'] appeals to [ancient] authors seem to compromise [the story's] claims to verisimilitude," Najemy, pp. 36–37); see also Doglio, *L'Exemplum nella novella latina del '400* (Torino: Giappichelli, 1973) pp. 7, 16; Tartaro, p. 693; and Di Francia, p. 311, who notes how the literary parallels make it difficult to draw the line between fact and fiction.

Both of these arguments make a convincing case against those who read *The History of the Two Lovers* strictly as a *roman à clef*. They do not, however, seem to completely undermine the idea that the romance was at least to some extent based on Schlick's own experiences. Aeneas' letter to the chancellor remains strong evidence in support of a historical reading of the text. The best interpretation would seem to lie between the two extremes, one which allows the story to be read as loosely based on historical truth while at the same time making use of rhetorical conventions.

[11] For the realism of the characters, see below on Boccaccio.

[12] This same image was typical not only of the various narrative forms out of which the *novella* grew, but also of a much longer tradition of European literature and thought — one that can be traced back to authorities of classical and early Christian culture, such as Juvenal and St. Jerome

History of the Two Lovers this image is pervasive. Sometimes it is
Lucrece herself who illustrates it, such as in the scene of outrage
she stages when the bawd delivers Eurialus' first letter;[13] and
when she pretends to deny her feelings in her early letters to her
lover; and again when she accuses her husband of infidelity only
moments after he has interrupted her adulterous tryst.[14] Elsewhere this image is presented by Eurialus who, significantly in
his most rational moments, criticizes not only Lucrece but also
the female sex more generally for the harm it brings upon men.[15]
The narrator also contributes to this general misogynistic vision
of women in long asides and implicit allusions which draw un-
flattering comparisons between Lucrece and other famous female

─────────────

(Di Francia, pp. 24–25). They continued, moreover, to dominate the
broader literary culture in which the new genre of the *novella* began to
flourish. In Tudor England, where the nature of women was the most
prominent issue of debate in the context of imaginative literature, this
negative sexual typology was particularly popular. Beecher explains:

> the question of women's natures had already settled into a formal polar-
> ized controversy [between virtue and vice, shrew and temptress] . . . .
> Together, these stories make up by far the most significant part of the
> Tudor literary creation, and together they form a complex forum on the
> nature of women, as potential redeemers and as potential destroyers."
> (pp. 67–68)

The interest in these issues reflected the concerns of contemporary society, where chastity was exalted, marriage considered "the sovereign
reward for right conduct" (p.65), and uncontrolled passion a serious
threat to social order.

13   What madness hath moved thee to come to my presence? Art thou so
     bold to enter the houses of noble men? Darest thou provoke great ladies
     to violate sacred marriage? (p. 151)

14   I fear lest thou have some other that thou lovest. These husbands be so
     false to their wives. (p. 188)

15   Oft have I heard the deceits of women, and I could not eschew it. If I
     escape now, there shall never no craft of women deceive me (p. 174)

     ah, fool that I was . . . I trusted a woman with my head. So was I counselled
     of my father when he taught me to trust the faith of no woman, for that
     they were cruel, deceitful, changeable, and full of divers passions (p. 179)

figures.[16] The overall impression that emerges from the text is that women are dangerous creatures.[17]

There is even a misogynistic resonance in the heroine's own name. To the reader of both Aeneas' day and Tudor England, the name Lucrece would have recalled the ancient Roman Lucretia, the wife of an influential Roman aristocrat in the time of the Etruscan kings. Raped by the son of the tyrant king, Tarquin the Proud, Lucretia took her own life out of shame for the outrage of her virtue. Her suicide led to a violent uprising against the monarchy, the overthrow of the Tarquin dynasty and the establishment of the Roman Republic.[18] Lucretia had been exalted as an *exemplum* of chastity and marital fidelity by both pagan and early Christian authorities,[19] and in fifteenth- and sixteenth-

---

[16] The most part of women be of this sort: that most they desire that most to them is denied, and when thou wouldest they will not, and when thou wouldest not, they would; and if they have the bridle at liberty, less they offend so that it is easy to keep a woman against her will as a flock of flies in the heat of the sun, except she be of herself chaste. In vain doth the husband set keepers over her: for who shall keep those keepers? She is crafty, and at them lightly she beginneth and when she taketh a fantasy, she is unreasonable, and like an unbridled mule . . . . See the deceit of women. Now trust them hardly; no man is so circumspect that cannot be deceived: he was never kindly deceived whom his wife never assayed to deceive. (pp. 164, 175)

For the allusions, see the notes to the text.

[17]Several scholars have acknowledged the negative dimension of Lucrece's image: Di Francia, pp. 307–09; Bottari, "Il teatro latino nell'Historia 'De duobus amantibus'," in *Classici nel Medioevo e nell'Umanesimo Miscellanea filologica* (Genova, 1975), p. 119, notes how Lucrece's "coquetry" tends to stifle her heroic nature; Giancarlo Borri, "La Storia di Due Amanti," *Pio II el la cultura del suo tempo. Atti del I convegno internazionale 1989*, ed. Luisa Rotondi Secchi Tarughi (Milano, 1991), p. 194; and Frugoni, p. 30.

[18]Livy, *Ab urbe condita libri*, I.lvii.

[19]See Valerius Maximus, *Factorum et dictorum memorabilium libri novem*, VI.i, where Lucretia is the first of six women identified as examples of "pudicitia," or chastity; Augustine (*De civitate Dei*, I.xix) dedicates an entire chapter to a comparison between Lucretia and various other

century Europe she was still one of the most common models of female virtue.[20]

As several scholars have pointed out, the choice of Lucrece as the name for a flagrant adulterer would have struck Aeneas' readers as a highly ironic one.[21] But in the context of the story's broader criticism of women, and of their sexual mores in particular, the link with Lucretia would also have underscored the hypocrisy and the deceitfulness which had come to define Aeneas' heroine. And while the parallels stain the particular figure of Lucrece, they also seem to reinforce the story's view of women more generally as creatures of uncontrollable passion: not even the purest, most virtuous woman—not even a Lucretia—can defend her virtue in the face of passion's temptations.

Just as specific elements within the story link *The History of the Two Lovers* to the *novella* tradition, so do the techniques of its composition. In writing this tale, Aeneas adopted the traditional approach of the *novellista*, drawing his characters, plots, and themes from well-known works of prose and poetry. Considered as a whole, the story is clearly an original piece, but its individual parts are largely borrowed from tales of classical and vernacualar cultures. While today such appropriation would be considered plagiarism, in the literary culture of the fifteenth century it was an accepted step in the process of composition. Indeed, it was not

---

Christian women who were forced by foreign men. Although Augustine condemns Lucretia's suicide as unchristian, he defends the purity of her motivations.

[20]Enrico Menesto, *Coluccio Salutati, Editi e Inediti Latini dal M.S. 53 della Biblioteca Comunale di Todi, Res Tudertinae*, vol. 12 (1971), p. 15. See also Viti, *Ecumenismo della cultura*, p. 260; and Boccaccio's exultation of Lucretia in *De mulieribus claris*, xlviii.

[21]Najemy, p. 37; Frugoni refers to the allusion as "playful" (*scherzoso*) and notes how Machiavelli does the same thing with the same ironic motive (pp. 29–30); Bigi speaks in general terms about the "strong humourous tension" in the contrast between the exemplary substance of the name and the not so exemplary reality of the figure in the story (p. 171). See Morrall, *Aeneas Silvius Piccolomini (Pius II) and Nikolaus von Wyle*, pp. 24–25, who suggests that the name is indicative of the good light in which Aeneas sees the heroine, since she is emblematic of virtue outraged.

the originality of the *novellista*'s ideas that would win him respect and popularity, but rather his skill at recasting the features of old and familiar stories into a new mould. A well-read audience would take pleasure in identifying the different sources from which a tale had been crafted, and in this way come to appreciate the creativity of its author.[22] As we go on to discuss the specific sources used in constructing *The History of the Two Lovers*, it will become clear not only how important this technique was to the structure of the tale, but also how clever a craftsman Aeneas was.

Most scholars who classify *The History of the Two Lovers* as a *novella* define it more specifically as one written in the style of Boccaccio, perhaps the most famous *novellista* of all time.[23] They point out the many details in Aeneas' story which seem to be drawn directly from Boccaccio's writings, and in particular from the *novelle* in his *Decameron*.[24] More often, however, they draw attention to parallels in the general approach the two authors take to writing their tales. Like Boccaccio — and unlike other *novellisti* before him — Aeneas peoples his story with strikingly human figures.[25] Both major and minor characters in *The History*

---

[22]Najemy, p. 36.

[23]Through translation, Boccaccio was becoming a familiar figure to audiences in England in the 1560's. Scholars have noted his influence on many of Aeneas' other writings besides the tale of Lucrece and Eurialus. See Bigi, p. 164.

[24]Di Francia (p. 307) and Borri (pp. 190–91) note parallels with the *storico* of Day VII; Borri with Day IV (pp. 190–91), Vili with Day VIII (p. 246). See Morrall, *Aeneas Silvius Piccolomini (Pius II) and Nikolaus von Wyle*, pp. 19–20, and *Aeneas Silvius Piccolomini (Pius II) The Goodli History*, pp. xxvii–xxxi, for a comparison with *Filostrato*. With the exception of the last, most scholars do not describe these parallels in any detail.

[25]On Boccaccio, see Bigi, *Poesia latina e volgare nel Rinascimento italiano* (Naples: Morano, 1989), pp. 68–79; Di Francia, pp. 95ff, 307–08; and Morrall, *Aeneas Silvius Piccolomini (Pius II) and Nikolaus von Wyle*, p. 18. Boccaccio was the first to introduce realistic characters into the *novella*. Traditionally, figures were sketched in broad and sometimes exaggerated strokes, and emerged more as types than as individuals. See also Vittore Branca, *Boccaccio medievale*, seventh edition (Florence, 1990). On Aeneas' characters, see Di Francia, who describes Lucrece as "profoundly and realistically human" (p. 308).

of the Two Lovers demonstrate real fellings, thoughts and concerns;
and at several points even their physical appearance is described
in fine realistic detail.[26] The figure of Lucrece has been linked to

---

[26]See, for example, the lengthy and detailed description of Lucrece
at the beginning of the tale (pp. 134–35). Here the traditional ideals of
female beauty are complemented by many untraditionally naturalistic
and individualized details (the hair pulled into a knot, the dimples in
her cheeks, even her height). On this, see Bigi, "La Historia de duobus
amantibus," p. 169; Bigi, *Poesia latina e volgare nel Rinascimento italiano*,
68–70; and Borri, p. 194. The realism of the characters has been the subject of recent scholarly debate. In the introduction to her edition of the
text, Doglio argues that the constant comparisons, direct and indirect,
to figures from literary and specifically classical culture have the effect
of distancing the characters from reality. Of Lucrece she writes: "the
parallels with Helen and Andromache betray a continuous process of
abstraction and transfiguration of reality" (*Storia di due amanti*, pp. 35–
36). The romance, she concludes, "transcends the real and hovers in a
sublime idealism . . . . It is not to the reality of a passion, or of a specific
or individual couple which [Aeneas] writes but . . . an alternative to
reality" (p. 44). Responding to this interpretation, Bigi argues that instead of attenuating the realism of the characters, the classical parallels
actually serve to enhance it, uniting them, as it were, with a universal
human experience as it is recognized by ancient authors ("La Historia
de duobus amantibus," pp. 171–72). The literary parallels in *The History of the Two Lovers* should be understood as an expression of human
experience (p. 174). See also his similar statements in *Poesia Latina e
volgare nel Rinascimento italiano*, pp. 68–70. Bigi's argument seems the
more plausible, especially considering that the allusions are to authors
who have been widely recognized precisely for their realistic portraits
of humanity (Ovid, Seneca, Terence; on Terence see Betty Radice, Introduction to *The Comedies* by Terence [London and New York: Penguin
Books, 1976]). For similar opinions, see also Tartaro, p. 692; and Morrall,
Aeneas Silvius Piccolomini (Pius II) and Nikolaus Von Wyle, pp. 17–18. Cf.
Givens on Boccaccio, p. 108. Aeneas himself seems to lend support to
this argument: in a letter to his close friend Piero da Noceto, written
some months before the tale of Lucrece and Eurialus, he remarks explicitly on the similarities between a comedy written by Terence and Piero's
own adventures: "illud autem mihi risum excussit, quod de Philorcio
scipsisti sive hanc volumus Antiphilam dicere. visus sum cum Terentio
loqui, dum tuas perlegi litteras. nunc mihi Pamphilus, nunc Heschinus,

Boccaccio in still other ways. Her psychological development,[27] her cleverness and quick wits,[28] and simply her prominence in the story specifically recall the heroines of Boccaccio's tales.[29] There is further evidence of his influence in the depiction of the romance between Eurialus and Lucrece. Love for Boccaccio is an irrational and irresistible natural force and a fundamental aspect of the human condition.[30] It was championed in the *Decameron* in particular as a law of Nature, and hailed as supreme over all social conventions and moral codes. In *The History of the Two Lovers*, the same vision of irrationality and overwhelming strength is acknowledged by both the story's characters and its narrator, while the idea of love as supreme law finds a champion in the figure of Eurialus.[31] Even the storyline of Aeneas' tale is

---

nunc Clinia videbaris" Rudolf Wolkan, *Der Briefwechsel des Aeneas Silvius Piccolomini*, Vol. 1, no. 1 (Vienna, 1909), p. 285, Ep. 119, 16 January, 1443). Far from seeing them as idealized abstractions, Aeneas seems to perceive the characters in classical literature as interchangeable with real human beings, and the line between art and life a very fluid one.

[27] The penetrating psychological portrait of Lucrece in the first part of the tale recalls Boccaccio's *Fiammetta*, a work which explores the intimate thoughts and emotions of a woman awaiting the return of her lover. The *Fiammetta* is often considered the first modern psychological novel (Givens, p. 104). See Di Francia, pp. 305–07, who also sees parallels in this dimension with Day VII of the *Decameron*; and also Tartaro, p. 690; Rossi, p. 194; Viti, p. 246; and Bottari, p. 114.

[28] Doglio, p. 39. Boccaccio puts intelligence on a par with the highest virtues, and in the *Decameron* in particular, he depicts women as sympathetic and clever ladies.

[29] Even the misogynistic tones with which Aeneas' heroine is coloured are not out of line with Boccaccian heroines: although Boccaccio is most famous as a champion of women, he was also at times a harsh critic of the female sex (see, for example, the *Corbaccio*).

[30] For a more detailed discussion of Boccaccio's views on love, see Aldo Scaglione, *Nature and Love in the Late Middle Ages* (Berkeley, 1963); Azzura B. Givens, *La Dottrina d'Amore nel Boccaccio* (Messina and Florence: G. D'Anna, 1968); Natalino Sapegno, *Il Trecento* (Milan, 1960); and McWilliam, pp. lxxix–cix.

[31] See Eurialus' opening monologue, where he points to the supreme law of love as justification for fulfilling his sexual desires (pp. 146–49).

said to be cast in a distinctly Boccaccian mould. The love triangle of husband, wife and lover was the classic premise for many of Boccaccio's stories.[32] So is the theatrical pattern in which the romance unfolds in the second half of the tale[33] and the tragic turns the story takes.[34] Together these parallels suggest that

Much of his speech is drawn directly from Seneca, whose ideas had also strongly influenced Boccaccio; see Morrall, *Aeneas Silvius Piccolomini (Pius II) and Nikolaus von Wyle*, pp. 26–27. Eurialus does not defend these views to the end of the story; the concluding speech demonstrates a very different opinion on the relationship between natural impulses and social ethics.

In addition to ideas about the nature of passion, Boccaccio is considered the source and inspiration for the conventions of courtly love which are woven into Aeneas' romance. The image of love entering the heart through the lovers' eyes, their sighs and tears of passion, Eurialus' inability to eat and sleep and his pledge to comply with Lucrece's every wish, and, in turn, her insistence on his fidelity are only some of the the many conventions of the tradition which Aeneas includes in his story. The conventions of courtly love had been developed in Provençal literature — prose romances, the works of troubadours, trouvères — and had been codified by Andreas Capellanus in the twelfth century in a work entitled *The Art of Courtly Love*. Boccaccio was the first to introduce them to the Italian narrative tradition. See McWilliam, pp. cvi–cvii; Givens, pp. 24–28; and Morrall, *Aeneas Silvius Piccolomini (Pius II) and Nikolaus von Wyle*, pp. 16–17.

[32]Bigi, "La Historia de duobus amantibus," p. 168; and Doglio, *ibid.*, p. 36.

[33]In developing his storylines, Boccaccio often used Roman comedy as a model, and is considered the first to have integrated it with the *novella* tradition. The two genres are, in fact, very similar. Like the traditional *novella*, ancient comedies typically centred on themes of illicit love and their stories were played out in a similar pattern of secret encounters, disguises and elaborate tricks. In general, classical culture seems to have had very little influence on the *novella* before Boccaccio. His tales introduce a broad range of Latin authors to the tradition, including Seneca, Livy, Cicero, Sallust, Plautus and Terence. See Bigi, *Poesia latina e volgare nel Rinascimento italiano*, p. 73; and McWilliam, p. lviii.

[34]The general tone of melancholy which permeates the story and the unhappy conclusion to the lovers' romance recall Boccaccio's love stories, especially those from Day IV of the *Decameron* (Borri, pp. 190–91).

Aeneas was influenced very stongly by the fourteenth-century *novellista* as he wrote his own tale of love.

As well as classifying *The History of the Two Lovers* with earlier states of the *novella*'s development, scholars have aligned it with the *novelle* of Aeneas' humanist contemporaries. Toward the beginning of the fifteenth century, humanists began to try their hand at the genre, making an exception to the general attitude of hostility they showed toward vernacular literary culture.[35] Aeneas had been educated in the *studia humanitatis*, and thus it is not surprising that *The History of the Two Lovers* has much in common with the humanist *novella*. The similarities begin with the very language in which the tale was originally written. Instead of a vernacular, Aeneas chose Latin, and more precisely, the classical Ciceronian Latin revived and revered in humanist culture.[36] Like most humanist *novellisti*, Aeneas also made use of his vast knowledge of ancient literature in shaping the story itself. His work is interwoven with literally hundreds of allusions

---

[35]Di Francia, p. 302. The humanists both translated *novelle* from Italian into Latin, and wrote original compositions, distinctive in the way they blended elements of classical learning with the traditional features of the genre. The Italian humanist *novellisti* included some of most distinguished figures in the intellectual world: Leonardo Bruni, Leon Battista Alberti, Bartolomeo Fazio, Luigi Passerini, Agnolo Poliziano (of whom the last two wrote *novelle* in Latin). Translations into Latin were done by Bruni, Fazio, Antonio Loschi, and Filippo Beroaldo. See also Tartaro, p. 690; Maria Luisa Doglio and Giuseppe G. Ferrero, eds., *Novelle del '400* (Torino: UTET, 1975), pp. 44–45; and Di Francia, p. 334. Bruni's translation of Boccaccio's first story from Day IV of the *Decameron* was mistakenly attributed to Aeneas by the editor of his *Opera Omnia* (Aeneas Silvius Piccolomini, *Aeneae Sylvii Piccolminiei Pii Pontificis Maximi II Opera quae extant omnia* [Basel, 1551], Ep. 410, pp. 954–59); see Doglio, *L'Exemplum nella novella latina del '400* (Torino: Giappichelli, 1973), p. 6. On Italian humanist *novelle*, see Bigi, *Poesia latina e volgare nel Rinascimento italiano*, pp. 70–72. Humanist culture also finds reflection in the *novelle* of sixteenth-century England, such as George Pettie's *Petite Palace of Pettie his Pleasures* and Barnabe Riche's *His Farewell to Military Profession*.

[36]There were, however, many humanists who chose to write their *novelle* in vernacular. See Di Francia, p. 303.

to classical texts, most of them in the form of direct quotations.
These allusions come from a broad range of works, from the
"high" authors of tragedy, lyric, and epic to the "low" ones of
comedy and satire. The quotations in the first part of the story are
taken mostly from tales of tragic love: Virgil's account of Dido
and Aeneas; Ovid's of Medea and Jason, and of Helen and Paris;
and Seneca's of Phaedra and Hippolytus. In the second half of
the tale, when the action proper of the romance begins, most
of the allusions are to the comedies of Terence and the satires
of Juvenal.[37]

The imprint of humanist culture is particularly evident in the
romance that develops between Lucrece and Eurialus. Their
illicit affair echoes ancient tales of abduction and abandonment,
and the tradition in classical literature of a woman falling in
love with a foreign man.[38] The lovers' epistolary courtship is
also shaped by Aeneas' humanist learning, and specifically his
knowledge of Ovid.[39] The images of love as sickness and disease,

---

[37]There is considerable discrepancy in the number of references which
scholars identify and editors note in the text. The most thorough philological study was done by the Hungarian scholar J.I. Devay in his now
rare edition of the work: *De duobus amantibus historia* (Budapest, 1904).
It is difficult for audiences of today to appreciate fully the significance of
these allusions and quotations. Readers well versed in classical literature, of whom there was a steadily growing number in fifteenth-century
Italy and sixteenth-century England, would have been able to identify
many of the sources of these references with ease. Admittedly, in the English version it would have been more difficult to recognize the specific
excerpts, since the linguistic clues so important for leading the reader
back to the original text would have largely been lost in the translation. For some of the more famous quotations, however, such as the
description of Dido in Book IV of Virgil's *Aeneid*, there may have been
no need for such hints. In any case, the more explicit references would
have made the story's dialogue with classical culture very clear, and
may even have encouraged the more curious learned readers to explore
further for other, more camouflaged allusions.

[38]Morrall, *Aeneas Silvius Piccolomini (Pius II) and Nikolaus von Wyle*,
p. 17, speaks specifically of the tales of Dido, Medea, and Helen.

[39]Scholars have identified the inspiration for their romantic correspondence in Ovid's *Heroides*, a collection of fictional letters exchanged

and as a force capable of changing man from a rational being to a passionate beast, are, in turn, a classical inheritance.[40] Even the "Boccaccian" idea of passion's overpowering strength and of love as natural law have their origin in ancient literature.[41]

Aeneas' classical education informs many other aspects of *The History of the Two Lovers* besides the romantic. Most of the characters in the story are named after famous men and women from the ancient world (Menelaus, Agamemnon, Eurialus, Lucretia, etc.),[42] and are further linked to these figures through both explicit comparisons and more subtle allusions.[43] Aeneas also introduces into his tale one of the most popular topics of humanist

---

between famous heroes and heroines of classical literature. Eurialus and Lucrece's letters themselves incorporate ideas drawn from another of Ovid's works, the *Ars amatoria*, which, as the title suggests, discusses the art of love (it is interesting to note that in April, 1444, a few months before he wrote the tale of Eurialus and Lucrece, Aeneas wrote a letter to a friend, asking him if he could borrow his copy of this work, together with the plays of Terence [Wolkan, pp. 310–11, Ep. 135]). Some scholars have also suggested Abelard's letters to Eloise as a model for the correspondence between Lucrece and Eurialus. See Doglio, *Storia di Due Amanti*, p. 38; and Najemy, p. 34. See also Morrall, *Aeneas Silvius Piccolomini (Pius II). The Goodli History*, pp. xxx–xxxi, for parallels between Lucrece and Eurialus' exchange and that of Troilus and Creseide in Boccaccio's *Filostrato*.

[40]On lovesickness, see Scaglione, pp. 60–26. At one point in the story the narrator makes direct reference to Ovid as his source.

[41]In the discussion of love as a natural law, Aeneas' specific source is Seneca's *Hippolytus*. Because of Boccaccio's knowledge of classical texts, it is difficult at times to determine whether a reference in Aeneas' story to ancient literature is inspired by the fourteenth-century *novellista* or by Aeneas' own humanist education. In general, though, Aeneas' story reflects both a broader and a more intimate knowledge of classical literature than do Boccaccio's *novelle*, and expresses it with more direct and literal links to the ancient texts themselves. On this see Bigi, *Poesia latina e volgare nel Rinascimento italiano*, p. 69.

[42]The significance of these names will be treated in a subsequent section of this introduction.

[43]Several scholars have tried to identify Lucrece with a single classical heroine, some suggesting Helen of Troy (Morrall, *Aeneas Silvius Piccolomini (Pius II) and Nikolaus von Wyle*, p. 18, and *Aeneas Silvius Piccolomini*

debate, namely the minor but important theme of the struggle between fortune and intelligence (*ingegno*).[44] In the story's misogynistic subtext, moreover, not only does he echo a common humanist attitude towards women, but he does so by using the very words and images that ancient authors — Ovid and Juvenal in particular — had used to do the same thing.[45] Finally, the elements of ancient theatre incorporated into the tale enhance associations with the humanist *novella*. Given the number of direct quotations from Terence's *Eunuchus* and the *Heautontimorumenos* in particular, Aeneas goes beyond Boccaccio in integrating Roman comedy with the *novella* tradition.[46] In this dimension of the story as in others, Aeneas' humanist culture builds on the foundations of his medieval predecessor.[47]

There are thus many reasons which justify the traditional classification of *The History of the Two Lovers* as a *novella*. The story's theme, characterization, plot and compositional technique are all developed according to a pattern typical of the genre, and

---

(Pius II). *The Goodli History*, p. xxxv), and others Dido (Bottari, p. 118). Rather than emphasizing an equation with a single figure, however, Aeneas seems more interested in developing a composite portrait of his heroine, and thus, in creating a more original figure. In general, the imprint of ancient literature is perhaps most evident on the figure of the heroine. Her physical description is largely inspired by Petrarch's vision of ideal female beauty (golden hair, sunlike eyes, coral lips, crystal teeth). See Doglio, *ibid.*, p. 35; and Bottari, p. 114, who suggests that she is also modelled to some extent on Suetonius' description of Augustus.

[44]The complex portrayal of how the two forces interact seems to align more closely with the humanist vision than with the "medieval perspective" of Boccaccio, in whose *novelle* this issue is also very prominent. For one of the few discussions of Fortune in *The History of the Two Lovers*, see Bigi, "La Historia de duobus amantibus," pp. 69–70.

[45]On Ovid, see Di Francia, pp. 308–09. See the notes to the text for various examples.

[46]The works of Terence served as inspiration for the action, dialogue and even the names of Aeneas' characters. See especially Bottari, pp. 122–26, who offers the most detailed consideration of the role of theatre in *The History of the Two Lovers*; and also Tartaro, p. 690; Firpo, pp. 12–13; Doglio, *ibid*, pp. 38, 40; and Viti, pp. 246–47.

[47]See Bigi, *Poesia latina e volgare nel Rinascimento italiano*, pp. 69–71.

in particular of the *novelle* of Boccaccio and of the humanists. The story's precise relationship to the *novella* tradition could be described as a union of these two types in a way that enhances the specifically humanistic elements of Boccaccio's stories. But while the *novella* in its various forms clearly had a significant impact on the shape of Aeneas' narrative, there are still other dimensions of the tale which are wholly foreign to this tradition. To define the story simply in terms of this genre is to simplify what is a much more complicated relationship to contemporary literary traditions.

The most obvious way in which Aeneas' story diverges from the *novella* tradition is the context in which it was originally presented. When Aeneas completed the story in 1444, he incorporated it into a letter to his teacher and friend, Mariano Sozzini—a letter that Sozzini had asked Aeneas to write him a story of love, and that the tale of Lucrece and Eurialus that follows is Aeneas' fulfillment of this request. As well as explaining the circumstances surrounding the story's composition, Aeneas' letter also serves as a kind of preface to the tale, outlining its background, main theme and even its moral message. Rather than a kind of wrapping, the letter to Sozzini should thus be thought of as an integral part of the tale itself.

It is precisely this interconnectedness that makes *The History of the Two Lovers* such a difficult text to classify. The early editors and publishers of Aeneas' works offered their own opinions on the issue by including the story in his private correspondence. Modern scholars have tried to resolve the question in another way by describing it as an "epistolary novella."[48] The English translator eliminated the dilemma altogether by simply excluding the letter from his version of the story.[49] If the generic tension has been resolved in this particular edition of the tale, its existence as part of the story's history should not, however, be forgotten. Whether intentionally or not, the English version of

---

[48]Najemy (pp. 33, 36) also acknowledges its "generic instability"; see also Doglio, *ibid.*, p. 33.

[49]Sections about the moral intent of the story were largely reworked into a poem which concludes the text.

the story fits more closely into the category of *novella* than Aeneas had originally intended.

The other elements in *The History of the Two Lovers* which stand outside the *novella* tradition are still very evident in the English translation. Perhaps the most obvious is the psychological development of the story's characters. The traditional focus of the *novella* was action, not characterization; very little time was spent describing the thoughts and feelings of the characters, or explaining the motivation for their behaviour.[50] Aeneas, in contrast, devotes almost the entire first half of his story to a detailed exploration of the mental and emotional landscapes of his hero and heroine; and while the second half of the tale may be dominated by action, there are still frequent pauses to illuminate the psychology behind it. So continuous, so extensive and so detailed is the exploration of the lovers' thoughts and emotions, that the action of their romance seems to play a distinctly subordinate role. Thus, while it cannot be denied that the typical storyline of the *novella* is present in *The History of the Two Lovers*, it should also be recognized that its role is far less important than that which was traditionally assigned.[51]

Aeneas' interest in the psychology of romance is usually described as part of the story's "Boccaccian heritage," but the parallel with this medieval author can be taken only so far. There is, for example, no precedent in Boccaccio's writings (or in any other *novella*, for that matter) for the combination of a

---

[50]Beecher explains how the focus on action in Italian *novelle* was to

the detriment of more complete characterizations . . . . Novellas rarely proceeded with sufficient leisure to permit a full development of the inner lives of the protagonists. Dialogue could be terse and colloquial as well as ceremonial, but tended to serve the advancement of an action rather than the exploration either of ideas or of sentiments." (p. 31).

[51]Cf. Tartaro:

In Piccolomini's narrative . . . the facts, and thereby the swift-moving chain of events in the plots of the *Decameron*, are willingly sacrificed to the emotions and the erotic psychology of the text . . . with the aim of enriching the emotional dimension of the *Historia* — in a context dense with tensions and emotions, fears and throbbing sensuality — more than to push forward the action (pp. 692–93)

See also Firpo, pp. 11–12; Di Francia, pp. 307–08; and Rossi, pp. 194–95.

fundamentally static psychological study with the more traditionally action-oriented plot.[52] Moreover, Boccaccio's explo-
rations of psychology are essentially limited to women (Fiammetta, most notably), whereas Aeneas' are directed to both men
and women equally, and are specifically aimed at distinguishing
them along the boundaries of gender. In *The History of the Two
Lovers* men and women in love are shown to act very differently
from one another.[53] Lucrece's feelings of passion are intense and
unshakeable, and her devotion to Eurialus develops almost into
a kind of fanaticism. In surrendering to her romantic desires,
she seems to eliminate altogether her identity as a wife, so that
Eurialus becomes her only reason for living. Her behaviour,
moreover, is identified as being typical of all women: she writes
in one of her letters to Eurialus: "I know myself. If I begin to
love, I shall neither keep measure nor rule . . . . A woman when
she beginneth to love only in death maketh an end. Women rage;
they do not love, and except they be answered with love, nothing
is more terrible." The heroine goes on to generalize about the
very different behaviour of men: "You men are of more stronger
mind, and sooner can quench the fire," and though Eurialus
denies this outright, his actions suggest otherwise. While expe-
riencing the same, if not more intense, feelings for Lucrece, the
hero is considerably more unstable in his devotion to her than
she is to him. Throughout the story his attitude remains ambivalent, shifting from blind devotion and obsession to resentment,
frustration and even disgust.[54] The psychological portraits that
emerge from Aeneas' tale should thus be recognized as a more

---

[52]Tartaro, p. 692.

[53]Many scholars have remarked on the differences in the romantic psyches of hero and heroine: Viti, pp. 262–63; Di Francia, p. 309,
although he considers Eurialus to be a comparatively undeveloped
character; Bigi, "La Historia de duobus amantibus," pp. 169–71; Frugoni, pp. 30–32; and especially Borri, pp. 192–93.

[54]Some scholars have interpreted these differences in character in
terms of Aeneas' own judgment. Di Francia considers Aeneas' portrait
of Eurialus as a sign of his disapproval: he is cowardly and selfish, almost as though he were a caricature (p. 309); Morrall also reads Eurialus'
unstable devotion to Lucrece as a sign of the author's critical attitude
toward the hero (although at the same time he approved of Eurialus'

complex and more complete study of romantic psychology than what exists in the earlier *novella* tradition. If Aeneas can be said to have drawn inspiration from Boccaccio, it seems clear that he developed these ideas further, into something new and original.[55]

The story's relationship to classical culture also differs from what was typical in the *novella* tradition, and specifically in the *novelle* of the humanists. *The History of the Two Lovers* contains an extraordinarily large number of direct quotations from ancient texts: the most extensive philological analysis of the tale identifies well over a hundred — sixty from Terence alone.[56] The first part of the story is particularly thick with allusions — so much so, in fact, that at points Aeneas' narrative seems to consist simply of pieces of other texts cobbled together. Also unusual is the length of the individual citations. In some instances Aeneas quotes passages of several lines without changing a word. Lucrece's first monologue, for example, is drawn almost verbatim from Medea's opening speech in Ovid's *Metamorphoses* VII, 12–152 (pp. 153–58). Moreover, her subsequent conversation with Yosias, her servant, is almost identical to that which Seneca reports between Phaedra and her nurse at the beginning of his tragedy *Hippolytus*.[57]

---

ultimate decision to uphold the principles of social decorum). He sees a more ambivalent attitude toward Lucrece: critical, but at the same time sympathetic with the strength of Lucrece's love (*Aeneas Silvius Piccolomini (Pius II) and Nikolaus von Wyle*, p. 24). Aeneas' sympathies, he concludes, are more with the heroine than the hero (pp. 21, 24–27; and *Aeneas Silvius Piccolomini (Pius II). The Goodli History*, p. xxii).

[55]Cf. Tartaro, who talks of Aeneas' "original connection" with Boccaccio (p. 692).

[56]See Devay. Most modern editions of the work provide only a selection of these quotations (and some are misleading in their tallies, such as Najemy, who reports only three references to Seneca, p. 36). Di Francia notes the unusual nature of his approach to classical sources (pp. 315–16).

[57]This is the most extensive quotation. The passage spans 150 lines, about 60 of which are quoted word for word (pp. 102–103). In turn, Eurialus' lengthy opening monologue, which is drawn from the same text, essentially reproduces most of a speech pronounced by the Chorus

The epistolary framework, strongly psychological characterization, and distinctive appropriation of classical texts in Aeneas' story demand a reconsideration of its classification as a *novella*. If it is to be defined as such, it should be recognized as a more original interpretation of the genre than has so far been emphasized, as more of a dialogue with the tradition than an example of it in its purest form. But given the prominence of these exceptional features in the story, it also seems worth considering whether there is another more appropriate rhetorical category into which *The History of the Two Lovers* could additionally, or even alternatively, be placed. The three elements of the story which diverge from the *novella* tradition all serve in one way or another to explain the moral conflict in Lucrece and Eurialus' romance. The letter in the humanist tradition was a genre specifically used as an arena for an open discussion of ethical issues which grew out of real human experiences.[58] The significant psychological dimension in the text reinforces the conception of the tale as a moral discussion still further. The interior portraits of Lucrece and Eurialus explore almost exclusively the moral dilemma of their romance, describing the minds of the hero and heroine engaged in a struggle between their natural desires and moral conscience.[59] Moreover, the classical allusions — and the lengthy excerpts, in particular — play an essential role in this moral debate: both Eurialus and Lucrece articulate their thoughts and feelings in the very words which Virgil, Ovid and Seneca had used in depicting other figures faced with similar ethical conflicts: Medea, as she confronts her feelings for Jason; Dido hers for Aeneas; and Phaedra hers for Hippolytus. If, as scholarship has generally maintained, Aeneas' classical references have an ornamental purpose and present a kind of literary game for the

---

(146–49). Here, once again, *The History of the Two Lovers* pushes beyond the traditional boundaries of the *novella*.

[58] Bigi identifies Petrarch as the one who initiated this tradition (*Poesia latina e volgare nel Rinascimento italiano*, pp. 70–71). See also Doglio, p. 35.

[59] Bigi notes this in Eurialus ("La Historia de duobus amantibus," p. 170); Di Francia (p. 303), Doglio (p. 36) and Viti (p. 262) in Lucrece. Firpo states that "what really weighs on the author is the secret movements of the soul troubled by torments of love" (pp. 11–12).

reader, they also, and more importantly, provide a critical vehicle for the communiction of ethical ideas.[60]

It should be remembered that the *novella*, for the most part, did include a moral dimension. The genre was meant to provide entertainment as well as edification — just as Aeneas had defined his tale in his letter to Carolus. But while *The History of the Two Lovers* has the same component parts of the *novella*, it does not develop them in the traditional way. Not only does it incorporate new elements into the narrative in order to explore moral issues, it also gives this dimension a pre-eminence which in the *novella* was traditionally reserved for the action. The balance has, in a sense, been reversed. With this in mind, we should turn back to the letter of Carolus and reconsider the relationship between the moral and narrative dimensions of the story as Aeneas had outlined them. Perhaps the key to this interpretation lies in the very first word he uses to describe the text. Rather than a *novella*, *The History of the Two Lovers* should be read as essentially a moral tract — *tractatus* — which adopts and adapts the genre of the *novella* as a means of presenting its themes.[61]

As we turn our attention now more fully to the moral dimension of the story, the definition of the tale as an ethical treatise will become still more convincing. At the same time,

---

[60]The role which these ancient voices play in articulating the moral dilemma of the romance has yet to be given adequate consideration. For a long time the unusual number and density of classical quotations was simply dismissed as an "excessive exercise in erudition," or an abuse of literary knowledge, their only impact being to leave the reader exhausted, even irritated, by the text (Di Francia, p. 315). While recent scholarship is more admiring than it is critical of such a demonstration of learning, it continues to view these references from an essentially rhetorical standpoint, and see their role as more decorative than substantive (see Firpo, p. 10; Tartaro, p. 692; and Doglio, pp. 43–44). There are, however, some scholars who recognize the more complex role of these references and allusions, such as Bigi, who emphasizes how they contribute to the humanity of the characters ("La Historia de duobus amantibus," pp. 168–72; and *Poesia latina e volgare nel Rinascimento italiano*, pp. 67–71). Cf. Devay's comment: "propter moralem usum multas pulchritudinis poeticas et admixtas res historicas," p. ix.

[61]Tartaro, p. 692.

the tale's alignment with humanist culture suggested by its epistolary framework will be confirmed and still further refined. The moral ideas in *The History of the Two Lovers* align closely with a minor but significant group of early Italian humanists who not only developed new ideas of moral pedagogy, but also criticized more traditional approaches. Aeneas' anti-traditional ideas would have had a different resonance in fifteenth-century Italy than they would in sixteenth-century England, but in both cultures they were significant statements and represent an important contribution to ethical thought in early modern Europe.

* * *

The "edifying lesson" in *The History of the Two Lovers* has seen a broad range of interpretations over the years. Scholars in the first half of this century seem to have been as blind to the story's message as fifteenth-century audiences supposedly were. Indeed, Aeneas would probably have been still more exasperated with their attitude to the text than with that of his contemporaries: not only did they fail to perceive the tale's edifying moral, they even denied that one existed at all: "It would be a close and attentive reader," remarked one of his early biographers, "who should easily glean a moral from a tale whose sole object was to amuse."[62] If anything, they considered Aeneas' story immoral, Boccaccian, a reflection of his "corrupt" nature, or more precisely, a statement of the "liberal sexual mores" which he is judged to have adopted in that particular period of his life.[63] The "coarseness" and sexual explicitness of Lucrece and Eurialus' affair as well as the image projected of love as natural law formed the basis of these readings, and were also used to explain the feelings

---

[62]Boulting, p. 139; see also Flora Grierson, whose suggestion that the tale's only intellectual value lies in its literary charm and eloquence echoes this opinion (p. vi).

[63]Ady describes Aeneas' habits when he first arrived in Germany as "of the lowest order . . . . He was frivolous, profligate, pagan, and apparantly without vestige of shame or reticence" (pp. 98–99). See also Boulting, who posits that the novel may have been written at some moment when Aeneas took an "attitude of defiance and bravado toward sexual scruples" (pp. 137–38).

of shame and remorse which Aeneas confessed years later in his letter to Carolus.[64]

For the most part, however, scholars have revised these interpretations considerably. While they continue to acknowledge the story's crudeness and lasciviousness, they do not view these features as the message of the tale.[65] Newer interpretations have been based on a re-evaluation of what had once been dismissed as a "moral tag" appended to the story to serve as a kind of excuse for its erotic content.[66] In the original Latin text, this statement appears in the letter to Sozzini, in both the prefatory comments to the tale and again in the remarks which follow the narrative proper. In the English translation, Aeneas' message is given a somewhat more explicit interpretation and is recast into a poem of twenty-eight lines. Both of these alterations are in keeping with trends in contemporary English literary culture. Lyric poetry was becoming an increasingly popular genre in the late sixteenth century, and verses were often inserted into the context or conclusion of short romance prose fiction.[67] The emphasis on the tale's moral intent reflects the uneasiness and suspicion with which English audiences and moral authorities in particular looked upon bawdy tales of Italian

---

[64] Ady, p. 98; and Boulting, p. 137.

[65] See, however, Morrall, *Aeneas Silvius Piccolomini (Pius II) and Nikolaus von Wyle*, where he states that "Aeneas adopted, at least temporarily, from Boccaccio's *Decameron* the view formulated by Francesco de Sanctis in the words, 'Nature, that in Dante's world had meant sin, has now become law . . . .'" He goes on to argue that by the end of the story Aeneas changes his mind, demonstrating "perhaps his own skeptical view of the message which the *Decameron* contained" (p. 28); see also Najemy: "We need not take too literally or seriously . . . Aeneas' expressed wish that from his story the young should learn to flee the sorrows of love and to dedicate themselves to a life of virtue" (p. 34).

[66] See Boulting, p. 140; and G. Papparelli, *Enea Silvio Piccolomini* (Bari, 1950), who refers to his "feigned moralism" (p. 93). Both see this as part of a broader phenomenon in medieval and Renaissance literature.

[67] George K. Anderson and William E. Buckler, eds., *The Literature of England*, Vol. 1 (Glenview, Ill.: Scott, Foresman and Co., 1968), pp. 390–92.

origin.[68] Translators typically responded to these concerns by adding a moral commentary to the tale so as to make its instructional value as explicit as possible. In a sense, they were hoping to prevent the one-sided readings of which Aeneas had accused his audience and which twentieth-century scholars have to some extent sustained. The translator begins the poem:

> By this little book thou mayest perceive my friend
>> The end of love not fained nor fortunable,
> By which right plainly thou mayest intend
>> That love is no pleasure but a pain perdurable,
>> And the end is death which is most lamentable,
> Therefore, ere thou be chained with such care
> By others' perils, take heed and beware.
> First by Eurialus, by whom perceive thou mayest,
>> The best it is to eschew shortly
> To drink of the cup, or of it to taste
>> That savoured more of gall than of honey.[69]

Aeneas' message is very clear. In part it is a statement that love brings long-lasting suffering and pain so strong that it can

---

[68]The outcry was particularly strong towards the middle of the century, when the Italian *novella* was just beginning to make its appearance in English literary culture—and precisely when *The History of the Two Lovers* was first translated. Roger Ascham's well-known criticism of the corrupting influence of Italian literature in his work *The Schoolmaster* (1567) symbolises this attitude of moral suspicion and distrust. See Beecher, pp. 32–38.

[69]Cf. with the Latin original: in the prefatory remarks, he writes:

> Instruit haec historia iuvenes, ne militia se accingant amoris, quae plus fellis habet umquam mellis sed obmissa lascivia, que homines reddit insanos, virtutis incumbant studiis, quae possessorem sui sola beare potest. In amore autem quot lateant mala, si quis nescit, hic poterit scire
> (And this will be a kind of warning to the young, to shun such trifles. So let all maidens attend and, profiting by this adventure, see to it that the loves of young men send them not to their perdition. And this story teaches youths not to arm themselves for the warfare of love, which is more bitter than sweet; but putting away passion, which drives men mad, to pursue the study of virtue, for she alone can make her possessor happy. While if there is anyone that does not know from other sources how many evils love conceals, he may learn from this) (Grierson, p. xxi).

and at the end:

even take the lover's life; and that if there are any pleasures to be found in it, they are far outweighed by its perils. It is a warning that the reader learn from the tale to beware of passion and to stay away from its dangers.

While scholars generally agree that the above statement represents the story's "edifying lesson," they remain divided over the precise meaning of Aeneas' words. On the basis of the adulterous nature of Lucrece and Eurialus' affair, one scholar has suggested that the author's warning is directed specifically at illicit love.[70] In the opinion of another, who notes the story's emphasis on issues of honour, the reference is to love of a dishonourable nature.[71] Still another argues that Aeneas' conclusion is meant to relate to the very specific situation of the tale's hero and heroine, and should in no way be understood as a general statement.[72] For the most part, however, the message has been read as a sweeping condemnation of love — with love being understood as sexual passion or lust; and given the very general nature of the statements made throughout tale, this last interpretation would seem the most appropriate. The more complicated part of Aeneas' statement is the nature of the sufferings which love is said to bring. Over the course of the tale, hero and heroine endure many different kinds of pain, some physical and psychological, others social and moral. It is in the context of these sufferings that the specifically ethical meaning of Aeneas' message emerges, and the story's relationship to moral culture begins to become more clear.

Perhaps the most obvious pains which Eurialus and Lucrece experience over the course of the story are the physiological and psychological ones: hero and heroine are described (and

---

quem qui legerint, periculum ex aliis faciant, quod sibi ex usu siet, nec amatorium bibere poculum studeant, quod longe plus aloes habet quam mellis.

(And may all who read [this story] take a lesson from others that will be useful to themselves: let them beware to drink the cup of love, that holds far more of bitter than of sweet) (Grierson, p. 135).

[70]Mitchell, p. 47.

[71]Morrall, *Aeneas Silvius Piccolomini (Pius II) and Nikolaus von Wyle*, pp. 23–24, 27–28.

[72]Bigi, "La Historia de Duobus Amantibus," pp. 163–65.

describe themselves) as being burned, wounded, weakened, and blinded by love. They also appear to undergo almost a mental breakdown, which makes them rage in a kind of furor or madness. Their emotional pain, moreover, is almost constant: they are anxious, at times to the point of desperation, when they are separated; and when they are together, they are troubled by the fear that their love will be discovered. As the poem at the conclusion of the story suggests, the pain is most severe when passion is brought to an end: the story reaches a powerful climax of emotional, psychological and physical agony at the scene of the lovers' parting. It is ultimately Lucrece who experiences the greatest physical suffering, but, as the narrator observes, for anyone who truly loves, the end is death: "If any man doth not know the dolour of death, let him consider the departing of two lovers, which hath more heaviness and more painful torment."[73] The vision of love as suffering and pain and the images with which these ideas are articulated had played a significant role in love literature since ancient times. It is not always evident from which period in this long literary tradition Aeneas draws his inspiration, but to a large extent the origin can be traced to classical authors. The words of Ovid, Virgil, Seneca, Terence and Juvenal among others are constantly interwoven with his own to create an unhappy and painful language of love.[74]

As well as hurting them in body and mind, passion carries moral consequences for the lovers, leading them to violate their vows of loyalty and to neglect their rightful duties. Lucrece, whose loyalty lies with her husband, family and country, recognizes these repercussions explicitly in her opening monologue: "Shall I betray, alas, the chaste spousels . . . . Shall I than forsake my mother, my husband and my country?" Further on in the tale her betrayal is emphasised symbolically in the ring she sends to Eurialus. The ring had originally been a gift from Lucrece's mother to Menelaus, and thus by entrusting it to her lover, Lucrece seems to violate both her family and her marital obligations. The immorality of her actions resonates still further

---

[73]Throughout the tale, both lovers allude constantly and overtly to death as the end of love.

[74]See the notes to the text for specific citations.

in the defensive attitude she takes to questions of her chastity, and in Eurialus' exaltation of female virtue in one of his early letters.[75] Passion also leads the hero to compromise his own very different vows of loyalty and fidelity. Inflamed by his passion for Lucrece, Eurialus is clearly distracted from his duties to the Emperor. Indeed, from the way he is portrayed in the story, he seems to devote all of his energy and attention to his lover. The language he uses to describe their affair reveals just how seriously his feelings of passion have interfered with his work: Lucrece is his ruler and commander, and he her obedient and loyal servant.[76] As the person to whom he feels his greatest loyalty, Lucrece has effectively taken the place of the Emperor. But passion causes Eurialus to neglect his responsibilities in still another way: in a desperate attempt to meet with Lucrece, he bribes Pandalus with a political office in exchange for his assistance in arranging a rendezvous for the lovers. Rather than to carry out his duties, Eurialus uses his authority as a means of fulfilling his own irresponsible desires. The conflict between the hero's passion and political duty is further reinforced by comparisons made between him and figures of antiquity who had also neglected their duties in order to pursue their desires — Julius Caesar, Alexander, Hannibal. The most significant of these parallels, however, is implied in the hero's name. Eurialus was the name of a handsome young Trojan warrior who appears as a minor character in Virgil's *Aeneid*.[77] In Book IX, he and his companion volunteer for a dangerous mission that will take them

---

[75]Summarizing Eurialus' letter, the narrator explains:

> The cause of his sending was his love, desiring no dishonesty. He believed her very honest and chaste, and so much more to be beloved, and that unhonest women and overliberal of their honour he did not only not love but also greatly hate. For, chastity lost, nothing is in a woman to be praised.

[76]In the Latin, the equation with the emperor is still more obvious (*imperium*).

[77]There are, in fact, two characters in classical literature who share his name, the other being the gladiator in a satire by Juvenal, *Satire* VI, 81ff. The fact that Eurialus, like Virgil's hero, has a companion named Nisus who is often introduced with the Virgilian epithet of "faithful" seems to suggest that the parallel is intended to be with the character from

through the enemy's camp. Eurialus is overcome with desire for the rich spoils of armour and weapons and abandons the mission to collect more booty.[78] The Trojan figure is admittedly driven by greed rather than by lust, as is the Eurialus of *The History of the Two Lovers*, but the parallel seems significant nonetheless: in the case of both figures, their strong feelings of passion lead them to neglect their political duties.[79]

Of all the many pains with which passion afflicts the lovers, there is one which is given particular prominence: the pain of dishonour and bad reputation.[80] For both hero and heroine, the indulgence of their desires stains both their honour and that of their families, and carries the threat of public disgrace in the event that their affair is disclosed. For Lucrece, honour and reputation are bound up in her chastity and fidelity to her husband; for Eurialus they are won through faithful service and obedience to the Emperor. Throughout the story, both lovers identify the dangers of a romantic liaison in terms of dishonour and disgrace. In the climax of her opening monologue, the lovesick Lucrece asks herself incredulously, "but shall I so lose my fame?" And in the subsequent conversation with her servant, Yosias, she is reminded explicitly of the dishonour her actions will bring: "Oh,

---

the *Aeneid*. Cf. Morrall, *Aeneas Silvius Piccolomini (Pius II). The Goodli History*, p. xxi.

[78]*Aeneid*, IX, 176–445. While the name would have been enough to recall the Virgilian hero, other aspects of his character seem to strengthen the alignment: both are soldiers, and faithful and close servants to their leaders; both are on missions to ensure that their leader is installed as head of Rome; and both are described as good looking and intelligent.

[79]The political consequences of passion are suggested by numerous other images. The story is full of allusions to classical tales in which love leads to political upheaval. The resonance is particularly strong in the names of the two other figures involved in the love triangle. Menelaus, king of Sparta, launched a long and bloody war against the Trojans when the son of the King of Troy abducted his wife, Helen. The rape of Lucretia, recalled in the name of the heroine, brought war and political upheaval to Rome.

[80]Cf. the slightly different interpretation of Morrall, *Aeneas Silvius Piccolomini (Pius II) and Nikolaus von Wyle*, p. 28, that "love with honour is morally degrading."

unhappy . . . thou shalt shame thy house, and only of all thy kin thou shalt be adultress."[81] Eurialus, in turn, considers the loss of honour a high price to pay for his fleeting moments of romantic pleasure. Again and again when the lovers are in danger and the threat of discovery is suddenly made very real, he becomes aware of the suffering such dishonour would bring: "Ah, fool that I am, I am taken; I am ashamed. I shall lose the Emperor's favour". And shortly after, he expresses similar concern at what could happen to his reputation: "What if any man had known me . . . ? what shame; what slander had both I and mine forever. The Emperor would have refused me and, as light and mad brained, might have esteemed me." It is in his letter to Lucrece at the end of the tale, however, where he reveals most clearly how painful this transgression of social mores will be for both him and for his lover. Here, the consequences of dishonour and disgrace are singled out as the specific reasons for bringing an end to their affair. Eurialus explains:

> Thou sayest thy taking away should be the greatest pleasure that could be to me. It is truth, and greater delight I could not have than thee always at my desire. But I must rather take heed to thy honour than to my lust . . . . If I take thee away (beside my shame that for thy sake I set little by) what dishonour shouldest thou do to all thy friends? What sorrow should thy mother take? What should be then spoken of thee? What rumour should all the world hear of thee? . . . If I should carry thee about with me and have thee in my tent as a follower of the field, what reprefe and shame should it be both to thee and me. For these causes, I beseech thee, my Lucrece, put away this mind and remember thy honour . . . .

Presenting the narrator's opinion as much as his own, Eurialus makes it very clear in these comments that dishonour and a bad reputation represent very dangerous and unpleasant consequences. And while he recognizes the physical and emotional pleasures of his romance with Lucrece, he sees at the same time that they are far outweighed by the sufferings they bring.

The social repercussions of the romance are also emphasized in more indirect ways. They are underlined in the constant

---

[81]Yosias reiterates these ideas later on in the story: "my mistress is undone, and the house shamed forever".

allusions, direct and indirect, to classical figures who also jeopardized their honour and reputation by deciding to pursue their desires (Dido, Phaedra, Helen). They resonate in the irony of Eurialus' conversation with Pandalus, in which he ingeniously presents a rendezvous with Lucrece as the only way to preserve the honour and reputation of the heroine and her house.[82] The shame which their love brings them is also emphasized symbolically. In order to pass unnoticed into the house of Lucrece, Eurialus must dress in sackcloth and blacken his face as though he were a servant. The narrator is the first to point out the shamefulness of his actions, but later, upon reflection, Eurialus himself feels embarassed by his behaviour and realizes how humiliated he would have been had his identity been revealed. In dishonour and public disgrace lies much pain for both the hero and the heroine of Aeneas' tale.

It should be pointed out that interspersed with these various images of pain and suffering are other ones of the joys of love. Lucrece and Eurialus' rendezvous, and their sexual encounters in particular, are consistently described as exceptionally pleasurable. But in the words of the concluding poem, there is clearly more gall to their romance than there is honey. The moments of delight are few and fleeting, while those of suffering seem only to grow stronger as the story moves towards its climax and conclusion.

The very negative vision of love which emerges from *The History of the Two Lovers* fits smoothly into the intellectual currents both of Aeneas' day and of Tudor England. As well as sustaining the traditional images of love's physical and psychological torments, thinkers and writers of both cultures, and the humanists in particular, tended to present passion as a dangerous threat to female virtue, to men's civic interests and duties and, in

---

[82] What if she determined to follow me? What dishonour should it be to your kin? What mock among people? What shame as well to all the town as to you? . . . For first thou shalt save the honour of the house, and hide the love that in no wise can be published without your shame . . . . Help therefore both her and me and save thy house from shame . . . . I commit unto thee both Lucrece, we, our love and fame, and the honour of thy kin.

particular, to the pursuit of honour.[83] Perhaps more important, however, is the fact that these intellectual issues aligned with the values of their society. In both fifteenth-century Italy and sixteenth-century England the control of female chastity represented the very key to social order; involvement in civic and public duties was a source of esteem; and honour was one of the most important values in the code of social morality, the basis of success in public life, and the definition of a good reputation.[84] Thus, while the conception of love in Aeneas' tale aligns with the ideals of literary and intellectual culture, it should also be recognized as a reflection and indeed promotion of the morals of his contemporary society as well as that of Tudor England.

With this in mind, we have come full circle from the interpretation of the story put forth in the first half of this century. Far from a profligate and social rebel, Aeneas appears to be a supporter of the morality of his day. While the Boccaccian concept of love as natural law does find an advocate in his tale, it is not Aeneas' voice that is exulting such "liberal sexual mores." It is true, as several scholars have pointed out, that Lucrece, in her complete and unshakable obedience to love's rule, and in her willingness to sacrifice everything for her desire, even her own life, does indeed represent the portrait of a true Boccaccian heroine,[85] but it is Eurialus, who ultimately turns away from this attitude to embrace morality as his supreme law, that is the true hero of Aeneas' tale.[86] His final letter to Lucrece represents the

---

[83]Beecher, pp. 32, 42, 43, 68; and Olga Pugliese, "La nouvelle conception de l'amour," in *L'Epoque de la Renaissance* (Budapest, 1988), pp. 215–18. It should also be noted that, like Aeneas', their skeptical views often went hand in hand with a misogynistic attitude towards women.

[84]See Beecher, pp. 32–34; and Morall, *Aeneas Silvius Piccolomini (Pius II) and Nikolaus von Wyle*, pp. 23–24.

[85]Firpo, p. 12; Viti, p. 263; and Morrall, *Aeneas Silvius Piccolomini (Pius II) and Nikolaus von Wyle*, p. 19.

[86]Cf. Morrall, *Aeneas Silvius Piccolomini (Pius II) and Nikolaus von Wyle*, p. 23:

> His conduct was in no way discreditable. On the contrary, the hero chooses duty to his royal master and refuses to destroy the good repute of his

turning point in both the development of his character and of the story as a whole, and articulates explicitly the ethical signifi- cance of the tale's edifying message: "But he were no true lover that would regard rather his own lust than thy fame." It is these words which define the story's conception of the proper relation- ship between passion and moral convention. In the same way as it does at the level of narrative, *The History of the Two Lovers* does not so much reiterate Boccaccio as it does engage him in dialogue, and in this case in particular, overturn his views.[87]

---

mistress and ruin her marriage. It is a sensible choice, entirely appropriate in a society which accepted illicit love-matches and the hypocrisies which accompanied them as long as the rule was observed that no challenge was offered to social decorum.

[87] Aeneas adopts the same critical and cautious attitude towards love in his private correspondence as he does in the tale of Eurialus and Lucrece. Scholars point often to a pair of letters written almost two years after he wrote *The History of the Two Lovers* (and, perhaps significantly, after he had entered the priesthood), which present a still more intense diatribe against love, and against women, in particular (the letter to Johann Vrunt, 8 March 1446, Wolkan, Vol. 2, Ep. 6, pp. 30–33; the letter to Ippolito da Milano, 3 January 1446, Wolkan, Vol. 2, Ep. 7, pp. 33–39. The latter one is often referred to as his "Remedia amoris"). Aeneas' discussion of these issues is actually considerably more extensive, and begins long before he wrote the tale of Lucrece and Eurialus. In the years leading up to the composition of the story, Aeneas was writing almost constantly on the subject of love, usually in the form of comments on the romantic adventures of friends and family. In the context of these letters, he articulates and defends the same opinions seen in *The History of the Two Lovers*, and uses, moreover, the same images, allusions and turns of phrase to do so. Writing to his nephew, Antonio Tedeschi, who seems to have abandoned his studies to pursue a romantic interest, he warns him of the brevity of love's joys ("aliqua fortisan formosa puella, tuo capta nitore, te cepit teque quasi catenis ligatum retinet. tu eius delicias sequeris beatumque te putas, dum in amplexus venis illius. sed longe deceptus es" [Wolkan, Vol. 1, Ep. 37, p. 113]). He remarks to his friend Niccolo Amidano on the pain and suffering of romantic passion, which has "multum fellis parumque mellis" (Wolkan, Vol. 1, Ep. 63, July 1443, pp. 163–64). And in a letter to Kaspar Schlick, Aeneas expresses his concern at the chancellor's idea of bringing his wife on his travels for imperial business: "regis negotia curare habetis, non bene conveniunt

* * *

The position which *The History of the Two Lovers* occupies in moral culture cannot be determined, however, simply on the basis of this philosophy of love. It is also necessary to consider the approach which Aeneas uses to communicate this message. Several scholars have identified in the tale a traditional approach to ethical instruction, while others have pointed — more indirectly than directly — to several elements which clearly stand outside this tradition. It has not yet been determined how to reconcile these two lines of interpretation but the solution seems to lie in a closer examination of the text in the light of moral traditions. The differences between Aeneas' tale and standard methods of instruction are in this way revealed to be considerable. In fact, not only does *The History of the Two Lovers* diverge from traditional ethical discipline, it also criticizes it, questioning the effectiveness of its methodology and undermining the validity of its ideals. The image of the tale as a moral rebellion is therefore justified — but not in the terms in which it was originally conceived: rather than the morals themselves, it is the methods of teaching them which Aeneas' story challenges.

The ethical culture in which *The History of the Two Lovers* was composed, and was translated over a century later, was grounded in the tradition of the *exemplum*, the short moralizing fable out of which the *novella* had originally evolved. The aim of the *exemplum* was to illustrate abstract ideals of moral behaviour using concrete examples from life. The characters who people its stories are either models of moral perfection or the very essence of moral depravity; indeed, sometimes they seem little more than personifications of a particular virtue or vice. Their moral integrity, or lack thereof, is suggested primarily by their actions as they confront a series of temptations, and is reinforced by the narrator's concluding maxim, either exulting virtue or condemning vice. Though the tales themselves often claim to be based

---

nec in una sede morantur rerum publicae et amor uxoris" (Wolkan, Vol. 1, Ep. 94, 1 November 1443, p. 213). *The History of the Two Lovers* thus represents not only part of a larger current in Aeneas' thought, but also a reflection of his own personal attitudes towards love, forged in the context of real experience.

on historical events from a distant past, the morality which they celebrate belongs to an ideal world; the *exemplum* is designed to represent how men and women ought to behave, rather than how they usually do in reality. At the same time, however, the morality they describe is held up as an ideal well within the reach of humanity: the exhortation that typically followed these moralizing tales was for imitation, not approximation, of the virtue illustrated therein. Thus, through the *exemplum*, moral perfection became a realistic goal to which men and women were taught to aspire, and the standard against which their actions were ultimately measured and judged.[88]

The *exemplum* tradition had been the foundation of Christian ethics in Europe since the Middle Ages, and continued to be the most significant component in moral persuasion well into the time when *The History of the Two Lovers* was published in England.[89] It represented the cornerstone of the sermon, the fundamental vehicle by which the Church communicated its code of ethics to its flock. Preachers typically instructed their audiences by parading out incarnations of virtues and vices, exhorting their listeners to embrace the same rigours of moral purity exemplified in their stories.[90] The *exemplum* also informed much of secular literature of the same period, and most notably the *novella*. The edifying message woven into these stories was often a very traditional one of ascetic ideals. The characters in the *novella* were thus often represented as embodiments of specific ethical qualities, while the narrative itself was typically punctuated with moralizing statements and concluded with a kind of maxim. Whether in sacred or profane contexts, the *exempla* used for instruction for

---

[88]S. Battaglia, "L'esempio medioevale," *Filologia romanza* 6 (1959) pp. 60ff; J.Th. Welter, *L'exemplum dans la littérature religieuse et didactique du moyen âge* (Paris, 1927); Carlo Delcorno, *L'exemplum e letteratura tra medioevo e rinascimento* (Bologna: Mulino, 1989).

[89]Curtius, *European Literature in the Latin Middle Ages* (Princeton, 1973), pp. 59–61; J.Th. Welter, p. 423; and Beecher, p. 37.

[90]The Franciscan and Dominican orders were particularly well known for their mastery of this form of preaching. The most famous among them was San Bernardino of Siena (1380–1444), who travelled extensively throughout Italy, attracting vast audiences for his sermons.

the most part were not original. As it had been in the previous centuries, the voice of morality was that of the *magni auctores* of ancient pagan and early Christian cultures. Sermons and moral treatises drew heavily on the Church Fathers such as Ambrose, Jerome, and Augustine; on classical authors, especially Ovid; and on the catalogues and collections of *exempla* which had been compiled both recently and in the distant past.[91] One of the most popular sources, in fact, was the first-century *Factorum et dictorum memorabilium libri novem* of Valerius Maximus, a veritable encyclopaedia of moral precepts. In many ways this volume also carries a symbolic importance as well: its encyclopaedic format, authoritative tone, and paradigmatic understanding of morality embodies the very essence of ethical culture in Aeneas' day.

The clearest link between *The History of the Two Lovers* and the *exemplum* tradition lies in the closing line of the tale:

> Therefore, ere thou be chained with such care
> By others' perils, take heed and beware.
> First by Eurialus, by whom perceive thou mayest,
> The best it is to eschew shortly
> To drink of the cup, or to of it taste
> That savoured more of gall than of honey.[92]

---

[91]Riccardo Fubini, *Umanesimo e Secolarizzazione da Petrarca a Valla* (Rome: Bulzoni, 1990), pp. 145–49, 154–59; Salvatore Battaglia, "La Tradizione di Ovidio nel Medioevo," *Filologia Romanza* VI (1959), fasc. 1, pp. 185–204; Ovid was considered "bonorum morum instructor, malorum vero extirpator" (p. 200). The encyclopaedic mentality is also reflected in the new codifications and compilations of *exempla* that continued to appear steadily throughout the fifteenth century, particularly in Northern Europe. See, for example, Meffreth (d. 1447), *Hortulus reginae*; Jean Gritsch (d. 1449), *Quadrigesimale*; Gottschalk Hollen (d. 1481), *Sermonum opus* (J.Th. Welter, pp. 418–23). Besides being distinguished for his skill and popularity as an orator, Bernardino was also distinguished from his contemporaries by his tendency to introduce original *exempla* into his sermons and relate them to his contemporary setting.

[92]See above, n. 69 for the Latin version and translation. The list of classical figures which follows these lines is an embellishment of the translator.

There are two things in Aeneas' words which recall traditional moral instruction: the identification of Eurialus' actions as a kind of model by which readers should take heed; and the final three lines which resonate like the moral maxims that typically conclude *exempla*. More than one scholar has stated on the basis of these similarities that Aeneas' tale should be seen as a kind of new *exemplum* (or even a *novella* in the "*exemplum* style") and thus fundamentally in line with traditional methods of moral instruction.[93]

The story's relationship to ethical tradition, however, is far more complicated than what is illustrated in these concluding lines. In the narrative itself there are several significant points at which Aeneas diverges from the standard *exemplum*, and to such a degree that his approach to teaching ethics can only be defined as untraditional. In fact, when considered in the context of the story, what appears to align with the *exemplum* tradition actually represents a criticism against it.

Perhaps the most obvious divergence is at the level of characterization. In *The History of the Two Lovers* moral integrity is not painted in extremes of virtue and vice, but rather as a more complex blend of moral strength and weakness. Hero and heroine are described throughout the story as stumbling back and forth between vice and virtue.[94] It is true that one does eventually end up choosing the "right" way, and the other the "wrong," but the path that leads to these destinations is a very long and winding one. Rather than providing absolute models of moral behaviour, the tale of Eurialus and Lucrece represents the real experience of typical human beings who are attempting to imitate such models. If in some sense they are *exempla*, they are *exempla* of a very

---

[93]Doglio, *La storia di due amanti*, pp. 43–44; Viti, pp. 248–49; and Borri, pp. 189–91. Borri also mentions in passing the "exemplary" quality of the characters; and describes the warning as having a "punitive component" typical of the *exemplum* tradition, although he goes on to say that the idea of punishment seems less direct and less severe than what was traditional (p. 191).

[94]Eurialus does so even more than Lucrece.

different kind from that of tradition: they are witnesses of human experience rather than behavioural ideals.[95]

As well as changing the traditional moral make-up of his characters, Aeneas adds a new dimension to the study of their behaviour. As mentioned earlier, morality in the *exemplum* tradition was viewed almost exclusively through action, with only passing references to the characters' interior. The psychological portraits so foreign to the *exemplum*-based *novella* not surprisingly, were also largely absent in a moral pedagogy of similar foundations. It was considered more important to provide a clear outline of the goals of moral behaviour than of the journey necessary to reach them. The tale of Eurialus and Lucrece, in contrast, shows in great detail exactly how and why its characters act the way they do. The human psyche is represented as a battlefield between passion, encouraging the indulgence of desires, and reason, which urges the respect of social morals. The pattern of struggle is different for Lucrece and Eurialus, but for both of them it is equally difficult. Again and again, passion emerges as an inconquerable force, while reason, in contrast, is shown to be fragile and unreliable. In the conclusion of the story, Aeneas assures his audience that reason, weak though it may be, is in fact capable of conquering passion, and that virtue can ultimately be attained. But he also leaves the very vivid impression of what a difficult road it is to follow, and how, by the very nature of the human condition, it is almost impossible not to stumble along the way.[96] The explicit warning at the end of the story to stay away from love is thus qualified implicitly with Aeneas' acknowledgement that he is asking of his readers a formidable task.

Finally, it should be noted that, although the concluding lines of Aeneas' tale are written in a moralizing tone, the story itself

---

[95]See Bigi, *Poesia latina e volgare nel Rinascimento italiano*, p. 70.

[96]This message is made all the more emphatic by the fact that Eurialus and Lucrece seem such unlikely candidates for making such errors: Lucrece is famed for extraordinary virtue, and Eurialus particularly dedicated to his career as an imperial soldier.

is distinctly not.[97] There is little evidence of such an attitude in the author's many intrusions into the narrative. His comments are not so much criticisms of individuals' actions as they are general and somewhat cynical observations (and exclamations) about human nature.[98] Many scholars, moreover, have even claimed to detect a tone of sympathy in the general portrayals of hero and heroine. Indeed, even Lucrece, whose misogynistic descriptions represent perhaps the closest thing in the story to moral judgment, seems to win the admiration of the author on account of the strength of her love, tenderness of her passion and her ardent sensitivity.[99] The same effect is achieved more indirectly by the image of love which the story conveys. So strong, so overwhelming, and so involuntary are their feelings of passion that at times hero and heroine seem to be more victims of destiny than culprits. Rather than condemnation, they rouse the reader's pity and compassion, and nowhere more so than in the powerful scene of their parting, where their pain is made very real.

It would be wrong to read this sympathy and absence of judgment as indifference to, or even less, a condonement of the lovers' behaviour.[100] From what has been discussed above, it is clear that Aeneas very much upheld the social mores of his day, and that it was Eurialus', not Lucrece's, decision of which he approved. It should also be clear, however, that Aeneas had a profound

---

[97]See Borri's qualified interpretation of the story as an *exemplum*: "in Aeneas Silvius Piccolomini the educational *exemplum* is not concerned with the direct and drastic punishment of sin" (p. 191); see also Di Francia, pp. 313–14.

[98]Di Francia, pp. 312–13, describes his comments as "judicious," "wise" and "noble." He concludes that "it should not be thought that Aeneas Silvius was excessively concerned with morality . . . . It would be a mistake" (p. 313). Cf. Viti, "Mandragola," p. 248.

[99]Morrall, *Aeneas Silvius Piccolomini (Pius II) and Nikolaus von Wyle*, p. 24; *Aeneas Silvius Piccolomini (Pius II). The Goodli History*, p. xxii; and Bigi, "La Historia de duobus amantibus," p. 169.

[100]See, though, the curious comment early on in the tale, in which the narrator seems to justify the lovers' affair: Lucrece's husband is introduced as "unworthy to whom such beauty should serve at home, but well worthy of his wife to be deceived."

understanding of the human condition, and it is this which represents the key to unlocking the tone of the story. Neither indifference nor approval, Aeneas' attitude should be understood instead as one of acceptance and forgiveness, reflecting his recognition of the sad inevitability of human error.

The History of the Two Lovers thus seems to represent a significant break with the *exemplum* tradition, and thereby with moral culture more generally. By making his characters realistic human beings instead of incarnations of virtue and vice, Aeneas redefines the traditional basis of moral instruction. Moreover, by exploring the long and winding path that leads to virtue, he introduces new dimensions into traditional discussions of moral behaviour. And while he continues to maintain the same high ideals as did the *exemplum*, he balances or perhaps "humanizes" these expectations with a sense of realism and a compassionate understanding of failure. What distinguishes this untraditional approach to ethical teaching at all levels is its fundamentally human quality, a reflection of Aeneas' profound understanding of human nature, and his faithful adherence to real experience.

The story's relationship to moral tradition is, however, still more complicated. If *The History of the Two Lovers* can be described as turning away from the *exemplum* tradition, it also turns against it. At various points in the story, Aeneas seems to call into question the effectiveness of the *exemplum* as a means for teaching ethics. He does so indirectly, using the hero and heroine of the tale as his mouthpiece. In confronting the moral issues involved in their affair, both Eurialus and Lucrece turn for guidance to their traditional moral educations. Instead of choosing the path of virtue, however, they end up embracing vice, largely as a result of misinterpretations and misuse of *exempla*. While their approach casts the two characters in a bad light, it also exposes a series of problems inherent in the *exemplum* tradition itself, and still others that emerge when this instruction is put into practice in the real world.

The first to apply the lessons of traditional moral education is Lucrece. In her opening monologue, the heroine vacillates back and forth, now listening to the temptations of passion, now to the interrogations of her reason. Towards the end of the battle, when her reason reminds her of the impact any involvement

with Eurialus would have on her reputation, she counters with
the example of a trio of ancient literary figures, famous in particular from Ovid, an important source for *exempla*: "Nothing
shall he dare," she states, "that feareth the threatening of fame,
many others have done the same. Helena would be ravished.
Paris carried her not away against her will. What shall I tell of
Diana [Ariadne] and Medea?"[101] The examples to which Lucrece
makes appeal are hardly the models of moral excellence which
preachers would have exhorted their audiences to imitate. On
the contrary, they seem much more like those which would have
been held up as examples to avoid. What seems important to
Lucrece is not so much what she is imitating as the very action of
imitation itself. Precedent alone becomes the authority by which
she steers her actions. As a preface to her list of *exempla*, Lucrece
introduces her point in a distinctly proverbial manner ("Nothing
shall he dare that feareth the threatening of fame"); and in the
triumphant cry with which she concludes her speech she takes
the same approach: "No man blameth the faulter who faulteth
with many."[102] From a moral perspective Lucrece's maxims are
absurd, and the second one in particular, which claims for her
a kind of immunity to moral judgment. As in the case with the
exempla themselves, the form rather than the substance of ethical
teaching becomes the authority by which she sanctions her actions, and absolves herself of guilt. Lucrece's words clearly reveal
her own failure to grasp some of the most basic principles of the
exemplum tradition. At the same time, however, they illustrate
how easily these tools of moral instruction can be misunderstood
and manipulated in real life. Whatever its intentions may be, the

---

[101]It should be noted that here, and in all places where Lucrece and
Eurialus reason with *exempla*, Aeneas is not quoting from another text.

[102]Cf. Morrall, *Aeneas Silvius Piccolomini (Pius II) and Nikolaus von Wyle*,
p. 19:

> [Lucrece] fortifies her determination with an utterance which has the ring
> of a proverb, and she recalls other classical models, Ariadne and Medea,
> for the choice she is about to make . . . . At the end of the story she pleads
> to be allowed to accompany Eurialus . . . . Like Helen she would willingly
> be abducted by force.

exemplum clearly has the dangerous potential to defend vice as much as virtue.

In her conversation with Yosias which follows this monologue, Lucrece adopts the same method of reasoning. Troubled by her servant's reminder of the shame which adultery will bring, and yet still feeling the fires of passion within her, Lucrece, exasperated, concludes that suicide is the only way to save her virtue. When Yosias tries to dissuade her from taking such action and vows to stop her should she try, she declares his efforts futile, and defends herself by pointing to two more *exempla*: "I am determined . . . to die. Collatinus' wife [Lucretia] venged with a sword . . . . Who that determineth to die cannot be let. Portia, at the death of Brutus, when weapon was taken from her did eat hot coals." Like Lucretia, the figure of Portia was a famous *exemplum* singled out by Valerius Maximus for her extraordinary virtue.[103] It was not, however, their "determination in death" that had earned them recognition and respect, but rather the reason behind their suicide: they took their lives in the name of chastity and marital fidelity. Lucrece appears to understand the exemplary value of these figures by their actions, rather than by their motivations. Thus, while in her earlier speech she chooses the wrong examples, this time she chooses the right ones, but for the wrong reasons. As before, Lucrece lends authority to her position by phrasing her argument in a maxim: "Who that determineth to die cannot be let." Here, once again, she seems to have learned only half of what moral instruction intended, and what she has learned she uses to fulfill and defend her immoral desires. Instead of counselling prudence and moral rectitude, her knowledge of *exempla* continues to lead her down a dangerous path of imprudent action.

At the end of the story Lucrece is still using the same approach, and indeed, the very same Ovidian models which she used in her first speech reappear in this final illustration of her moral reasoning. In her last letter to Eurialus, as she begs him to carry her off with him to Germany, she recalls the figure of Helen: "take

---

[103]In the *Factorum et dictorum memorabilium libri novem*, the suicide of Portia is included in Book IV, chapter 6, as an example of conjugal love ("De amore coniugali").

me away. It is no great pain to take one away that would be gone, nor think it no shame. For Paris the son of a king did likewise." Lucrece's argument seems grounded in a variation on the maxim which concluded her first speech: "No man blameth who faulteth with great and important people." Again, the model of another not only lends authority to her actions but also absolves her from moral responsibility. But while Lucrece may be convinced that such behaviour brings no shame, society would not have been of the same opinion. Having led her to compromise her virtue, the *exemplum* tradition drives her, here, at the very climax of the story, toward destroying what were considered among her most precious possessions: her honour and her good name.

That Lucrece's behaviour is not simply part of the story's broader misogynistic polemic is evident from the fact that Eurialus demonstrates the very same kind of reasoning. In his opening monologue, he too finds justification for surrendering to his passion in a series of precedents — famous warriors (Julius Caesar, Alexander, Hannibal), poets (Virgil), philosophers (Aristotle), and legendary heroes (Hercules) — all of whom indulged their sexual desires. As were Helen, Medea and Diana, Eurialus' gallery of *exempla* are more appropriate as models to avoid than to follow. He appears, moreover, to be taking the same line of reasoning as Lucrece when, in her final letter, she finds justification and moral reprieve for her actions in the overall greatness of the figure rather than in the moral merit of his behaviour. The hero concludes his argument slightly differently from the heroine, however: rather than making up an absurd maxim of his own, he rejects one that is "said commonly" — and one, significantly, which articulates the very essence of the story's moral message: "It is not true that is said commonly: honour and love accord not together." Ironically, what leads Eurialus to make this bold statement is his earlier misinterpretation of the role of precedent. One misunderstanding leads to another in a dangerous pattern of reasoning, leaving the hero feeling fully justified in proceeding down an immoral path. Like Lucrece, Eurialus has managed to use the *exemplum* to clear rather than challenge his conscience.

The problems of the *exemplum* tradition are illustrated most thoroughly and explicitly, however, in the debate that takes place between the two lovers in the course of their literary courtship. In her third letter to Eurialus, Lucrece reveals that she is reluctant to become involved with a foreigner for fear of being abandoned upon his return home. To justify her concern, she cites a series of literary women whose lovers had left them behind, again calling up *exempla* from Ovid's *Heroides*: "Many examples do move to refuse a stranger's love; Jason, . . . Theseus, . . . Aeneas . . . ." Significantly, the stories she uses to argue against an affair are the very same ones which she had brought up in an earlier speech to sanction the pursuit of her desires: Medea, Ariadne, Dido are the counterparts respectively of Jason, Theseus and Aeneas. For Lucrece, there is no absolute value in these *exempla*. Rather than using them as a guide to virtue, she manipulates them so as to support a previously established position. In response to her list of classical figures, Eurialus presents a formidable list of his own, both of women who betrayed men ("But more are to be brought, my Lucrece, whom women hath deceived: Troilus by Cressida, Deiphus by Helena; and Circe by her enchantments deceived her lovers") and of foreign men who had abandoned their homes to live with their lovers ("it is read that the Greeks returning from Troy . . . tarried with their loves, content rather to want their friend, their houses, their reigns, and other dear things of their country than to forsake their ladies"). While soothing Lucrece's fears, Eurialus' gallery also exposes the flaws in her approach to the *exemplum* tradition: for every example there can be found an opposite, so that any argument that is rooted in the concept of precedent alone is a fundamentally precarious one. Eurialus makes this explicit in his reproach of Lucrece: "But it were not according by the deeds of a few to judge all the rest. Shouldest thou for a certain ill man abhor and accuse all men? Or I, for many ill women, hate all the rest?".[104] But while the hero is able to identify the problems inherent in this technique of

---

[104]Cf. Najemy, who describes the hero's reaction to Lucrece's citation of Medea, Ariadne, and Dido:

> Eurialus responds, as if in a debate, with a barrage of literary learning and counterexamples. . . . Eurialus is "enflamed" and, it seems, challenged by Lucretia's appeal to *literary tradition* . . . . His promise never to leave Siena and in any case never to abandon Lucretia seems motivated more *by a mimetic attachment to his literary example of the Achaeans than*

argumentation, he shows no intention of discarding it himself. Indeed, his comments on the *exemplum* seem hypocritical after he takes advantage of the very same technique to convince Lucrece of his noble intentions. Immediately after pronouncing these criticisms he goes on: "Nay, rather let us take other examples, as was of Anthony and Cleopatra." Whether unwilling or unable, the heroine does not perceive the contradiction in his arguments, and it is only in Eurialus' final letter, when he admits to her his plans for his imminent return to Germany, that his statements about the *exemplum* will begin to make some sense, and in a very painful way.

It is in the context of this broader discussion that we can now turn back to the moral maxim at the conclusion of Aeneas' tale. As well as in the closing remarks, the statement appears in the narrative itself, and more precisely in the mouth of the hero. In the lovers' final rendezvous, Lucrece, weakened by love, swoons into the arms of Eurialus, leaving him frightened and concerned for his own safety. He chastizes himself, recalling what he has apparently known all along about love: "Alas, unhappy love that has in thee more gall than honey." Eurialus' words, however, have little effect on his behaviour. When Lucrece revives moments later, he suddenly forgets his wise reminder and resumes his lovemaking, unconcerned. With the hero's experience as a dramatic illustration of the ineffectiveness of these words, the readers should think twice before they take to heart a moral maxim which paraphrases the same statement. In the context of the story, Aeneas' concluding maxim is far more ironic than it is moralizing. Rather than a valuable tool for moral guidance, the final lines of the tale are an invitation for reflection on an ethical culture which relies on the *exemplum* as a means of inculcating morals.[105]

> *by any practical assessment of how he could really leave the emperor's service* (p. 38–39; italics mine)

[105]This attitude to the *exemplum* tradition may also be reflected in a passage in the letter to Sozzini, which so far has only been read in the context of the debate over the story's realism:

> Nec vetustis aut obliteratis utar *exemplis*, sed nostri temporis ardentes faces exponam; nec Troianos nec Babilonios sed nostre urbis amores audies

While Aeneas' tale challenges the methodology of traditional moral instruction, it also seems to question the validity of one *exemplum* in particular: the figure of Lucretia. Her association with Lucrece has already been discussed from the point of view of the heroine, but the relationship between the two women has yet to be considered from the perspective of the Roman figure. While the name Lucretia underlines the hypocrisy of Aeneas' heroine, there are more subtle links between the stories of the two women which cast a shadow instead over the *exemplum* of Lucretia, and more specifically over her claims to chastity.

Lucretia's purity is first called into question by the pattern of connections between the two stories. There are many aspects of Lucrece's situation apart from her name which recall that of Lucretia: both women are young wives of noblemen, and both are renowned for their extraordinary beauty and virtue.[106] Their lovers, moreover, are attracted by their chastity as well as their physical appearance. In the scene preceding their first (and for the Roman Lucretia, also the last) rendezvous, the women are found at their sewing; and when their lovers announce their intentions, they put up a struggle, and are quickly overpowered.[107] Finally, they both take their own lives as a result

---

. . .

(Nor shall I make use of old forgotten types, but I'll bring forth torches that burned in our own days. You will not hear the loves of Troy and Babylon . . .) (Grierson, p. xx)

[106]For this and most of these similarities, see the detailed account of Lucretia in Livy I.lvii.

[107]The sixteenth-century English version presents Lucrece's resistance as genuine: "And taking her garment, the striving woman that would not be overcome, he overcame." According to the Latin text, however, Lucrece's struggles were only an act: "Acceptaque mulieris veste pugnantem feminam, que vincere nolebat, abs negotio vicit." ("And having taken off her clothes, without effort he overcame the struggling woman, who did not want to overcome him" [Doglio, *La storia di due amanti*, p. 108]). Such behaviour is entirely consistent with the dissimulating mask of disinterest and disgust she shows Eurialus at the beginning of their correspondence.

of their encounters.[108] Lucrece's experience does not, of course, represent a re-enactment of the story of Lucretia; but it does, nevertheless, present parallels with the Roman figure at key points in the situation and plot, and ones which audiences of fifteenth- and sixteenth-century Europe would have recognized as similar to the *exemplum*. Behind these familiar actions, however, are strikingly unfamiliar motivations: while Lucretia is moved by the purest feelings of chastity, Lucrece is driven by an almost uncontrollable passion. Equally important is the different way in which their motivations are presented: in keeping with the traditional style of the *exemplum*, the accounts of the Roman figure provide only a cursory sketch of the psychology of her response; the reader must accept on faith the authorities' interpretation of her underlying motives. Aeneas' story, in contrast, illuminates the thoughts and feelings of his heroine in intimate detail, and, indeed, even allows her to speak directly to the reader. From the standpoint of Lucretia, the pattern of similarities and contrasts between these two stories has some disturbing implications: suddenly, it seems very dangerous to assume that her motives must necessarily have been purity and chastity. Unless her own thoughts and feelings are unveiled, it seems impossible to determine whether she was truly motivated by virtue. Given what *The History of the Two Lovers* presents as the very natural and very powerful feelings of passion in Lucrece, it begins to seem very plausible that the supposedly perfect model of purity and marital fidelity is, in fact, a hypocrite and a fraud.

The purity of Lucretia's intentions is again called into question in what appears to be the narrator's allusive dialogue with Augustine, the most important authority on Lucretia's exemplary status in the Christian tradition. In *De civitate Dei*, Augustine

---

[108]While some of these parallels could refer to any number of different stories, the presence of linguistic connections with the accounts of this ancient *exemplum* makes it still more plausible that Aeneas had the story of the Roman Lucretia specifically in mind (cf., for example, Valerius Maximus' description of Lucretia: "Dux Romanae pudicitiae Lucretia, cuius *virilis animus* maligno errore fortuna e *muliebre corpus* sortitus est"; and Aeneas' of Lucrece: "sed temperatum verecundiae metum,*virilem animum femineo corde*gerabat"). The English translation varies from the Latin: "but under the dread of shame she cared in a woman's heart".

defends Lucretia's innocence of adultery on the basis that she
had submitted unwillingly to her seductor. He argues that while
their bodies were joined, their souls remained distinct, and with
this spiritual division her chastity must necessarily have been
preserved. He explains:

> "There were two and only one committed adultery." Very striking
> and very true! For he, taking into consideration in this intermin-
> gling of two bodies the utterly foul passion on the one side and
> the utterly chaste will of the other, and paying attention, not to the
> union of the bodies, but to the variance of the souls says: "There
> were two . . . ."[109]

The History of the Two Lovers defines the relationship between
Lucrece and Eurialus in precisely the opposite terms. In the very
significant and powerful passage which describes the lovers'
parting, Aeneas uses the same division of corporal and spiritual
to describe the relationship of the hero and heroine of his story.
But rather than the division of their souls, he emphasises their
union, and in so doing undermines the point which represents
the very key to Augustine's defense:

> But when two souls be joined together, so much is the division
> more painful, in so much as the delight of either of them is more
> sensible. And surely here was not two souls, but surely as weeneth
> Aristophanes, one soul in two bodies. So departed not one mind
> from another, but one love and one mind was in two divided; and
> the heart suffered partition.[110]

That Aeneas was making in this passage a deliberate allusion to
Augustine is confirmed by a comparison of the two texts in their
Latin original.[111] The same words appear in both passages, only
in *The History of the Two Lovers* they are twisted in such a way as to

---

[109]Translation by George McCracken, *The City of God Against the Pa-
gans*, Vol. 1 (Cambridge, Mass.: Harvard University Press, 1958), p. 85.

[110]In the English translation *animos* is rendered as "minds"; to demonstrate the consistency with Augustine's words, it is translated as "souls".

[111]Italics mine:

> Mirabile dictu, *'duo fuerunt, et adulterium unus admisit.'* Splendide
> atque verissime. Intuens enim *in duorum corporum commixtione unius*
> inquinatissimam cupiditatem, alterius castissimam voluntatem, et non

argue the opposite point. If the pattern of parallels and contrasts in the two stories leaves room to doubt Lucretia's purity, the allusion to Augustine represents still more of a direct challenge to such a claim. By reusing the words of this Church Father, the passage seems to be describing Lucretia as much as it does Lucrece, and in so doing, offers a dramatically different interpretation of her tale. What makes this allusion still more significant, however, is the level at which Aeneas directs his criticism. In its dialogue with Augustine, *The History of the Two Lovers* appears to question one of the most respected and revered *auctores* of Christian culture, and one who stood at the very foundations of traditional moral teaching.

The undermining of Lucretia as a model of chastity is more than simply an attack on a single *exemplum*. In a tale which emphasizes the weakness of human will in the face of passion, it resonates as a powerful statement of how unrealistic models of perfect virtue really are, how claims to moral perfection are fundamentally hypocritical, and how the expectation for such behaviour, such as traditional morality encouraged, can only lead to similar hypocrisy. In the complex figure of Lucrece, *The History of the Two Lovers* exposes the gap that exists between the demands of moral culture and the capabilities of human nature, and the crisis of ethics that results.

The criticisms of moral culture put forward in the tale of Lucrece and Eurialus are thus many and varied. Aeneas' tale exposes several flaws at the theoretical level of traditional ethical discipline — the establishment of unrealistic ideals, the use of irrelevant models of behaviour — and at the same time, reveals a series of other problems which develop in the context of applying this discipline to real situations. However well intentioned the traditional methodology may be, the experience of Eurialus

---

quid coniunctione membrorum, *sed quid animorum diversitate ageretur* adtendens: 'Duo fuerunt . . . .'

and Aeneas writes:

At cum *duo invicem conglutinati per amorem sunt animi,* tanto penosior est separatio, quanto sensibilior est uterque dilectus. Et hic sane iam *non erant spiritus duo,* sed quemadmodum inter amicos putat Aristophanes [Aristotle] *unius anime duo corpora facta erant.* Itaque non recedebat animus ab animo, sed *unicus animus scindebatur in duos.*

and Lucrece suggests over and over again that, in reality, it helps to bring about moral crisis rather than moral order. Instead of learning virtue from the *exempla* placed before them, the hero and heroine learn vice. Through misunderstanding and manipulation, they succeed in justifying their immoral behaviour with the authority meant to sanction virtue. And if they do take away any useful lessons from these teachings, they seem to forget them at the very moment when they are needed the most. If at times this moral crisis seems more the failure of the "students" than of their education, there is no sense from the story that the solution lies in reforming their attitude toward traditional techniques. It seems instead that the resolution is to be found in a reformation of the goals and methodology of moral education itself, such that it will be more compatible with both human nature and individual situations of ethical conflict.

While *The History of the Two Lovers* is very specific in terms of its criticisms of traditional moral culture, it is considerably more vague and elusive with regard to its suggestions for reform. There are, nevertheless, some hints, both in the hero's ethical reorientation at the end of the tale, and in the nature of Aeneas' story as a work of moral instruction. When Eurialus explains to Lucrece the reasons behind his decision to return to Germany, there is no evidence that his arguments are based on models of virtue or *sententiae*, as they had been so clearly before. Instead, his approach is to evaluate all the particulars of their own specific and very real situation in relation to the general moral principle that honour and reputation should take precedence over passion. It is a much more independent and individual approach to ethics than tradition allowed, free of both authoritative voices and the baggage of models and maxims. The only tool, in fact, that Eurialus seems to need is his own reason. Given the tale's emphasis on the weakness of this aspect of human nature, Aeneas' vision is a remarkably optimistic one, and would seem to demand some explanation of what is needed to galvanize reason effectively, though not infallibly, against the powers of passion. Perhaps some answer can be found by stepping back from the details of the narrative and turning instead to the previous discussion of how Aeneas himself seeks to teach morality through his tale. If *The History of the Two Lovers* represents Aeneas' vision of effective moral instruction, reason's best guide along the path toward virtue is an intimate familiarity with the human condition and experience of real life. Given the extent to which the story's representation of humanity is articulated in the rhetoric and imagery of classical authors, it seems a fair conclusion to draw that he identified this moral education at least to some extent with a humanistic one, recognizing the ancient authors not so much as *auctores* but rather as valuable witnesses and eloquent reporters of the reality of human ethical experience.

While the moral philosophy expressed in *The History of the Two Lovers* clearly does not align with traditional ethical discipline, it does overlap with a smaller but extremely important counter-current in fifteenth-century Italian moral culture. The origins of this movement can be traced back almost a century earlier to the writings of Petrarch (1304–1374), widely considered the founder and father of humanism.[112] Petrarch attacked the very foundation of Christian medieval ethics — the use of *exempla* and *sententiae* as tools for ethical education, its general encyclopaedic mentality and its reverence for the opinion of authorities, which resulted in a system of ethics based on selections from "approved" texts.[113] While his criticism was fundamentally aimed at the Church as the institution which embodied moral culture, he directed his attacks at any authority, Christian or pagan, which represented these views.[114] Favourite targets were Valerius Maximus, who became the very symbol of medieval trends of compiling and cataloguing knowledge, and even Augustine, in his most doctrinaire texts, and specifically *De civitate Dei*.[115] It is easier to identify what Petrarch opposed than what he presented as an alternative to ethical discipline, but there does emerge from his writings a general sense of his own very

---

[112]Riccardo Fubini develops this interpretation of fifteenth-century moral culture at length in a series of articles. The more important of these are published in a collection, *Umanesimo e Secolarizzazione da Petrarca a Valla* (Rome: Bulzoni, 1990).

[113]Fubini, "Intendimenti umanistici e riferimenti patristici da Petraca a Valla," in *Umanesimo e Secolarizzazione*, pp. 145–61.

[114]Fubini, "Introduction" to *Umanesimo e Secolarizzazione*, p. xi.

[115]Fubini, "Intendimenti," pp. 147, 150–60.

different approach. Inspired largely by the moral thought of Seneca, Petrarch advocated a more independent approach to ethics, free of rigid norms, restrictive authorities, and established canons. Moral discourse was, in his eyes, an ordering or preparing of the soul, not the attainment of perfection, and it was best achieved not through learning selected precepts but rather through a real understanding and evaluation of classical texts.[116] Petrarch concealed these radical new ideas and attacks on ethical authorities in rhetoric and anonymity, sometimes camouflaging them to look like the very ideas he was criticizing.[117]

While such disguises have made his criticisms largely invisible to modern scholarship, they were perceived and embraced in the generation that followed him by several very important humanists, Poggio Bracciolini and Lorenzo Valla among the most important.[118] In response to the general crisis of institutions — and of the Church in particular — in the first half of the fifteenth century, Poggio and Valla went forward with Petrarch's criticism of Christian ethics, levelling subtle attacks at specific authorities, contemporary and past, as well as at the ideology and methodology of ethical discipline in general. Like Petrarch, they spoke out quietly, experimenting with new forms, such as the dialogue, in which they concealed their statements, and using the same technique of anonymous allusion as the medium for their polemic.[119] Each of the humanists developed his own distinct version of criticism and new ethical ideas, with Valla offering the most radical attacks and solutions.[120] But if the range of ideas makes it impossible to describe their thought in terms of a single unified ideology, both the common aims and extensive dialogue among

---

[116]*Ibid.*, pp. 155, 158–59.

[117]*Ibid.*, pp. 149, 153–54, 159–61.

[118]Fubini, *Umanesimo e Secolarizzazione, passim.*

[119]Fubini, "Intendimenti," p. 161.

[120]On Poggio, see *ibid.*, pp. 145–72; and in the same volume, "Poggio Bracciolini e San Bernardino: temi e motivi di una polemica," pp. 183–219; "Il teatro del mondo nelle prospettive morali e storico-politiche di Poggio Bracciolini," pp. 221–314. On Valla, see "Intendimenti," pp. 172–82; and in the same volume, "Indagine sul 'De voluptate' di Lorenzo Valla," pp. 332–94.

them suggest that their thought should be recognized collectively as parts of a whole that evinced both parallel and oppositional patterns to traditional moral philosophy.[121]

The moral thought in *The History of the Two Lovers* bears a striking resemblance to this ethical movement at many different levels. Its attitude of criticism toward traditional moral culture, and its attack on the *exemplum* and moral maxims in particular, echo the ideas at the very foundation of these humanists' position. In its criticism of Lucretia, the tale follows their typical pattern of attacking specific authorities (Valerius Maximus and Augustine in *De civitate Dei*) and concealing the polemic in anonymous allusion. It is perhaps this atmosphere of caution and camouflage that explains the narrative element of Aeneas' work which, as was argued earlier, has a secondary, subordinate role to the moral issues in the story. The *novella* offered the kind of environment in which Aeneas could present his polemical ideas safely; indeed, as a genre so integrally connected to the *exemplum* tradition, it represented the ideal form of camouflage, and an opportunity to launch an internal attack. Given the fact that the very similar expression of Petrarch's ideas has only just recently been uncovered, it is perhaps not so surprising that Aeneas' has remained concealed for a similarly long time.[122]

Of the various humanists involved in this intellectual movement, the one who seems to come closest to Aeneas' ideas in *The History of the Two Lovers* is Poggio Bracciolini, especially in his role as critic of the *exemplum* tradition.[123] Aeneas' attacks sound very much like those which Poggio had made more directly in his dialogue *On Avarice* (1428), the *Facetiae* (1438–1452) and throughout his private correspondence. Poggio argues that *exempla* were too obscure and irrelevant to provide any useful moral guidance. He points out that instead of instructing virtue

---

[121]Fubini, "Introduction," *Umanesimo e Secolarizzazione*, pp. 7, 12–13.

[122]To our knowledge, there has been no study which connects *The History of the Two Lovers* to this particular intellectual movement.

[123]On Poggio, see especially Fubini, *Umanesimo e Secolarizzazione*, "Poggio Bracciolini e San Bernardino: temi e motivi di una polemica," pp. 183–219; and "Il teatro del mondo nelle prospettive morali e storico-politische di Poggio Bracciolini," pp. 221–314.

they seem to teach vice. Finally, he observes that people seem incapable of recalling the precepts they had learned when the situation demands they do so.[124] Poggio also shared Aeneas' skepticism concerning the capacity for *exempla* to provide realistic ideals for human beings. Moral perfection was, in his eyes, an unattainable goal, and to make it, as did traditional ethical culture, a rigid requirement in human behaviour was merely to open the door to hypocrisy.[125] The questioning of Lucretia's claims to moral purity has much in common with Poggio's attack on what were essentially the Church's contemporary models of virtuous behaviour — the clergy — in which he accused them of hiding their greed, lust, gluttony and other vices behind the purity of their vestments.[126] Like Aeneas, moreover, Poggio couches his criticism in a form very similar to the *exemplum*, the *facetiae*, which were almost an alternative or even inversion of the genre.[127] Many of the anecdotes represented polemical variations on specific *exempla* used by the famous Franciscan preacher Bernardino of Siena.[128] Poggio also adopted the opposite rhetorical style of the *exempla*, teaching his audience by seeking to entertain them rather than preaching sternly to them. It is to this end that he writes so many of his *facetiae* in the language of Roman comedy.[129] Here again Aeneas' tale seems to align closely with Poggio's approach and the dozens of quotations from Terence scattered throughout his story suddenly take on polemical significance. Indeed, if there is a narrative with which *The History of the Two Lovers* can be grouped, Poggio's *Facetiae* seem a very logical choice, from both a rhetorical and an ideological perspective.

In more general terms, the tale of Lucrece and Eurialus suggests an approach to ethical reform similar to Poggio's. Like

---

[124]Fubini, "Poggio Bracciolini e San Bernardino," pp. 190–91.

[125]Fubini, "Intendimenti," p. 162; "Il teatro del mondo," pp. 235–39, 247–51.

[126]Fubini, "Intendimenti," p. 137; "Poggio Bracciolini e San Bernardino," pp. 214–15; "il teatro del mondo," pp. 243–44, 247–49.

[127]Fubini, "Poggio Bracciolini e San Bernardino," pp. 190–94.

[128]*Ibid.*

[129]Fubini, "Poggio Bracciolini e San Bernardino," pp. 192–95, 199.

Aeneas, Poggio recognized the inherent weaknesses in human nature and emphasized the difficulty of attaining virtue. Moral failure, he wrote, was a natural and inevitable part of human existence. Poggio set his ethical standards according to specifically human limitations, encouraging an attitude of approximation rather than imitation of virtue, and a greater willingness to accept weakness and error.[130] He also maintained that the guide to virtue lies in reason and in real human experience. In contrast to Bernardino and other traditional preachers, Poggio sought a rational form of moral persuasion, recognizing, though, at the same time, that reason is necessarily a limited power. The best education lies in concrete examples of real life, from which could be learned not precepts and absolute norms but rather discretion and prudence — tools that could be applied to all moral issues, regardless of place, time, or situation. The search for virtue thus became an independent and an individual process, and the discipline of ethics fundamentally relativized.[131] There is much more to Poggio's moral philosophy than finds resonance in *The History of the Two Lovers*, and it would be incorrect to regard Aeneas' text simply as a recasting of his ideas. Nevertheless, it is clear that in both the substance and form of its attacks on traditional moral culture and in its ideas for renewal, the tale of Lucrece and Eurialus takes up a position in moral culture very close to the works of this important thinker and moral philosopher.[132]

While the ethical views expressed in *The History of the Two Lovers* stand in opposition to traditions in fifteenth-century Italy,

---

[130]Fubini, "Intendimenti," p. 162; "Il teatro del mondo," pp. 235–39, 247–49, 256.

[131]Fubini, "Intendimenti," p. 170; "Poggio Bracciolini e San Bernardino," pp. 200–01, 216; "Il teatro del mondo," pp. 228, 245–46, 250–51.

[132]*The History of the Two Lovers* can also be aligned on a more specific level with another figure who had a less direct connection to this movement, Coluccio Salutati (1331–1406). Salutati had been Poggio's teacher and, significantly, the one on whom Poggio had modelled his teaching that precepts can only be approximated (Fubini, "Intendimenti umanistici e riferimenti patristici dal Petrarca a Valla," p. 162). His connection with the tale of Lucrece and Eurialus is through the figure of Lucretia. Sometime before 1368, Salutati wrote a declamation entitled *De Lucretia* in which he presents Lucretia's own, very untraditional explanation for

in sixteenth-century England their position would have been somewhat more ambiguous. English moral culture had also been built on the *exemplum* tradition, and a general respect for the same moral authorities. The separation from the Roman Church, moreover, does not seem to have resulted in a significant break with this approach to moral teaching or general organization of moral culture. The traditional method of exalting virtue and condemning vice in the *exemplum* is apparent even in the ethical interpretations within which English translators so frequently framed their stories.[133] If they were eager to emphasize the ethical value of the tales' somewhat ambiguous moral messages, they were also clearly determined to present it as part of traditional moral culture. Aeneas' tale thus represented as much a criticism of English ethical tradition as it did of Italian.

The moral resonance of the tale is complicated, however, by the author's relationship to the Church. Though he was not in holy orders when he wrote the story, Aeneas was eventually to become not only a priest but also the very head of the Roman ecclesiastical hierarchy, as Pope Pius II. In a climate hostile to the Roman Church, and to the pope in particular, as was England in the mid-sixteenth century, the erotic nature of the love story

---

her suicide. In the presence of her husband and a fellow soldier, Lucretia confesses that in the course of his attack Sextus Tarquinius had aroused in her feelings of passion and that she fears her experience will kindle still more powerful desire. It is not out of shame that she commits suicide but out of the conviction that if she does not, she will begin to carry out her shameful desires (Menesto, pp. 39–43). The *De Lucretia* was well known among Salutati's contemporaries and, given Aeneas' intellectual circles, it would not seem improbable to suppose that he had read it too. The fact that it was first published among his own letters in his *Opera Omnia* (Aeneas Silvius Piccolomini, *Aeneae Sylvii Piccolminiei Pii Pontificis Maximi II Opera quae extant omnia* [Basel, 1551] p. 969) makes his familiarity with it all the more plausible. It is unclear from the text whether or not he drew direct inspiration from Salutati's work. Whatever the connection, however, it is clear that the tale should be classified with it as part of a broader debate on the validity of this specific *exemplum*. See Morrall, *Aeneas Silvius Piccolomini (Pius II). The Goodli History*, pp. xxiv–xxv, who also notes the similarity between Salutati's Lucretia and Aeneas' Lucrece.

[133] Beecher, pp. 36–37.

alone would have represented fuel for religious fires. But its criticism of ethical tradition, which lay at the very foundation of Christian culture, would have done so even more, confirming English accusations of a serious crisis in moral leadership at the very heart of the Roman Church.

It is difficult to know whether English audiences would have read Aeneas' tale in these terms. So far scholars have not turned up even a single English equivalent of the letter to Carolus which would provide evidence for contemporary reader reception. Indeed, even the views of the translator are unclear. The interpretive remarks with which he concludes the tale do not articulate the ethical criticisms as part of the tale's edifying message. They do, however, present an interpretation that seems more along the lines of the story's very different approach to ethical instruction than the traditional one. To Aeneas' warning to take heed of Eurialus, the translator adds a series of other figures whom he considers to illustrate the same message presented in the tale of Lucrece and Eurialus — Troilus and Cressida, Pyramis and Thisbe, Dido — that love brings "pain perdurable" and ends in death. The figures he chooses are all in some sense *exempla*, in so far as they are concrete illustrations of an abstract idea, but they are not the models of virtue and vice so integral to traditional religious ethics. If the translator seeks to define the story as a guide to virtue, he does not try to frame the adulterous affair in traditional terms as the very incarnation of vice. The story thus remains outside the *exempla* tradition, and if not explicitly defined as such, there is still room for such an interpretation by an attentive reader.

* * *

A general survey of Aeneas' other writings from the same period as the tale of Lucrece and Eurialus reveals that the story represents part of a broader trend in his own intellectual development. In the same year that he wrote *The History of the Two Lovers*, Aeneas finished a comedy entitled *Chrysis*, and a satirical tract, *De miseria curialium*. Both of these texts are dominated by images of moral dislocation and crisis, where men and women are constantly falling victim to the overwhelming power of their passions. The vision finds a different expression in each of the works: *Chrysis* depicts an imaginary world of exaggerated depravity where men and women indulge, defend and even celebrate their passions. The satire *De miseria curialium* describes the moral decay, corruption and hypocrisy in the context of the court. In both of these texts, as in *The History of the Two Lovers*, Aeneas seems particularly interested in exploring the psychology of human behaviour; indeed, if action is subordinated to such investigations in the tale of Lucrece and Eurialus, in *Chrysis* it is even more so: the entire play consists of a series of monologues and dialogues, with essentially no action at all. Drawing his images and allusions from a similar repertoire of classical texts, Aeneas illuminates a familiar picture of the difficult struggle between human passion and reason. The audience is left with the same impression as it is after reading of Lucrece and Eurialus' struggle, that the road to a virtuous life is a difficult one to follow. In *Chrysis* this message is articulated explicitly in the closing lines of the play: "virtutibus insudandum est" — "you must sweat to be virtuous." Both Aeneas' comedy and his satire are on the whole more cynical than *The History of the Two Lovers*, their humour more biting and their outlook more bleak. The portraits they present, moreover, seem more of a caricature of human beings than realistic figures like Eurialus and Lucrece. The three works are nevertheless fundamentally related, so much so, in fact, that they are perhaps best defined as variations on a common theme. With this in mind, the traditional emphasis on the narrative element of Aeneas' story as its defining essence once again seems misplaced, and the value of the *novella* classification still more limited.

The same issues and ideas emerge in the context of Aeneas' private correspondence. To a large extent, his letters from this period consist of a moral commentary on day-to-day life at the imperial court of Frederick III. The world which he describes in these three literary pieces is clearly a reflection of the real one around him. In his letters, Aeneas expresses his frustration with the emperor's ministers and other officials who seem driven more by their own interests and ambitions than by any commitment to a common or higher good. He notes the hypocrisy in the behaviour and attitude of the courtiers who surround him. He constantly laments the weakness of human nature and remarks with concern on the moral laxity and corruption he sees at every level of society. Interspersed with these commentaries on the court are other letters which focus instead on issues brought to him by his friends and which, as described earlier, deal most often with their problems in love. While Aeneas adopts an attitude of exasperation and contempt in describing the unremorseful behaviour at court, his tone is significantly different in these other letters, in particular when his friends approach him with a moral dilemma. Aeneas does not try to preach to them, nor does he condemn them for their weaknesses or mistakes. What he concentrates on instead is helping them to understand their behaviour and the nature and causes of the moral issue. Nowhere is there the sternness and severity so characteristic of traditional moral preaching. Indeed, Aeneas lightens the weight of his comments with gentle humour; and if he does reprimand his friends, he does so with compassion and a sincere willingness to forgive. Like his ideas on love, Aeneas' ethical thought in *The History of the Two Lovers* seems thus to be a sincere reflection and product in large part of his own very real experiences.[134]

Of all his writings in this period, however, there is none which expresses his moral philosophy more explicitly or more powerfully than the letter he wrote to his father almost a year before he penned the tale of Lucrece and Eurialus.[135] The background to this letter is an event which happened several years earlier while Aeneas was at Basel attending a Church council. During his brief stay he formed a liaison with an English woman who, sometime after he returned to Vienna, bore him a son. From what is written in his letter, it seems that Aeneas had at an earlier time called on his father to help take care of the child, and that his father, displeased with his son's behaviour, had refused to honour his request. Aeneas makes no attempt here to justify his actions; on the contrary, he readily admits that what he did was wrong:

---

[134]See Wolkan, Vol. 1, *passim*. This interpretation is based on a reading of some 120 letters, dating from 1442 to 1445.

[135]*Ibid.*, Ep. 78, 20 September 1443, pp. 188–91.

"I frankly confess that it is a fault."[136] But while Aeneas accepts and agrees with his father's judgment, he criticizes his father's harsh and unforgiving attitude and does so using arguments which seem strikingly similar to the tale of Lucrece and Eurialus. What he seems to want to impress on his father most of all is that his actions were perfectly natural, indeed, inevitable for a human being. He explains: "Certainly you yourself are made of flesh and did not beget a son of stone or iron . . . . I, also, am no eunuch, nor one of the frigid sort";[137] and he reminds his father that he too was guilty of similar behaviour: "surely you must remember what kind of a spark you have been in your time."[138] Aeneas then points to other figures who made the same mistake — including one which Eurialus mentions — but rather than using them as justification for his behaviour, as the hero of his story does, he presents them as witnesses to the weakness of the human condition: "I am no holier than David nor wiser than Solomon," and he concludes, "I know of none that are free of it."[139] In his attempt to describe his feelings of sexual passion, Aeneas reveals the fundamental contradiction between nature's intentions and society's attempts to restrict them, and confesses his own frustration with this paradox: on the one hand, he points out, it makes no sense to condemn sex "since Nature, that does nothing amiss, has implanted this instinct in all creatures";[140] but on the other, he recognizes the validity of what he considers his

---

[136] fatebor ingenue meum errorem.

The English here and in following translations is taken from Boulting (pp. 142–43).

[137] Certe nec lapideum nec ferreum genuisti filium cum tu esse carneus . . . nec castrarus sum neque ex frigidorum numero . . . .

Aeneas says the same thing of Schlick, in the letter he sent him in July 1444: "And do not be ashamed to recollect, if ever anything of this kind happened to you; for you too were a man. He who has never truly felt the flames of love is but a stone, or a beast" (Grierson, p. xvi).

[138] Scis qualis gallus tu fueris . . . .

[139] nec sanctior sum Davide rege, nec Solomone sapientior . . . . nec scio, quis hoc careat.

[140] natura, quae nichil perperam operatur, omnibus ingenuerit animantibus hunc appetitum . . . .

father's very strict observance of social mores: " 'there are limits within which this is lawful; outside wedlock it is not lawful.' "[141] Unlike Eurialus in his opening speech on natural love, Aeneas does not conclude that passion should be obeyed as supreme law. Instead, by affirming his father's statement, he acknowledges once again the validity of this morality: "That is true."[142] But after he makes this statement, he immediately points out how difficult it is to put these ideals into practice: "But who regards [these bounds]? Who is so upright as not to fall seven times a day?"[143] If his father is expecting perfection of him, he does so in vain: "I am no hypocrite who wishes only to appear to be good."[144] Aeneas does not think much of himself for his behaviour, but as a weak human being, repentant of his mistake, he defends his right to mercy and forgiveness: "I am quite unaware of any such merit in myself, and Divine Compassion alone gives me hope of pardon. God is aware that we are all weak and prone to sin, nor will His fountain of forgiveness cease, that flows to all."[145] With this last comment Aeneas accuses his father's moral ideals of being not only incompatible with human nature, but also fundamentally unchristian, and in so doing makes a still stronger attack on the Christian traditions he represents.

Aeneas' letter continues with a narrative description of what happened the night his son was conceived, focussing on the battle between passion and reason that went on inside of him. The more he describes, the more parallels emerge with the tale of Lucrece and Eurialus, and between Aeneas and Eurialus in particular. He explains:

---

[141] certos esse limites intro quos hoc licet nec extra legitimas matrimonii faces progredi debet hic appetitum.

[142] Ita sane est.

[143] Sed quis servat illos, quis tam virtus, ut septies in die non cadat?

[144] nec sum ypocrita, ut videri bonus quam esse velim. (lit. "Nor am I a hypocrite, so as to wish to seem rather than be good.")

[145] ego nullam in me scio, solaque mihi divina pietas spem facit misericordiae, qui nos labiles scit et ad lasciviam proclives, nec nobis qui patet omnibus fontem venie claudet.

I was delighted by the wit of the woman, in whose mouth was great charm. Soon the eloquent Cleopatra came to my mind, who enticed not only Anthony but also Julius Caesar by her eloquence. "Who would reprimand me," I said to myself, "if I, a nobody, were to do the same thing for which the greatest men are not despised?" I looked to Moses, then to Aristotle, and sometimes to Christians as my examples. What more? Desire was victorious . . . .[146]

In the same way as he does in *The History of the Two Lovers*, Aeneas explores the psychological dimension of moral decision, and reveals the practical problems of traditional ethical discipline: as in the case of Lucretia and Eurialus, *exempla* lead Aeneas toward vice instead of virtue.

When read in the context of this extraordinary personal confession, *The History of the Two Lovers* is revealed to be far more autobiographical than it has ever before been recognized. If the circumstances of the affair find closer parallels with the situation of his friend, the chancellor Kaspar Schlick, the moral struggles of the characters, and of Eurialus in particular, are very much Aeneas' own. The Aeneas looking back on the incident at Basel and admitting his error is the Eurialus at the end of the story who, having returned to the road of virtue, rides off to Germany. The letter seems to suggest, however, that it is only a matter of time before the weak Eurialus returns once again in some form or other. "But who regards [these bounds]? Who is so upright as not to fall seven times a day?" With these words Aeneas articulates the ideas at the very core of *The History of the Two Lovers*: a profound awareness of human weakness and a dramatic plea that these imperfections be acknowledged in the context of Christian ethics.

* * *

---

[146] oblectatus sum facetiis feminae, cuius in ore maximus lepor erat, moxque in mentem venit Cleopatra facundia, que non solum Antonium sed Julium Caesarem quoque eloquentia inescavit, mecumque quis reprehendat, inquam, si ego homuncio id faciam, quod maxime viri non sunt aspernati. Interdum Moysen, interdum Aristotelem, nonnumquam Christianos in exemplum sumebam. quid plura? vicit cupido . . . .

The "edifying lesson" expressed in *The History of the Two Lovers* finds confirmation in still another letter which Aeneas wrote considerably later in life. It is the letter with which this discussion began. Surprisingly, while scholars have often referred to and quoted the first few lines of it in their discussions, they have made no mention of what else it contains. Aeneas' point is not simply to confess his shame and remorse for the lascivious nature of his story, and to express frustration with his contemporary audience at their failure to find its moral meaning. The primary aim of the letter seems, in fact, to be something quite different: to salvage the tale's edifying message by articulating more explicitly what had been illustrated in the experiences of Lucrece and Eurialus.[147] The interpretation which he goes on to present sounds very much like the one which this analysis has tried to argue.

Aeneas begins his explanation with a poem of 44 lines in which the muse Calliope explains the traditional image of Cupid as an allegory of lascivious love. He is a boy because lovers, like children, lack reason. He is naked, because they are not mindful of protecting their chastity. He is blind to show that they do not perceive virtue very well, and do not know how to distinguish it from vice, or because they believe their sin to be secret. A lover is oblivious to all other things except the beloved — advice, public opinion, bonds and responsibilities, and the laws of God. His wings represent the flightiness and fickleness of passion, and its tendency not to follow a straight course. He shoots an arrow to symbolise that love pierces the heart like iron, and carries a torch to show that its sensation is like a burning fire. The poem concludes: "Learn this image of lascivious love . . . so that you may beware of the wretch [Cupid] until you become acquainted with love, and return to your senses, as you read my verses."[148] Thus, according to Aeneas' own interpretation,

---

[147]Several scholars have described this letter ambiguously as a retraction. See Doglio, *L'Exemplum nella novella latina del '400*, p. 2; Ady, p. 99; and Mitchell, p. 47.

[148] Accipe lascivi quaenam sit amoris imago . . . / Ut melius miserum caveas, dum noris amorem / Et redeas ad te, dum mea metra leges. (Aeneas Silvius Piccolomini, *Aeneae Sylvii Piccolminiei Pii Pontificis Maximi II Opera quae extant omnia* [Basel, 1551], Ep. 395, pp. 870–71).

The History of the Two Lovers represents a dramatization of the many different sufferings of lascivious love — moral, physical and psychological — as a warning to his readers, as it is here to Carolus, to stay away from such danger.

The letter then continues in prose with another allegory, which Aeneas explains as an illustration of love's extraordinary power, quoting directly from Lactantius' *Divine institutiones*:

> It was not without wit that a certain poet wrote of the triumph of Cupid. In his book he makes Cupid not only the most powerful of gods but also their victor. Having ennumerated the loves of each one, by which they have come under Cupid's power and sway, he described a procession in which Jupiter, with the other gods, is led in chains before the carriage of the triumphant Cupid.[149]

Rather than a separate message, this second allegory is more of a qualification of the first, implying that it will be difficult to put these words of warning into practice. Even the strongest are weak in the face of passion's powers.

The second half of the letter is devoted exclusively to pointing out the problems that result from establishing standards of morality that do not take these weaknesses into account. He begins with the classical world, criticising Cicero for condemning a fellow citizen's adultery as incongruous with his acceptance of similar behaviour by the very gods he worshipped: "Marcus Tullius then was a fool in charging Gaius Verres with his adulterous crimes, because Jupiter, whom he worshipped, committed the same actions . . . ."[150] More generally he argues that moral

---

[149] Non insulse igitur . . . quidam Poeta triumphum Cupidinis describens, non modo potentisssimum deorum Cupidinem, sed etiam victorem facit. Enumeratis enim moribus singulorum quibus in potestatem cupidinis dictionemque venissent, instruxit pompam in qua Iupiter cum caeteris diis ante currum triumphantis ducitur cathenatus. (trans. Sr. Mary Francis McDonald, OP, Lactantius, *The Divine Institutes* [Washington: Catholic University Press, 1964])

Cf. in the letter to Schlick: "Ipse nanque vel per deorum medullas, non lateat igneam favillam." ("It is no secret that into the very marrow-bones of the gods has crept the fiery particle"), Grierson, p. xvi.

[150] Stultus autem M. Tullius, inquit Lactantius, qui Caio Verri adulteria obiecit, eadem enim Iuppiter, quem colebat, admisit . . . .

philosophers adopt similar double standards when they exalt ethical principles they themselves do not practice: "Look also at the philosophers, the teachers of life, . . . and you will find with few exceptions that they are wrathful, avaricious, lustful, arrogant, violent, and cloaking their vices beneath the pretext of wisdom, since they do at home what they censure in the classroom."[151] They are guilty, in short, of transgressing the very virtues which they demand their pupils imitate, and none more so than chastity. The result is hypocrisy and general moral breakdown:

> Therefore, those who only teach these things and do not do them take away from their authority with the very precepts themselves. For who would obey them, since the teachers themselves instruct them not to obey? It is good to teach upright and honest things, but unless you also do them yourself, it is a lie. And it is unsuitable and foolish to have goodness on your lips, but not in your heart.[152]

On the one hand, Aeneas is criticising the moral philosophers for their failure to live up to their own standards; but on the other he seems to suggest that the problem lies not so much with the philosophers as with the very standards themselves.

The letter to Carolus thus lays out in very specific terms the criticisms of ethical culture to which Aeneas had given more subtle and allusive expression in the tale of Eurialus and Lucrece. It does so, moreover, in a way that illuminates still more clearly the links between Aeneas' own moral philosophy and the positions of Petrarch and his followers. In support of his argument, he cites among others Seneca and Lactantius, two of the most important influences on this group of thinkers. Moreover, in his references to "moral philosophers" Aeneas is adopting their standard

---

[151] Aspice quoque Philosophos vitae magistros . . . et invenies paucis exceptis iracundos, cupidos, libidinosos, arrogantes, protervos, et sub obtentu sapientiae sua vitia palliantes, cum domi faciant ea quae in scholis arguissent.

[152] Igitur qui docent tantum nec faciunt, ipsis praeceptis suis detrahunt pondus. Quis enim obtemperet, cum ipsi praeceptores doceant non obtemperare? Bonum est recta et honesta praecipere, sed nisi et facias, mendacium est, et est incongruens atque ineptum non pectore sed in labiis habere bonitatem.

technique for camouflaging what were dangerous criticisms directed at the teachers of Christian ethics. Indirect though they may be, Aeneas' attacks were aimed not only at ancient philosophers but also against those of his own day — the clergy, and more generally, the institution of the Church.

* * *

On 26 April 1463, Aeneas, now Pius II, issued from his papal throne a Bull, "In minoribus agentibus," in which he retracted several of the works which he had written in his earlier years.[153] Among them were his erotic writings, and though he makes no specific mention of it, it is generally believed that they included the tale of Eurialus and Lucrece. Scholars have interpreted the retraction from the point of view of the story as a narrative: it was wholly inappropriate for a man who had dedicated his life to God, and even more so for the very leader of Christendom, to be associated with such an erotic work. But in the tale's "edifying message," Aeneas had still another, and perhaps stronger motive for his actions. As Pope Pius II, he now found himself in the very uncomfortable position of being the head and symbol of the ethical culture which in his earlier work he had opposed and attacked. It would have been necessary, therefore, for him to protect himself from the accusations of hypocrisy and treason which the work might have incited both within the confines of the Church and without. Whether his retraction represents simply a cautionary tactic or a sincere change of heart is a question that has yet to be answered; indeed, in the context of his ethical development it has not even been posed. Aeneas' moral philosophy has not been studied systematically in any detail, either for the period during his papacy or for that previous to it. Yet the letter to the mysterious Carolus, which in so many ways has proven to be the key to unlocking this fascinating text, seems to point to an answer, and in so doing, opens up a series of other very different but important issues on religious ethics in the context of the papacy, and the figure of Aeneas as moral philosopher.

---

[153]See C. Fea, *Pius II a calumniis vindicatus* (Rome, 1823), pp. 148–64.

The History of *The History of the Two Lovers*:
The Role of Translation
EMILY O'BRIEN

Even as he was writing the Bull of Retraction, Aeneas seemed to recognize the futility of asking that his works be put aside. He writes in despair: "But what shall be done? The word once written, takes wing; it cannot be called back. Oh that what has been published could be blotted out . . . ."[154] And indeed, Aeneas' predictions came true. Far from being blotted out, *The History of the Two Lovers* became one of the most popular and best-selling works in early modern Europe and had a considerable impact on the development of love literature in the same period.[155] The text was circulated first in manuscript form, and after the middle of the fifteenth century in printed versions as well. It was first published in Cologne in 1468, and by the end of the century more than 30 editions of the tale had been produced — an exceptionally high number in these early days of print culture.[156] The work was to become still more popular in the century that followed, for by 1700 another forty editions had been published.[157] As Aeneas had expected, the tale of Lucrece and Eurialus did take wing, and to all corners of Europe: by the end of the sixteenth century it had been translated into Italian,[158]

---

[154]Boulting, pp. 181–83.

[155]See Di Francia, p. 316; and Morrall, *Aeneas Silvius Piccolomini (Pius II) and Nikolaus von Wyle*, p. 35.

[156]Doglio, *L'exemplum nella novella latina del '400*, p. 21; Doglio also notes that the earliest printing of the text in Italy was in 1476.

[157]Najemy, p. 39.

[158]The oldest translation is Alessandro Braccesi's version of 1489, *Traductione de una Historia de due Amanti composta dalla felice memoria di Papa Pio II*. It is available in several modern editions (*Storia di due amanti di Enea Silvio Piccolomini in seguito papa Pio secondo col Testo latino e a la Traduzione libera di Alessandro Braccio* [Capolago, 1832]). Another Italian translation was done around the same time by Almanno Donati. This version was never printed. See Doglio, *L'exemplum nella novella latina del '400*, pp. 17–18.

French,[159] German,[160] Spanish, Polish and Hungarian[161] as well as English, and all of these versions went through multiple editions. Aeneas' retraction thus had very little effect. Whether he liked it or not, he has the very distinguished reputation of being one of the most popular figures in the literary world of early modern Europe.

A brief consideration of the various translations of the tale suggests that Aeneas would in many cases have found it difficult to recognize his original work. *The History of the Two Lovers* was altered, sometimes considerably, over the course of time. In Alessandro Braccesi's 1481 translation, for example, the more explicit sexual passages and obscure classical references have been omitted from the text. Moreover, instead of writing letters to Lucrece, Eurialus sends her poems — eleven sonnets, two madrigals and a series of other verses. The tone of the tale is also transformed, from a sense of melancholy, anxiety and suffering to one of optimism and serenity. The most striking change of all, however, comes at the story's dramatic conclusion: shortly after Eurialus departs for Germany, Lucrece's husband, Menelaus, suddenly dies. The two lovers, free from all moral restraints, reunite and marry, have eight children, and live happily ever

---

[159] *l'Ystoire de Eurialus et Lucresse, vrays amoreux, selon pape Pie. Traict tres recreatif et plaisant de lamour indicible de euriaus et de lucresse compose par le pape avant la papaute nome enee silvye et translate de latin en francois* (Paris: Antoine Verard, 1493), attributed to Octavien de Saint-Gelais. See Doglio, pp. 17–18. On this and other French translations, see Marie Francoise Piejus, "Une traduction française de la 'Historia de Duobus Amantibus' d'Eneas Silvius Piccolomini," in *La Circulation des Hommes et des Oeuvres entre la France et l'Italie à l'Epoque de la Renaissance. Actes du Colloque International (22–23–24 novembre 1990)*, pp. 103–17; and Michel Bideaux, "'L'Histoire de Duobus Amantibus' nel '500 francese," in *Pio II e la cultura del suo tempo. Atti del I convegno internazionale 1989*, ed. Luisa Rotondi Secchi Tarughi (Milano, 1991), pp. 175–88.

[160] The first translation, by Nikolaus von Wyle, was done in 1463; the first printed version in 1477. See Morrall, *Aeneas Silvius Piccolomini (Pius II) and Nikolaus von Wyle*, pp. 28ff.

[161] See Doglio, *L'exemplum nella novella latina del '400*, pp. 17–18.

after![162] While Braccesi's very radical reinterpretation of Aeneas' tale should not be considered representative of all translations, it nonetheless serves to illustrate an important point: rather than a single work, the tale of Lucrece and Eurialus is best considered from a historical perspective as a series of different texts.

The evolution of *The History of the Two Lovers* was perfectly normal in the context of fifteenth- and sixteenth-century European literary culture. The role of the translator was much more broadly defined than it is today. Not simply limited to reproducing the work of another, he was empowered to make considerable emendations to the original text, and to do so anonymously, so that the changes blended seamlessly into the original work. The underlying motives for such a technique can to some degree be understood as personal ambition: whether he received credit or not, a translator had the opportunity to parade his own talents before a captive audience, as did Braccesi with his poems and madrigals. For the most part, however, he saw his job as that of a cultural assimilator, one who made a text enjoyable, accessible, and acceptable to a new audience with very different values and experiences, literary heritage and intellectual and political interests. As a result, it is important to approach these alterations, additions, and omissions — and, of course, the lack thereof — in these translations from the point of view of the cultural context in which they were made.

Compared to many other translations, the English version of Aeneas' text produced in 1550 represents a very faithful reproduction of the original. The storyline is essentially unaltered, the characters remain untouched and the moral message is preserved. The prose is, moreover, remarkably close to the Latin in both language and syntax; so much so, in fact, that at times it may be difficult for twentieth-century readers to construe. There are, of course, some alterations (many of which are pointed out in the previous discussion), some more significant than others. Nevertheless, had Aeneas been able to read this translation,

---

[162]See Di Francia, pp. 316–17; on Braccesi see, Paolo Viti, "I vogarizzmenti di Alessandro Braccesi dell' 'Historia de duobus amantibus' di Enea Silvio Piccolomini," *Esperienze Letterarie* 7 (1982), pp. 49–68; and Alexander Perosa, ed., *Alexandri Braccii Carmina* (Florence, 1943).

he would have found it a very familiar work.

The translator's decision to leave the text largely in its original form would seem to find an explanation in the fact that it fit so well as it was with rhetorical and ideological trends in sixteenth-century English society. Indeed, it may have been its natural affinity to this culture which made it such an appealing prospect for translation in the first place. From the point of view of narrative, *The History of the Two Lovers* offered a tale similar on many levels to the *novella*, a genre with which English audiences were becoming increasingly familiar and for which there was a growing demand. The story discussed issues particularly relevant to their own society and often prominent in the context of their own native literature — chastity, loyalty and the social repercussions of sexual desire. It upheld values that were fundamental to its culture — honour, sexual purity, marital fidelity — while its criticisms of Christian moral teaching echoed English attacks on the Roman Church. Finally, the language and imagery of classical literature which permeate Aeneas' story would have been familiar to audiences which were becoming more exposed to humanist education. Different though the two cultures may have been, the fifteenth-century Italian tale had much to say to audiences in sixteenth-century England.

For the most part, the changes and omissions that do occur in the text seem to align the story still more with English culture. By omitting the tale's original epistolary framework, the translator presented his audience with a very familiar and popular packaging. His inclusion of a poem at the end of the tale reflects contemporary interest in lyric, while its didactic intent illustrates the general concern to counter the corrupting influence of racy, lascivious tales of Italian origin. In addition to changes in the story's framework, there are a series of minor modifications to the tale itself which also seem to tailor it to particularly English audiences. The translator's tendency to generalize the more detailed descriptions of Italian custom or indeed even Anglicize them (thus *saturnalium* becomes "Jubilee", *magistratus* becomes "alderman", *Lex Iulia* becomes "civil law") was appropriate for an audience which, although curious and increasingly more familiar with Italian culture, would nonetheless have lacked the knowledge to understand and appreciate all of

Aeneas' allusions. Finally, the decision to make Eurialus' sufferings more bitter and long-lasting than they are presented in the original story seems to fit with the other efforts to appease English concerns by underlining still further the edifying message of the tale.

Not all the emendations made to the translation, however, serve to bridge the cultural gap between England and Italy. The decision to simplify or even eliminate some of the story's many references to classical literature, for example, accommodated not so much an English audience as it did a broader one. There were undoubtedly readers who could have appreciated some of Aeneas' more obscure allusions, but the vast majority would have brought to the text a far more general understanding of humanist culture. There are other cases in which the significance of the changes is less — the variations in the names of several characters (Sosias becomes Yosias, for example), incorrect translations of individual words, abridgements or minor alterations of descriptive passages or dialogue (such as when Eurialus is made to hide in a closet instead of under Lucrece's bed when Menelaus interrupts their tryst). The omission of a lengthy diatribe against the abuse of selling noble titles is particularly puzzling, given that it would have fit very smoothly into contemporary English discussions on the same issue. It is in these situations that the scholar can only offer a series of possible explanations — the demand of a specific audience, scribal error, or variations in the edition which was being copied or translated.[163] The confirmation of these theories depends on finding further evidence about the translator, the production of his text, and the history of its circulation.

The final product, with all of its emendations and adjustments, proved to be a successful formula: *The History of the Two Lovers* went through several editions in the latter sixteenth-century and still others in the following two hundred years.[164] Although we

---

[163]It is not clear whether the translator of the 1550 edition was himself responsible for these mistakes, or whether he was working from a translation in which they were already present. See the apparatus to the text for specific examples.

[164]There was another English edition in 1669 and still another in 1741; J.J. Jusserand, *The English Novella in the Time of Shakespeare* (London, 1901), p. 82.

cannot be certain of the specific reasons for its success, the story clearly had much to offer to the audiences of Tudor England: a dramatic tale of desire and physical passion; a penetrating study of the psychology of love; a lesson in morality told with realism and compassion; a dramatization of current social issues and tensions; an impressive display of humanist learning; and a sharp criticism of the Roman Church. Surely it is the spirit of humanitiy, tolerance and psychological comlexity of character—traits that shine through both in the original and in the English translation—that has allowd *The History of the Two Lovers* to transcend so successfully the barriers of place and time and continue to win audiences even today.

The Reception of Italian Renaissance Models in England in the Mid-Sixteenth Century
KENNETH R. BARTLETT

The anonymous translation of Piccolomini's *De duobus amantibus* reached an English audience early in the history of the Italian Renaissance influence on vernacular prose. The traditions of the Middle Ages had culminated in Chaucer who died in 1400. The use by Chaucer of Italian sources must be seen not as an English attempt to naturalize the early Renaissance styles and models of trecento Italy but as part of a European movement of shared culture. England remained powerfully part of the *respublica christiana* as manifested in its integration into continental literature, vernacular as well as Latin. There is a clear indication that Chaucer saw his material as fully applicable to his countrymen, despite the distance of his sources, such as Boccaccio.

The century which followed the death of Chaucer saw almost no translation of Italian imaginative literature into English. Indeed, the very absence of significant attempts to transport Italian models, whether popular or humanist, is remarkable, given the opportunities which existed. For example, in 1418 Poggio Bracciolini, one of Florence's great scholars and a humanist whose influence was to culminate in his appointment as Chancellor of the Florentine Republic, visited England and stayed for four years. His experience in that farthest outpost of the Roman *imperium* was disappointing, to say the least. He found little by way of undiscovered classical texts and few sympathetic friends. If anything, this point of contact between fifteenth-century English and Italian culture might have had a negative influence, because of Poggio's unhappy memories of his time in Cardinal Beaufort's service.[165]

Similarly, other moments might have linked the culture of Italy and England in the fifteenth century in a continuing way; but these, too, were curiously infertile. The humanist colleague of Leonardo Bruni, Tito Livio Frulovisi, produced no sustained intellectual or imaginative connections, aside from his important royal biography in the new humanist manner, his *Vita Henrici quinti* (c. 1438).

Much the same conclusions can be made about the English scholars and churchmen who studied in Italy, some resident with luminaries of the level of Guarino of Verona. Even the celebrated library of manuscripts collected by Henry V's brother, Humphrey, duke of Gloucester, created only a splendid library of classical texts which largely went to Oxford University to endow the collection which still bears his name. Their influence was not realized in the fifteenthcentury. Ironically, when Italian influence became a powerful engine after the Reformation, it was not Oxford but Cambridge which led the movement.[166]

English scholars continued to frequent the Italian universities, especialy Padua, and many spent periods of time in Rome. Equally, Italians held English sees and important positions within the English Church. Some, like the two Gigli bishops of Worcester, spent very little, if any, time in their sees; others, like Polydore

---

[165]See R. Weiss, *Humanism in England in the Fifteenth Century* (Oxford: Blackwell, 1967); and P.W.G. Gordan, *Two Renaissance Book Hunters: The Letters of Poggio Bracciolini to Nicolaus de Niccolis* (New York: Columbia University Press, 1974), especially letter XI: "You had better give up hope of books from England, for they care very little for them here" (p. 48).

[166]This conservatism of Oxford had much to do with the power of the theology faculty and the memory of the Archbishop Arundel's attempts to root out Lollard heresy in Wyclif's university. New ideas were not received with the enthusiasm they engendered at Cambridge.

Vergil, who began his long English residence at the beginning of the next century (1502) as papal subcollector, had a broad influence on English historiography but little in terms of popularizing Italian imaginative fiction, vernacular or Latin.[167]

Thus, the century of Duke Humphrey, John Tiptoft, Robert Flemmyng, John Free, Thomas Linacre, William Grocyn[168] and so many others remained empty of interest in the imaginative culture of Renaissance Italy. Certainly, important links were forged and connections to the spiritual, commercial, medical and classical humanist world of Italy were made; but the ability to mediate between the world of the Yorkists and Lancastrians and that of the muscular, imaginative culture so ably captured by Chaucer the century before is absent.

Part of the explanation for the lack of currency of Italian Renaissance ideas in England in the fifteenth century had been the effects of the Wars of the Roses and the collapse of central authority and aristocratic patronage in a period of desperate upheaval. Other factors had important consequences as well: the attraction of other, northern, cultural models, especially the court culture of Burgundy; and the desire for orthodoxy in the English Church, which equally contained much of the professional intellectual class of the kingdom, making it less curious about other, different imaginative forms.

The succession of the Tudors changed this situation to some degree. Henry VII was a new king from a new dynasty with only success in trial by battle as a claim to the throne. He needed to restore the prestige and authority of the monarchy and the royal court, and he recognized the power of culture to assist in his state building. Italian influences became established and institutionalized under his reign. The royal librarianship and the Latin secretaryship were created, initally filled by Italians. Italians took appointments as letter writers at the universities, and one of these, Pietro Carmeliano (who had actually been in England since 1481), began to teach at Oxford University, as well as

---

[167]See D. Hay, *Polydore Vergil: Renaissance Historian and Man of Letters* (Oxford: Oxford University Press, 1952).

[168]See Weiss, *op.cit.*; and G.B. Parks, *The English Traveler to Italy* (Rome: Edizioni di storia e letteratura, 1954).

assist in the preparation of Latin titles for printers. At Cambridge, Caius Auberinus fulfilled a parallel function, rising to giving the "Terence" lectures in humanities.[169] The fact that it appears that Auberinus at least was not paid for his teaching functions by the Unversity until 1507–8 indicates that his status was irregular. But his role had become important, as Carmeliano's had at Oxford.

The connection with printing, including with John Caxton who employed Carmeliano, is also important in the reception of Italian Renaissance literature. From the earliest years of printing, romances and novellas from the continent were popular. Many of these texts were from French originals; others, such as Malory, were indigenous English works. However, there were equally direct or indirect translations from the Italian which linked the literary cultures of the two nations in significant ways. For example, 1481 saw the printing of John Tiptoft's translation of Buonaccorso di Pistoia's *The Declamation of Noblesse*.[170] This availability of printed editions did not result in an explosion of Italian Renaissance titles during the late fifteenth and early sixteenth centuries, but it did prepare the ground for the remarkable interest in Italian titles at mid-century.

The reign of Henry VIII witnessed the flowering of interest in Italian culture. Court poets of the 1520s and 1530s in particular made Italian models and sources their own. Sir Thomas Wyatt the Elder, for example, took the poetry of Petrarch, Aretino and

---

[169]This humanist lecture derived its name not from the Latin playwright but from the text of Terentius Varro, *De Lingua Latina* in the 1471 edition of Valla's distinguished pupil, Pomponius Laeto. See K.R. Bartlett, "The Decline and Abolition of the Master of Grammar: An Early Victory of Humanism at the University of Cambridge," *History of Education*, (1977), pp. 3–4. See also D.R. Carlson, *English Humanist Books: Writers and Patrons, Manuscripts and Print, 1475–1525* (Toronto: University of Toronto Press, 1993).

[170]See H.S. Bennett, *English Books and Readers, 1475–1557* (Cambridge: Cambridge University Press, 1952), p. 289. It is interesting that the first English secular play, Henry Medwall's (fl. 1486) *Fulgens and Lucrece* was a translation from the Italian Buonaccorso da Montemagno's (d. 1429) *Controversia de vera nobilitate*. It is also interesting that Aeneas Silvius includes a discussion of nobility in *De duobus amantibus* which is omitted in the English translations.

Serafino dell'Aquila and fashioned it into English verse of the highest quality. A traveller to Italy himself, Wyatt had a sophisticated appreciation for the form and meaning of the original. His contemporary, Henry Howard, earl of Surrey, also wrote Petrarchan poetry, although he did not visit Italy.

Henry Parker, Lord Morley, was older than Wyatt and Surrey and not as gifted a writer. However, Morley's translations are important, not just because of their content but because of their intention. Morley is best known for his English version of Petrarch's *Trionfi*, printed between May and July 1554, although completed much earlier, in the reign of Henry VIII to whom it was originally dedicated in manuscript.[171] He also, moreover, translated Paolo Giovio's *Commentario delle cose de'Turchi*, Lapo di Castiglionchio's Latin *Life of Theseus*, Donato Acciajuoli's *Scipio and Hannibal*, Poliziano's Latin version of St Athanasius' *Prologue to the Psalter*, and a novella of Masuccio. Morley tells us in his dedicatory letter to the printed version of the *Triumphs* that he began it because he witnessed the effect a French translation of Petrarch's work had on Francis I and concluded, "how, being an Englishman, might do as well as the Frenchman, did translate this said work into our maternal tongue".[172] Elements of nascent national feeling, then, motivated Morley as well as his appreciation for the original. He wanted to make the work available to his own king and to his countrymen in their own language, a gift he could provide through his knowledge of Italian Renaissance literature and his interest in translation from Latin and Italian sources.

The 1540s saw much in the way of Italian Renaissance materials made available in English, at least in comparison to the previous 150 years. The courtly poets saw their paraphrases and translations in print and available beyond the manuscript

---

[171]For the occasion of the printing and the dating of the work, see K.R. Bartlett, "The Occasion of Lord Morley's Translation of the *Trionfi*: The Triumph of Chastity Over Politics," in A.A. Iannucci, ed., *Petrarch's Triumphs, Allegory and Spectacle* (Ottawa: Dovehouse, 1990), pp. 325–34.

[172]Francesco Petrarca, *Triumphs*, trans. Lord Morley, ed. D.D. Carnicelli (Cambridge, Mass.: Harvard University Press, 1971), p. 78. Spelling has been modernized.

culture of the Henrician court. For example, Wyatt's version of Aretino's *Penetential Psalms* appeared in 1549. The same year saw printed the first edition of the popular anthology, *Tales and Quick Answers, Very Mery and Pleasant to Read*, containing a collection of anecdotes, many from Italian Renaissance sources, such as the *Facetiae* of Poggio,[173] material which had, significantly, influenced Aeneas Silvius' creation of *The History of the Two Lovers*.

However, the most powerful influence on the English knowledge of and interest in the vernacular culture of Renaissance Italy was ironically the Reformation of the Church. The creation of the Henrician Church did not in any significant way divorce the English from Italy.[174] English students continued to travel to the University of Padua; English travellers still visited the Republic of Venice; English merchants continued to have mercantile dealings with Italians. Nevertheless, there was an obvious conclusion which can be drawn about the relations between Italian and English culture after the 1530s: the separation of England from the Holy See and the propaganda surrounding the Supremacy drove English observers to see Italy and Italians as different, as a separate people with their own curious customs and habits — and their own indigenous culture which was increasingly understood as distanced from the English experience. The universals of *respublica christiana* and Roman Church were fragmented forever. The consequence was that the English had to look at Italians for what they were. Imaginative literature could certainly assist in this desire to know the true nature of the Italian, defined by a national culture which, however, could also quite easily be mediated by the Europe-wide experience of humanist, Latin learning.

A clear manifestation of this is the growth in the study of Italian culture and language from the perspective of "otherness". One of the most interesting — and unusual — manifestations of

---

[173]See M.A. Scott, *Elizabethan Translations for the Italian* (New York: Burt Franklin, 1969; original ed., 1916), p. 4.

[174]See K.R. Bartlett, *The English in Italy: 1525–1558: A Study in Culture and Politics* (Geneva: Slatkine, 1991); and "The Strangeness of Strangers: English Impressions of Italy in the 16th Century," *Quaderni d'Italianistica* 1 (1980), pp. 46–63.

this new attitude to Italy can be found in Andrew Boorde's *The First Book of the Introduction of Knowledge*. This odd book was written by an Oxford-educated physician and monk[175] who embraced the Reformation but seemed most to enjoy travelling throughout the continent. Italy was an important stop for him. Although he witnesses for his reformed faith in his description of Rome ("I did see little virtue in Rome and much abominable vice, wherefore I did not like the fashion of the people"[176]), he nevertheless ensures that his reader will be able to deal with written and spoken Italian by giving them set phrases to memorize. For example, he offers: "Good morrow, my sir" as "Bonus dies nu sir"; and "Est kela, vel kesta, via recta pre andare Rome?" as "Is this or that the right way to go to Rome?" although he warns that it is written: "Est quela vel questa a via."[177] Certainly, Boorde is not truly useful as a linguistic or a cultural guide; but, once it saw print by William Copland in 1547 it prepared the English literary community for William Thomas' *Italian Dictionary* of two years later.

William Thomas[178] is the most important of the mid-century interpreters of Italian culture and language to the English. His *Italian Grammar* of 1550[179] provides an introduction to the vernacular literature through a study of the language. Thomas' principle of selection for the words in his appended dictionary is that of Bembo: Dante, Petrarch and Boccaccio will be the authors whose language he will reveal; and, he continues, his grammar, together with the dictionary, will provide enough knowledge of Italian to read those authors in the original. Thomas, then, had

---

[175]Boorde was a very poor monk since he was accused in 1517 of having carnal knowledge of women, despite his vows.

[176]A. Boorde, *Fyrst Boke of the Introduction of Knowledge*, ed. F.J. Furnivall (London: Early English Text Society, 1870), p. 178.

[177]*Ibid.*, p. 179.

[178]For Thomas see, E.R. Adair, "William Thomas: A Forgotten Clerk of the Privy Council," in *Tudor Studies* (London, 1924).

[179]The full title reads: *Principal Rules of the Italian Grammer, with a Dictionarie for the better understandyng of Boccace, Petrarcha, and Dante, gathered into this tongue by William Thomas* (London: Thomas Berthelet, 1550).

learned enough in his years in Italy to recognize the victory of the language of the three crowns in the *questione della lingua*. And, he believes it sufficiently useful to make these sources available to his fellow Englishmen.

The History of Italy (1549)[180] is Thomas' other gift to his English reading public. It is not so much a history as it is a kind of guide through the states of the peninsula. It is full of interesting and sympathetic observations, many from other sources; but is also reflects Thomas' own advanced Protestantism and dislike of the Roman Church. Clearly, familiarity with Rome, Italy and Italian literature and culture — even vernacular culture — would not lead to apostasy for mid-century Englishmen, if Thomas is an example. With Thomas' *History*, in fact, the process of separation of England and Italy had been largely completed, ironically through the mediation of an italophile hot gospeller who divorced contemporary Italy from the Roman Church and the *urbs aeterna* from the Holy See.[181]

In Thomas, moreover, the classical world of ancient Rome becomes more important than the Christian city, the see of St Peter. The humanism of the previous centuries had created in the European imagination a place for Italy outside the hieratic structure of Church and papacy. Thomas reinforces this by discussing the monuments of Rome and other Italian cities as consequences of a secular history in which English participation is not mentioned. Certainly, Thomas remarks upon the fall of a proud, corrupt and wicked Rome from a Protestant perspective and draws parallels with the recent reform of the Church; but the respect and knowledge of the nation, its culture and its history mitigates his Protestant sententiousness. For the Protestants around the young King Edward VI, Thomas' Rome and Italy were palatable and worthy of knowing.

The connection between Italian Renaissance culture and literature and the progress of the English Reformation followed more

---

[180]W. Thomas, *The History of Italy*, ed. G.B. Parks (Ithaca: Cornell University Press, 1963).

[181]Thomas' other printed work appeared in Italian and printed on the continent, perhaps in Italy. It was a dialogue defending King Henry VIII and the English Reformation, titled *Il Pellegrino inglese* (n.p. 1552).

conventional theological avenues as well. Archbishop Cranmer, in his attempt to build a particularly English Church, was catholic in his attraction to theologians with varied intellectual experience. Many Italians came to England to assist in the reform of the Church, and many of these had a high degree of personal culture. Men such as Emanuele Tremelli, Pietro Bizzarri, Peter Martyr Vermigli,[182] among others, came to England to find favour at court, the universities and the Church. Furthermore, there was the Italian exile congregation of Michelangelo Florio, whose preacher was the brilliant apostate former General of the Capuchins, Bernardino Ochino.

Ochino's influence was felt far beyond his celebrated preaching. In 1547 *Five Sermons* of Bernardino Ochino were translated into English. The next year saw more sermons of Ochino translated by Richard Argentine[183] and his *Tragedy or Dialogue of the Unjust usurped Primacy of the Bishop of Rome*, translated by John Ponet, future bishop of Winchester, from the original Latin.[184] Ochino's fundamental appeal was, of course, his religious message. However, as was stated by pious English observers with some regret, the power of his Italian vernacular preaching attracted many to his sermons for the language rather than for the message. Again, as with Thomas' *History*, Ochino made Italian Renaissance culture in the vernacular as well as Latin not only accessible to godly, Protestant Englishmen but also acceptable from a moral, religious perspective, given that Italy had clearly produced good men and that its indigenous culture could manifestly be used for good as for ill.

In this environment, interest in Italian Renaissance imaginative culture exploded around mid-century. Knowledge of that culture was no longer just the preserve of a few *italianati* at court and in the universities. Men such as Cardinal Wolsey (d. 1529) had some deep—if distant—knowledge of the culture of the

---

[182]See M. Firpo, *Pietro Bizzarri: esule italiano del cinquecento* (Turin: Giappichelli, 1971); and P. McNair, *Peter Martyr in Italy* (Oxford: Clarendon Press, 1967).

[183]Scott, p. 246.

[184]*Ibid.*, pp. 246–48. Also, Ponet was the author of *A Short Treatise of Politic Power*.

Italian Renaissance, as his pattern of patronage reveals. However, his sometime servant and eventual successor as Henry VIII's chief minister, Thomas Cromwell (d. 1540), had another kind of experience. His time in Italy had been spent either in service to Cardinal Bainbridge and as a merchant's factor.[185] He knew the language and had some degree of knowledge of the vitality of the popular culture outside the rarified arena of cinquecento Latin humanism. Consequently, the place of Italy in the educated English imagination was able to grow; and with it grew the English curiosity about the culture of this remarkable and increasingly complex nation, and the powerful literature it produced.

It is not surprising, then, that knowledge of the Italian language began to spread to parallel the already wide familiarity with humanist Latin. The princess Elizabeth herself translated some sermons of Ochino and learned the language very well and exhibited often as queen a deep interest in the imaginative literature of Renaissance Italy. She was instructed in Italian by Giovanni Battista Castiglione who appears to have combined language lessons with court intrigue.[186] Similarly, Elizabeth's cousin, the unfortunate Edward Courtenay, son of the attainted Marquis of Exeter and himself future earl of Devon, learned Italian very well while imprisoned in the Tower where he had been since the execution of his father. Courtenay's mastery of Italian in the Tower was no small feat and it was illustrated by his translation of Benedetto da Mantova's *spirituale* tract, *Il beneficio del Gesu Cristo crocifisso*, which he dedicated to the wife of Protector Somerset, in hope of securing his freedom.

If an Italian *spirituale* tract was seen as a good vehicle for a pardon by the Protestant duchess of Somerset and if the princess Elizabeth had received careful lessons in Italian which yielded not only her versions of Ochino but also her youthful translations of Petrarch's *Triumphs*, then Italian Renaissance imaginative culture had become firmly established as a caste mark among the English intellectual aristocracy, regardless of religion. Latin

---

[185]See A.J. Slavin, "The Gutenberg Galaxy and the Tudor Revolution," in *Print Culture and the Renaissance*, ed. G. Tyson and S. Wagonheim (Newark: University of Delaware Press, 1986), pp. 90–109.

[186]See Bartlett, *The English in Italy*, pp. 91–95.

humanism and Italian reformers had made the English mind susceptible: it now took the work of translators around 1550 to begin the deep penetration of the English curiosity about contemporary Italy.

The translators of mid-century are a fascinating and important group. They represent both the learned university-trained scholar and the dilettante gentleman; they are both advanced Protestants and conservative Roman Catholics. They translated material from several genres, not just vernacular pieces but Latin works as well, given the substantial interpenetration of humanist Latin with imaginative Italian culture that had occurred by 1550. It was this group of translators who made the vibrant and immediate world of Renaissance Italy so vivid to their English readers.

William Barker is among the more important translators around the mid-century. He is best remembered as the faithless servant who led his master, the duke of Norfolk, to the block after implicating him in the Ridolfi Conspiracy.[187] However, long before he entered Norfolk's service he was resident in Italy, largely Tuscany, where he produced two significant translations from the original Italian, Lodovico Domenichi's *On the Nobility of Women* and G.B. Gelli's *The Fanciful Fancies of the Florentine Cooper* (*Dialoghi del bottaio*). Although not immediately destined for print, these works were finished in Italy. Barker knew the civilized life of the *villeggiatura* around Siena and the court culture of Cosimo I's Florence, where Domenichi was the ducal librarian and a major intellectual figure. He equally knew the racy dialect and pungent commentary of the *poligrafici*, such as Gelli. In addition, Barker produced a learned Latin work on funerary inscriptions and a translation of Xenophon, which were immediately put into print.[188] What Barker was doing in Italy is

---

[187]For Barker, see K.R. Bartlett, "William Barker," in *Dictionary of Sixteenth Century Non-Dramatic Authors*, Vol. 132, ed. D.A. Richardson (London: Bruccoli, Clark, Layman, 1993), pp. 48–52; and "The Making of an Englishman Italified: William Barker in Italy," *Bollettino del Centro Interuniversitario di Ricerche sul Viaggio in Italia*, 20 (1989), pp. 209–17.

[188]W. Barker, *Epitaphia et inscripiones lugubres A Guiglielmo Berchero . . . collecta* (London, 1554); Xenophon, *The Bookes of Xenophon Contayning the discipline, schole, and education of Cyrus . . . Translated out of Greeke . . . by M. Wylliam Barkar* (London, 1553).

not known; but the effect of his sojourn there was to bring the culture of Renaissance Tuscany to his own countrymen.

The other great translator of mid-century is, of course, Thomas Hoby. His translation of Castiglione's *Cortegiano*, one of the most influential of all the Tudor translations, was begun long before it saw print in 1561.[189] Hoby's first journey to Italy from 1547–49 was the initial occasion of his direct contact with Italian culture and provides a continuing link with past italianati and connections to those of the present and future. On his route into Italy he met Thomas Wyatt the Younger, the rebel son of the great Henrician poet; in Padua he spent time with John Tamworth, the Mr J.T. to whom William Thomas would dedicate his *Italian Grammar*. Before he reached the peninsula he had translated Negri Bassanese's *The Tragedy of Free Will*[190] from the Italian and in Italy he began the deep cultural immersion in that nation which is minutely recorded in his journal and ultimately reflected in his translation of Castiglione.

Hoby spent some time touring the peninsula on this first visit, but much of his time was invested in studies in the studio of Padua. He polished both his Latin and Italian there and formed friendships with other English residents as well as with Italians and Spaniards. His world intersected with Barker's and they knew one another in Siena, an interesting moment when the two great mid-century translators of contemporary Italian imaginative literature lived in close proximity, linked by their knowledge of and interest in Italy and its literature, despite the wide divergence in their class, religion and expectations. When Hoby returned home he was able to witness for his love of Italy and do so in the highest regions of the court and intellectual

---

[189]For Hoby see K.R. Bartlett, "Thomas Hoby" in Richardson, ed., *op.cit.*, pp. 187–91, and "The Courtyer of Count Baldassar Castilio: Italian Manners and the English Court in the Mid-Sixteenth Century," *Quaderni d'italianistica* 6 (1985), pp. 249–58.

[190]F. Negri Bassanese, *Tragedia di F.N.B. intitolata Librio Arbitrio* (1546) as translated by Hoby does not survive. However, an English version by Henry Cheke, son of Hoby's companion in Italy, Sir John Cheke, has left his version of this dialogue. I expect that there would be many similarities between these two texts.

society where his connections and personal qualities gave him instant access.

There was a broader context to this attraction to Italian Renaissance culture. Just before the first extant translation of *The History of the Two Lovers* appeared there was clearly a growing interest in Italian prose fiction and novellas. As early as 1525, there was an English version of *Les Cent Nouvelles Nouvelles*,[191] a work from the French but composed of stories of Italian *novella* origin. Similarly in 1549 Thomas Berthelet printed *Tales and quicke answeres, very mery, and pleasant to rede*, a collection of anecdotes culled from many sources, but, again, largely classical or Italian. This edition was probably the second printed by Berthelet, following a somewhat shorter collection produced about 1535, but without a date. This text was subsequently enlarged and reprinted by H. Wykes in 1567.[192] The sources of this collection read like a compendium of Italian Renaissance wit: Lodovico Domenichi, Cinzio (Giambattista Cinzio Giraldi) and Poggio Bracciolini, among others.[193]

It is obvious, then, that imaginative works of romance fiction were finding a ready market in mid-century England, an observation reinforced by other translations produced within a decade of the anonymous version of *The History of the Two Lovers*. Henry Iden, for example, produced a translation of Giovanni Battista Gelli's *Circe* which was printed by John Cawood in 1557. This story, based on Plutarch, was printed in Florence in Italian only in 1549, and was sufficiently popular in English to see two editions of the Iden translation in one year (1557). Such was the appeal of the poligraphico, Gelli, that William Barker brought out the translation of the *Dialoghi del bottaio* eleven years later, although he had probably completed the work while in Florence some twenty years before.

The 1560s witnessed the publication of William Painter's *The Palace of Pleasure* (London: Hebry Denham for Richard Tottell

---

[191]*A C. mery Tales* (London: John Rastell, 1525), 24 leaves.

[192]See Scott, pp. 4–5.

[193]For a brilliant discussion of allusive anthologies in Renaissance England, see M.T. Crane, *Framing Authority: Sayings, Self and Society in Sixteenth Century England* (Princeton: Princeton University Press, 1993).

and William Jones, 1566, with later editions in 1569 and 1575). This collection of stories from various authors would prove to be a mine of materials for later English authors. The Italian sources are again reflective of the growing fashion of Italian Renaissance fiction, whether in Latin or the vernacular. Writers such as Giovanni Boccaccio, Matteo Bandello, Giovanni Francesco Straprarola da Caravaggio, Ser Giovanni Fiorentino and Masuccio Salernitano appear in translation to share their wit and wisdom with their English audiences.

Boccaccio's *Philocopo* was translated and put into print in 1567 (London: H. Bynneman for Richard Smith and Nicholas England) by H.G., probably Henry Granthan, who translated in 1575 Scipione Lentulo's *Italian Grammar*.[194] Geoffrey Fenton produced in that same year an English version of selections from Bandello in *Certaine Tragicall Discourses* (London: Thomas Marshe, 1567). The market for novellas and Italian material was obviously brisk.

Equally, though, the middle decades of the century saw an interest in Italian Renaissance poetry and drama, again both Latin and vernacular, in translation. Barnabe Googe translated Pietro Angelo Manzolli's *Zodiac of Life* (*Zodiacus vitae*, Venice, c. 1534) to appear in print in 1560. Baptista Mantuanus' *Eclogues* were translated from the Latin by George Turberville and printed in 1567. Ariosto's *Gli Suppositi* (1519) became in George Turberville's English *Supposes*, and Lodovico Dolce's *Giocasta* (1549) became the English *Jocasta* in 1566 when they were played at Gray's Inn and printed in 1572 (London: for Richard Smith).

Indeed, every area of learning and art in Italy was being acknowledged by English translations by the reign of Edward VI. The Reformation not only influenced the nature of the relationship between England and Italy during that reign, but also resulted in many translations of theological works. Besides the works of Ochino already noted, Peter Martyr Vermigli's tract on the real presence was translated (by Nicholas Udall) about 1550. Thomas Norton, future co-author of *Gorboduc*, while still secretary to Protector Somerset, translated a letter of Peter Martyr to the Duke in that same year.[195] The Latin letter of the Paduan

---

[194] *Ibid.*, p. 17.

[195] *Ibid.*, pp. 254–55.

Protestant apostate lawyer Francesco Spera saw print in 1550 as well in a version by either Edward Aglionby of Warwick or Edmund Allen, bishop-elect of Rochester.[196]

In the area of practical knowledge, Italian sources were equally popular in the 1540s and 1550s. There were English versions available of texts on medicine, horsemanship, warfare (including Peter Whitehorn's translation of Machiavelli's *Art of War* printed in English in 1560), voyages of discovery (including Pietro Martire da Anghiera's *Decades*, translated by Richard Eden, printed in 1555). History is represented by Nicholas Smith's translation pf Angelo Poliziano's *Herodianae historie* (London: William Copland, 1550?) and John Shute's translation of Andrea Cambini's *Libro . . . della origine de'Turchi* as *Two very notable Commentaries* (London: B. Hall for H Toye, 1562). Shute is also a significant figure because it was he, after having travelled through Italy to inspect buildings at the expense of the Duke of Northumberland in 1550, who wrote the first English treatise on architecture, *The First and Chief Grounds of Architecture* (London: Thomas Marshe, 1563), which is in effect a paraphrase of Vitruvius and Serlio.[197]

It was in this atmosphere of rapidly expanding English fascination with Italy and the culture of the Italian Renaissance that the anonymous translator of Aeneas Silvius Piccolomini's *De duobus amantibus* began his work. It was, then, produced as part of a developing intellectual tradition by 1550, a tradition which established the foundations of the subsequent explosion of English texts from the Italian that characterized the reign of Elizabeth. The intellectual context of these early translations from the Latin or Italian originals of the Renaissance in Italy form a rather coherent reflection of the broad interest in that culture. Every area of human experience is represented; but particularly significant is the imaginative literature of the novella, illustrating as it does the shared nature of humanity and the appeal of romance, humour and wit. Add to this the common ground of classical learning brought to England with the humanism of the fifteenth

---

[196]*Ibid.*, p. 254.

[197]See K.R. Bartlett, "The Wondrous Monuments of Building: Italian Architectural Theory and Practice in England in the Mid-Sixteenth Century," *Bulletin of the Canadian Mediterranean Institute* 9 (1989), pp. 1–3.

century and there emerges an appreciation of the audience for whom *The History of the Two Lovers* was intended. These readers constituted several categories: those who could have read the Latin original and who could appreciate the complex classical allusions and historical environment; those who were seeking a mildly salacious prose romance written with great insight into human nature, both male and female; and those desirous of accumulating more anti-Catholic ammunition for their reformed beliefs by reference to a romance depicting adulterous love and deceit written by a succesor to St Peter. This audience had been prepared by the popularity of the English versions of the stories of Boccaccio and Bandello produced at the same time. Desiring more, they turned with pleasure to *The goodly history of . . . Lady Lucrece . . . and of her Lover, Eurialus.*

There was apparently a 1547 translation of *The History of the Two Lovers*,[198] but no copy of it survives. Thus, the 1550 edition (London: William Copland) is the first available. It was reprinted in 1560 by John Kynge, and again by William Copland in 1567. Thomas Norton seems to have produced another version in 1569. Despite the popularity of the first editions of *The History of the Two Lovers*, there is no indication whatsoever of the identity of the translator. Nor is there any certainty which of the many printed editions — or manuscripts — of the Latin original the translator used for a base text. The first printing of Aeneas' story was extremely early, 1468 (Cologne: Ulrich Zell), followed soon after in 1473 by the first Italian printing (Rome: Adam Rot). A great many editions were then forthcoming: 1475 (two editions), 1476, 1483. Between 1483 and 1500 some thirty imprints were issued with an additional forty between 1500 and 1600.[199] It was translated into Italian, French and German as well. Moreover, the text circulated very widely in manuscript all across Europe from the time of its composition, again reflecting on the extreme popularity of the story and the fame of its author.

It is clear from the very Latinate quality of the English prose and the very close relationship between the original and the

---

[198]Scott, p. 7.

[199]M.L. Doglio, ed. and trans. *Enea Silvio Piccolomini, Storia di Due Amanti* (Torino: UTET, 1973), pp. 47–48.

translation that the anonymous translator most probably worked from the Latin, rather than from a vernacular version. It is very faithful to the text of *De duobus amantibus* in most regards, although there are instances of some omissions, of which one — the discussion of the nature of nobility — is significant. Whether this passage was missing in the text the translator used or whether it was consciously omitted cannot be determined. The poetic addendum to the English translation appears to be the work of the translator, since it serves as a kind of moral commentary to the text. Its quality indicates, perhaps, that the translator was not himself a poet of talent and did well in restricting himself to prose translation.

Although the identity of the translator of the 1550 and 1560 imprints of *The History of the Two Lovers* will likely never be discovered, it is nevertheless important to place him in the environment of the reception of Italian Renaissance literature in England. This work is early in that rich tradition but appears at a moment when the English rediscovery of Italy as a separate culture was beginning. Italians were now recognized as distinct, separate and other as a result of the events of the Reformation. However, in that discovery resided the foundations of a new appreciation of the literature of that nation, freed from the baggage of a universal Church and the memories of a shared imperial past. The Italians were enriching the imaginations of the English during those critical years around mid-century and the efflorescence of an indigenous English literature of the highest quality which appeared later in the reign of Elizabeth owes much to the English reception of Italian models of literary expression.

A Note on the Text

KENNETH R. BARTLETT

The base text used for the English translation of *The History of the Two Lovers* is the first extant edition of 1553?, printed in London by John Day[200] or William Copland. This text is referred to as "A" in the notes. There are possible earlier phantom editions

---

[200]The argument for Day's printing of *The Goodly History* in 1553?, see *Aeneas Silvius Piccolomini (Pius II). The Goodli History of the Ladye*

(1547, 1515)[201] but no copies survive. For purposes of textual comparison, the 1567 printing of the text by William Copland has been collated with the 1553? edition and appears in the notes as "B". The 1553? printing used as a base text[202] lacks its last leaf containing part of an original poem by the translator. This missing material has been supplied from a complete 1567 edition.

The 1567 printing by Copland is a reprint of a 1560 edition by John Kynge. The number of signatures and pages, the catchwords and all essential features are similar in both the 1560 and 1567 texts. Moreover, both of these editions are derived from the 1553? printing, differing from it only in details such as decorated capitals and other insignificant elements.[203] The purpose of the collation of the 1553? and 1567 printings is to draw students' attention to the variations which can arise from careless compositors' errors, and to illustrate the liberties the translator took with Aeneas' text through comparison of both English translations to the Latin original.

The two English translations have consequently been compared with the original Latin text of Aeneas Silvius as found in Maria Luisa Doglio's edition of *The Two Lovers*. The Latin text is referred to in the notes as "C". When significant differences appear between the Latin and English versions, the variations in the text are compared in the notes.

A modern critical edition of the first English translations has been prepared for the Early English Text Society by E.J. Morrall.

Lucres of Scene and of her Lover Eurialus, ed. E.J. Morrall (Oxford: Oxford University Press for The Early English Text Society, 1996), xiii–iv. We are not convinced, however, by Morrall's contention that the translation was made from the Gerard Leeu 1488 Antwerp printing of the Latin text (ibid., xv–vi). There are more deviations than can be explained by the Antwerp text and it is not impossible that the English translator was working from a manuscript copy.

[201]Scott, *Elizabethan Translations from the Italian* (New York: Burt Franklin, 1969; originally published, 1916), 7. *S.T.C.* 19969.8.

[202]*Goodli History of the Ladye Lucres of Scene and of her Lover Eurialus* (London: John Day or William Copland, 1553?). British Library: C.21 c.65.

[203]E.J. Morrall, pp. xiii–xiv.

We have consulted this text with great profit in the preparation of our modern spelling edition.

Bibliographies and Works Cited

I

Specific Bibliography on
The History of the Two Lovers

Bideaux, M. " 'L'Historia de Duobus Amantibus' nel '500 francese." *Pio II e la cultura del suo tempo. Atti del I convegno internazionale 1989*. Ed. Luisa Rotondi Secchi Tarughi. Milano: Guerrini, 1991. 175–88.

Bigi, E. "La 'Historia de duobus amantibus'." Rotondi Secchi Tarughi 163–74.

——. *Poesia latina e volgare nel Rinascimento italiano*. Naples: Morano, 1989.

Borri, G. "La Storia di Due Amanti." Rotondi Secchi Tarughi 189–97.

Bottari, G. "Il teatro latino nell' *Historia de duobus amantibus*" *I Classici nel Medioevo e nell'Umanesimo. Miscellanea filologica*. Genova: Istituto di filologia classica e medioevale dell'Universita di Genova, 1975. 113–26.

Braccesi, A. *Storia di due amanti di Enea Silvio Piccolomini in seguito Papa Pio secondo col testo latino e a la traduzione libera di Alessandro Braccio*. Capolago: Tipographia Helvetica, 1832.

Devay, J.I. *De duobus amantibus historia*. Budapest, 1904.

Doglio, M.L. *L'Exemplum nella novella latina del '400*. Torino: Giappichelli, 1973.

Di Francia, L. *La novellistica dalle Origini al Bandello*. Milan: Vallardi, 1924.

Frugoni, A. "Enea Silvio Piccolomini e l'avventura senese di Gaspar Schlick." *Rinascita* 4 (1941): 25–48.

Morall, E.J., ed. *Aeneas Silvius Piccolomini (Pius II), The Goodli History of the Ladye Lucres of Siena and of her Lover Eurialus*. Early English Text Society. London: Oxford University Press, 1996.

Najemy, J. *Between Friends: Discourses of Power and Desire in the Macchiavelli-Vettori Letters of 1513–1515*. Princeton: Princeton University Press, 1993.

Perosa, A., ed. *Alexandri Braccii Carmina*. Florence, 1943.

Piccolomini, A.S. *Storia di Due Amanti*. Trans. and introd. M.L. Doglio, with an essay by Luigi Firpo). Torino: UTET, 1973.

———. *Aeneas Silvius Piccolomini (Pius II) and Nikolaus Von Wyle: The Tale of Two Lovers, Eurialus and Lucrece*. Ed., introd., notes and glossary E.J. Morall. Amsterdam: Rodopi, 1988.

———. *Aeneae Sylvii Piccolminiei Pii Pontificis Maximi II Opera quae extant omnia*. Basel, 1551.

Piejus, M.F. "Une traduction française de la 'Historia de Duobus Amantibus' d'Enea Silvius Piccolomini." *La Circulation des Hommes et des Oeuvres entre la France et l'Italie à l'Époque de la Renaissance. Actes du Colloque International* (22–24 novembre 1990, Universite de la Sorbonne, Institut culturel italien de Paris). Paris: Université de la Sorbonne nouvelle, 1992. 103–17.

Pugliese, O. "La nouvelle conception de l'amour." *L'Époque de la Renaissance: 14001600. L'Avènement de l'Esprit Nouveau (1400–1480)*. Ed. T. Klanczay, E. Kushner and A. Stegmann. Budapest: Akadémiai Kiadó. Budapest, 1988. 215–25.

Rossi, V. *Il quattrocento*. Milan: Vallardi, 1933.

Tartaro, A. "La prosa narrativa antica." *La forma del testo* II. *La prosa*. Vol. 3: *Letteratura italiana*. Torino: Einaudi, 1984.

Viti, P. "I volgarizzmenti di Alessandro Braccesi dell' 'Historia de duobus amantibus' di Enea Silvio Piccolomini." *Esperienze Letterarie* 7 (1982): 49–68.

Wolkan, R. *Der Briefwechsel des Aeneas Silvius Piccolomini, I. Abteilung: Briefe aus der laienzeit (1431–1445) I, Band: Privatbriefe*. Vol. LXI in *Fontes Rerum Austriacarum*. Vienna, 1909.

Zannoni, G. "Per la storia d'una storia d'amore." *La Cultura* 9 (1890): 85–92.

II

General Bibliography on
Aeneas Silvius Piccolomini
(Pius II)

Ady, C. *Pius II (Aeneas Silvius Piccolomini) the Humanist Pope*. London: Methuen, 1913.

Battaglia, F. *Enea Silvio Piccolomini e Francesco Patrizi, due politici senesi del '400*. Siena, 1936.

Boulting, W. *Aeneas Sylvius Piccolomini (Enea Silvio Piccolomini — Pius II) Orator, Man of Letters, Statesman and Pope*. London: Constable, 1908.

Casella, N. "Recenti studi su Enea Silvio Piccolomini." *Rivista di Storia della chiesa in Italia* 26 (1972): 473–88.

Cesarini, R. "Rassegna bibliografica di studi piccolominiani." *Giornale storico della letteratura italiana* 141 (1964): 265–82.

Garin, E. "Ritratto di Enea Silvio Piccolomini." *Bulletino Senese di Storia Patria* 65 (1958): 5–28.

Mitchell, R.J. *The Laurel and the Tiara.* London: Hamill Press, 1962.

Paparelli, G. *Enea Silvio Piccolomini (Pio II).* Bari: Laterza, 1950.

———. *L'Umanesimo sul soglio di Pietro.* Ravenna, 1978.

Pastor, L. *Storia dei Papi.* Vol. 2. Roma, 1911.

Totaro, L. *Pio II nei suoi commentarii. Un contributo alla letteratura della autobiografia di Enea Silvio Piccolomini.* Bologna, 1978.

Voigt, G. *Eneas Silvio de' Piccolomini als Papst Pius der Zweite und sein Zeitalter.* 3 vols. Berlin, 1856–63.

Widmer, B. *Enea Silvio Piccolomini Papst Pius II. Biographie und ausgewahlte Texte aus seinen Schriften.* Basel, 1960.

———. *Enea Silvio Piccolomini in der sittlichen und politischen Entscheidung.* Basel, 1963.

Enea Silvio Piccolomini. Papa Pio II. Atti del convegno per il quinto centenario della morte e altri scritti raccolti da Domenico Maffei. Siena, 1968.

Pio II e la cultura del suo tempo. Atti del I convegno internazionale. 1989. A cura di Luisa Rotondi Secchi Tarughi. Milano, 1991.

III
Other Works Cited

Adair, E.R. "William Thomas: A Forgotten Clerk of the Privy Council." *Tudor Studies.* London, 1924.

Anderson, G., and W.E. Buckler. *The Literature of England.* Vol. 1. 5th ed. Glenview, Ill: Foresman, 1968.

Andreas Capellanus. *The Art of Courtly Love.* Trans. J.J. Parry. New York: Columbia University Press, 1941.

Ascham, Roger. *The Scholemaster.* Ed. J.E.B. Mayor. London: Bell and Daldy, 1863.

Augustine. *The City of God.* Trans. G. McCracken. Loeb Classical Library. Cambridge, MA: Harvard University Press, 1958.

Barker, W. *Inscriptiones lugubres.* London: Cawood, 1566.

Bartlett, K.R. "The Courtyer of Count Baldassar Castilio: Italian Manners and the English Court." *Quaderni d'italianistica* 6 (1985): 249–58.

———. "The Creation of an 'Englishman Italified': William Barker in Italy, 1551–1554." *Bollettino del Centro Interuniversitario di Richerche sul Viaggio in Italia* 20 (1989): 209–17. Turin, Italy.

———. "The Decline and Abolition of the Master of Grammar: An Early Victory of Humanism at the University of Cambridge." *History of Education* 6 (1977): 1–8.

———. "The Occasion of Lord Morley's Translation of the *Trionfi*: The Triumph of Chastity Over Politics." Ed. A.A. Iannucci, *Petrarch's Triumphs, Allegory and Spectacle*. Ottawa: Dovehouse Editions, 1990. 325–34.

———. "The Strangeness of Strangers: English Impressions of Italy in the 16th Century." *Quaderni d'Italianistica* 1 (1980): 46–63.

———. "Thomas Hoby." Richardson 187–91.

———. "William Barker." Richardson 48–52.

———. "The Wondrous Monuments of Building: Italian Architectural Theory and Practice in England in the Mid-Sixteenth Century." *Bulletin of the Canadian Mediterranean Institute* 9 (1989): 1–3.

———. *The English in Italy: 1525–1558: A Study in Culture and Politics*. Geneva: Slatkine, 1991.

Battaglia, S. "L'esempio medioevale." *Filologia Romanza* 6 (1959): 45–82.

———. "La Tradizione di Ovidio del medioevo." *Filologia Romanza* 6 (1959): 185–224.

Beecher, D. ed. *Barnabe Riche: His Farewell to Military Profession*. Barnabe Riche Society. Ottawa: Dovehouse Editions, 1992.

Bellonci, G., ed. *Novelle italiane*, vol. 1. Roma: Lucarini, 1985.

Bennett, H.S. *English Books and Readers, 1475–1557*. Cambridge: Cambridge University Press, 1952.

Boccaccio, Giovanni. *Opere*. Ed. Bruno Maier. Bologna: Zanichelli, 1967.

Boorde, A. *Fyrst Boke of the Introduction of Knowledge*. Ed. F.J. Furnivall. London: Early English Text Society, 1870.

Braccesi, A. *Alexandri Braccii Carmina*. Ed. A. Perosa. Florence: Bibliopolis Libreria Editrice, 1943.

Branca, V. *Boccaccio medioevale*, 7th ed. Firenze: Sansoni, 1990.

Carandente, Giovanni. *I trionfi del primo Rinascimento*. Torino: Edizioni R.A.I. 1963.

Carlson, D.R. *English Humanist Books: Writers and Patrons, Manuscripts and Print, 1475–1525*. Toronto: University of Toronto Press, 1993.

Chiarini, G., ed. *Novelle italiane: Il Quattrocento*. Milano: Garzanti, 1982.

Chrétien de Troyes. *The Complete Romances*. Bloomington, Indiana University Press, 1990. [Trans. of *Le chevalier et la charette*.]

Crane, M.T. *Framing Authority: Sayings, Self and Society in Sixteenth Century England*. Princeton: Princeton University Press, 1993.

Curtius, E.R. *European Literature in the Latin Middle Ages*. Trans. W.R. Trask. Bollingen Series, 36. Princeton: Princeton University Press, 1973.

Delcorno, C. *L'Exemplum e letturatura tra medioevo e rinascimento*. Bologna: Mulino, 1989.

Di Francia, L. *Novellistica*, vol. 1. Milano: Vallardi, 1924.

Doglio, M.L., and G. Ferrero, eds. *Novelle del Quattrocento*. Torino: UTET, 1975.

Doglio, M.L., trans. Enea Silvio Piccolomini: *Storia di Due Amanti*. Torino: UTET, 1973.

Fea, C. *Pius II a calumniis vindicatus*. Roma, 1823.

Ferrand, J. *A Treatise on Lovesickness*. Trans. and ed. D. Beecher and M. Ciavolella. Syracuse: University of Syracuse Press, 1990.

Ficino, Marsilio. *Commentary on Plato's Symposium on Love*. Trans. Jayne Sears. Dallas: Spring Publications, 1985.

Firpo, Massimo. *Pietro Bizzarri: esule italiano ndel cinquecento*. Turin: Giappichelli, 1971.

Fubini, R. *Umanesimo e secolarizzazione*. Roma: Bulzoni, 1990.

Givens, A.B. *La dottrina d'amore nel Boccaccio*. Messina: G. D'Anna, 1968.

Gordan, P.W.G. *Two Renaissance Book Hunters: The Letters of Poggio Bracciolini to Niccolaus de Niccolis*. New York: Columbia University Press, 1974.

Hahn, S.F. *Collectio Monumentorum veterum et recentium*, vol. 1. Brunsvigae, 1724.

Hay, D. *Polydore Vergil: Renaissance Historian and Man of Letters*. Oxford: Oxford University Press, 1952.

Jusserand, J.J. *The English Novel in the Time of Shakespeare*. Trans. E. Lee. London: Penguin Books, 1972.

Juvenal. *Juvenal and Persius*. Trans. G.G. Ramsay. Loeb Classical Library. Cambridge, MA: Harvard University Press, 1979.

Lactantius. *The Divine Institutes*. Trans. Sr Mary Francis McDonald, OP. Fathers of the Church Series, 49. Washington: Catholic University of America Press, 1964.

Livy. *Ab Urbe condita*. Ed. R. Seymour and C.F. Walters. 5 vols. Oxford: Oxford University Press, 1960–69.

McNair, P. *Peter Martyr in Italy*. Oxford: Clarendon Press, 1967.

McWilliam, G.H. "Foreword" to Giovanni Boccaccio, *The Decameron*. London: Penguin Books, 1972.

Menesto, E. *Coluccio Salutati: Editi e Inediti Latini dal Ms. 53 della Biblioteca Comunale di Todi*. Res Tudertinae, 12. Todi: n.p., 1971.

Morrall, E.J., ed. *Aeneas Silvius Piccolomini (Pius II) and Nikolaus von Wyle: The Tale of the Two Lovers, Eurialus and Lucrece*. Amsterdam: Rodopi, 1988.

Ovid. *The Art of Love and Other Poems*, vol. 2. Trans. J.H. Mozley. London: Harvard University Press, 1979.

——. *Metamorphoses*. Trans. R. Humphries. Bloomington: Indiana University Press, 1981.

Parks, G.B. *The English Traveler to Italy*. Rome: Edizioni di storia e letteratura, 1954.

Petrarca, Francesco. *Triumphs*. Trans. Lord Morley, ed. D.D. Carnicelli. Cambridge, MA: Harvard University Press, 1971.

Piccolomini, Aeneas Silvius. *Aeneae Sylvii De Duobus Amantibus Historia*. Ed. J.I. Devay. Budapestini: n.p., 1904.

——. *Aeneae Sylvii Piccolominiei Pii Pontificis Maximi II Opera Quae Extant Omnia*. Basel: Marcus Hopperus, 1551.

——. *Der Briefwechsel des Aeneas Silvius Piccolomini*. Ed. R. von Wolkan. Fontes Rerum Austriacarum. Bd. 61–62, 67, 68. Vienna: A. Holder, 1900–18.

——. *Enee Silvii Piccolominei postea Pii PP. II Carmina*. Ed. A. van Heck. Città del Vaticano: Biblioteca Apostolica Vaticana, 1994.

——. *The Tale of the Two Lovers by Aeneas Sylvius Piccolomini (Pius II)*. Trans. F. Grierson. London: Constable, 1929.

Radice, B. "Introduction." *Terence: Ten Comedies*. London: Penguin Books, 1976.

Richardson, D., ed. *The Dictionary of Literary Biography: Sixteenth Century Non-Dramatic Authors*, vol. 132. London: Bruccoli, Clark, Layman, 1993.

Sapegno, N. *Il Trecento*, 2nd ed. Milano: Vallardi, 1960.

Scaglione, A. *Nature and Love in the Late Middle Ages*. Berkeley: University of California Press, 1963.

Scott, M.A. *Elizabethan Translations for the Italian*. New York: Burt Franklin, 1969.

Seneca. *Four Tragedies and Octavia*. Ed. E.V. Rieu. Harmondsworth: Penguin, 1966.

Slavin, A.J. "The Gutenberg Galaxy and the Tudor Revolution." *Print Culture and the Renaissance*. Ed. G. Tyson and S. Waggonheim. Newark: University of Delaware Press, 1986.

Tartaro, A. "I volgarizzamenti di Alessandro Braccesi dell 'Historia de duobus amantibus' di Enea Silvio Piccolomini." *Esperienze Letterarie* 7 (1982): 49–68.

Thomas, William. *Il Pellegrino inglese*. N.p. 1552.

Valerius Maximus. *Faits et dits memorables*. Trans. and ed. R. Combes. 2 vols. Paris: Les Belles Lettres, 1995.

Virgil. *Aeneid*. Trans. H.R. Fairclough. 2nd ed. Loeb Classical Library. 2 vols. Cambridge, MA: Harvard University Press, 1935.

Viti, P. "La 'Historia de duobus amantibus' di Piccolomini: fonte probabile della Mandragola." *Ecumenismo della cultura. Atti del XV Convegno internazionale del Centro di Studi Umanistici*. Montepulciano, Palazzo Tarugi, 1977. Vol. 3. Firenze: Olschki, 1981.

Weiss, R. *Humanism in England in the Fifteenth Century*. Oxford: Blackwell, 1967.

Welter, J. *L'Exemplum dans la Littérature religieuse et didactique du moyen âge*. Paris-Toulouse: Guitard, 1927.

The goodly history
of the most noble and beautiful
Lady Lucrece of Siena in Tuscany,
and of her lover,
Eurialus,
very pleasant and delectable
unto the reader

The goodli
history of the moste noble and beau-
tifull Ladye Lucres of Scene
in Tuskan, and of her louer
Eurialus, verye
pleasaunt
and delec-
table
unto the re-
der.
(*)
*

*
* *

Anno Domini.
M.D.L.X.vii.

[facsimile rendering of original wording and linebreaks]

The Emperor Sigismond, entering into the town of Siena[1] in Tuscany, what honours he received is already everywhere published.[2] His palace was prepared at Saint Martha's chapel in the street that leadeth to the postern° called Tophore.[3] After the ceremonies were finished, when Sigismond was come thither, four ladies in nobleness, fashion, age, and apparel semblable,° did meet him not like mortal women but as goddesses to every man's judgment, and if they had been but three they had been to be reckoned them that Paris saw in his dream.[4] Sigismond (though he were aged) was prone to lust and delighted much in desiring° with ladies, and rejoiced in blandishments of women nor nothing was to him more pleasant than to behold goodly women. Then in advising° them (unlike to the rest) he was received from his horse° among them and turning to his familiars° said, "saw ye ever any like to these women? I am in doubt whether these faces be mankind or angels, but surely they are heavenly." They, casting their eyes to the ground in blushing,[5] became fairer and the° ruddy flushing in their cheeks gave such a colour to their countenance as hath the Indian ivory° stained with the scarlet, or the white lilies among the purple roses.[6] But among all, Lucrece, the young lady, not yet of twenty years, shone in great brightness, young married into the family of the Camillis to a very rich man, named Menelaus, unworthy to whom such beauty should serve at home, but well worthy of his

postern B. strete.　　**semblable** similar.　　**desiring** B. deuysinge.
Then in advising . . . his horse C. (p. 64) *ut ergo has vidit, desiliens equo* [therefore as soon as he saw them, dismounting from his horse].
advising observing.　　**familiars** attendants, household, entourage; C. (p. 64) *comites*.　　**the** B. that.　　**ivory** A. ynd uery; B. ynde euery; C. (p. 64) *Indicum ebur* [Indian ivory].

wife to be deceived.° The stature of the lady Lucrece was more
higher than the others. Her hair plenteous° and like unto the
gold wire which hanged not down behind her after the manner
and custom of maidens but in gold and stone she had enclosed it;
her forehead high, of seemly space, without wrinkle; her brows
bent, fashioned with few hairs,° by due space divided; her eyes
shining with such brightness that like as the sun they overcame
the beholders looking: with those she might whom she would,
flee (and slain) when she would revive.° Straight as thread was
her nose, and by even division parted. Her fair cheeks — nothing
was more amiable than these cheeks nor nothing more delectable
to behold, wherein (when she did laugh) appeared two proper
pits which no man did see that wished not to have kissed. Her
mouth small and comely, her lips of coral colour handsome to
bite on, her small teeth, well set in order, seemed crystal through
which the quivering tongue did send forth (not words) but most
pleasant harmony. What shall I show the beauty of her chin,°
or the whiteness of her neck? Nothing was in that body not to
be praised[7] as the outward appearances showed token of that
that° was inward.° No man beheld her that did not envy her
husband;° she was in speech as the fame° is that the mother
of Gracchus° was,° or the daughter of Hortentius.[9] Nothing
was more sweeter nor soberer than her talk. She pretended not
(as doth many) honesty by heavy countenance, but with merry

deceived C. (p. 64) adds: *et sicut nos dicimus, cornutum quasi cervum
redderet* [and, as we say, that she should give him horns like a stag] (this
was, and still is today, the symbol of a cuckold in Italian culture).
plenteous plentiful.   few hairs C. (p. 64) adds: *nigrisque* [and
black].   with those ... she would revive C. (p. 64) *His illa et occidere
quos voluit poterat et mortuos cum libuisset in vitam resumere* [With these
she could kill whom she wanted and, when it pleased her, restore them
to life].   chin C. (p. 66) *mentis* [of her mind].   that (B. omits).
inward B. in warder.   husband; C. (p. 66) adds: *erant insuper eius
in ore multe facetie* [there were also many witty things in her mouth].
fame report.   of Gracchus C. (p. 66) *Gracorum* [of the Gracchi].
was C. (p. 66) adds: *Cornelia*[8]

visage showed her soberness, not fearful, nor overhardy, but under dread of shame, she cared in a woman's heart.° Her apparel was divers, she wanted neither brooches, borders, girdles, nor rings. The abiliments° of her head was sumptuous; many pearls, many diamonds, were on her fingers and in her borders. I think the day that the Greek Menelaus feasted Paris Helen was no fairer, nor Andromache no more gorgeous when she was married unto Hector.[10] And, among those was Katherine of Persia,°[11] that shortly after died, in whose funeral the Emperor was present (and though he were but a child) made her son [a] knight at her sepulchre, and of her the beauty was all so° marvellous, but nothing so great as of Lucrece.° Her did the Emperor Sigismond, and all other, praise and behold;° but one among them more than enough was set upon her.

Eurialus of the country of Franconia, whom neither shape nor riches caused to be unmeet° to love, he was of the age of two and thirty years, not very high of° stature, but of gladsome and pleasant fashion, with noble eyes, his cheeks ruddy and fair as the white lilies among the purple roses;° his other members (as who sayeth) with a stateliness of shape correspondent to his stature. The other courtiers by long war were but poor. He, besides his own substance, by familiarity with the Emperor, received daily rewards. He was more and more gorgeous in sight of men and

but under dread . . . woman's heart C. (p. 66) *sed temperatum verecundie metum, virilem animum femineo corde gerebat.* [but she carried in a woman's heart a manly spirit, ruled by a fear of shame.]. **abiliments** decorations. **Persia** B. Perusia; C. (p. 66) Petrusia. **all so** C. (p. 66) quoque [also]. **Lucrece** C. (p. 66) adds: *Omnis de Lucretia sermo audiebatur.* [Everyone was talking about Lucrece.]. **behold** C. (p. 66) adds:*Quocunque illa vertebatur, eo et oculi sequebantur astantium, et sicut Orpheus sono cithare silvas ac saxa secum fertur traxisse, sic ista homines suo, quecunque volebat, intuitu ducebat.*[12] [Wherever she turned, the eyes of the bystanders followed her, and like Orpheus, who is said to have drawn after him the woods and the rocks with the sound of his cithara, she led them wherever she pleased with her presence]. **unmeet** not right for. **of** (B. omits). **cheeks . . . roses** C. (p. 66) *malis ad gratiam tumescentibus* [with cheeks pleasantly puffed up].[13]

led a great train of servants after him,° and he had such a horse (as the tale reporteth) as Mennon[15] had when he came to Troy. Nothing he wanted to provoke the same heat of the mind° called love, but only idleness.[16] Yet, youth, lust, and the glad goods of fortune, with which things he was well nourished, overcame him out of his own power. Eurialus, as soon as he has seen Lucrece, he brent° in the love of the Lady, and fixing° his eyes in her face, never thought he to have seen enough, yet loved he not in vain. It is a wondrous thing: there were many goodly young men, but Lucrece had only chosen this; there were many goodly women, but Eurialus had chosen her only. Nevertheless, not at that° time knew Lucrece the fire of Eurialus toward her, nor he hers, but each one of them thought to have loved in vain.

The ceremonies unto the Emperor finished, she returned home, whole vowed unto Eurialus, and Eurialus, clean given unto Lucrece, remaineth. Who now should marvel of the tale of Pyramis and Thisbe betwixt whom both acquaintance and neighbourhood might be everything° of their love, and° in time grew their love.[17] These lovers, Eurialus and Lucrece, never saw nor heard afore° either of other, he a Franconian and she a Tuscan, nor in this° business they employed° not their tongues, but it was all done with eyes, sithens° that the one so pleased the other.[18] Lucrece then wounded with grievous care and taken with the° blind fire, forgetting already that she is married, hateth her husband, and with wounds nourishing the wound,° holdeth fixed

---

him C. (p. 68) adds: *Nunc auro illitis, nunc muricis Tyrii sanguine tinctis, nunc filis, que ultimi legunt Seres, textis vestibus utebatur* [the clothes he wore were either covered with gold, or dyed with Tyrian purple, or woven with the thread the Seres once used].[14]		**the same heat of the mind** C. (p. 68) *illum blandum animi calorem magnamque mentis vim* [that enticing heat of the spirit and great force of the mind].		**brent** burnt.
fixing B. fyryng.		**that** B. the.		**everything** A. entire.		**and** C. (p. 68) adds: *quia domos habuere contiguas* [because their houses were beside one another].		**afore** before.		**this** A. these.		**employed** A. occupied.		**sithens** since.		**the** B. they.		**with wounds nourishing the wound** C. (p. 70) *alens veneneum vulnus* [nourishing the poisoned wound].

in her breast the countenance and face of Eurialus, nor giveth no manner rest unto her limbs, and with herself sayeth,[19] "I wot° not what letteth° me that I can no more company with my husband, nothing delighteth me his embracings, nothing pleaseth me his kisses, his words annoy me, so standeth always afore mine eyes the image of the stranger[20] that today was next unto the Emperor. Cast, alas, O unhappy, out of my chaste breast that conceived flames if thou may, if I might, alas, I should not be as I am, evil at ease. A new kind of strength against my will draweth me, my desire and my reason moveth me diversely,° I know the best, and the worst I follow. O noble citizen, what hast thou to do with an unknown man? Why brennest° thou in a stranger's love? Why seekest thou thy lust° in a strange country? If thy husband loveth° thee thine own country may give thee that thou lovest. O, but what a manner of face hath he! What woman would not be moved with his beauty, youth nobleness and virtue? Surely I am — and without his help I despair. God grant us better. Shall I betray, alas, the chaste spousels° and betake me to a stranger I wot not whence, which when he hath abused me, shall depart and shall be another's and so leave me behind? But, by his countenance, it is not like to be so, and the nobleness of his mind seemeth not to be such, nor so pretendeth not the grace of his beauty that I should fear deceit or his forgetting of love. And he shall promise aforehand.° So, assured, why do I dread? I shall apply it without, farther abroad, parde. I am so fair that he will no less desire me, than I him. He shall be mine forever, if once I may receive him to my kisses. How many do woo me wheresoever I go? How many rivals do watch afore my door? I shall intend° to love. Either he shall tarry here, or at his departing carry me with him. Shall I than forsake my mother, my husband, and my country? My mother is forward°

wot know.   **letteth** prevents.   **diversely** in different directions. **brennest** burns.   **lust** C. (p. 70) *talamos* [bedchamber, marriage, marriage bed].   **loveth** C. (p. 70) *fastidis* [disgusts].   **spousels** wedding vows.   **aforehand** beforehand.   **intend** decide.   **forward** obstinate.

and always against mine appetites; my husband I had rather be without° than have, my country is there as I delight to dwell,[21] but shall I so lose° my fame? Why not? What have I to do with men's words which I shall not hear? Nothing shall he dare, that feareth the threatening of fame, many other have done the same. Helena would be ravished. Paris carried her not away against her will. What shall I tell of Diana° or Medea? No man blameth the faulter that faulteth with many." Thus said Lucrece. Nor within his breast nourished Eurialus no less flames.

In the mid way betwixt the emperor's court and Eurialus' lodging was Lucrece's house, and Eurialus might not go unto the palace, but showing herself out of the high windows, was in his eyes,° but always Lucrece blushed when she saw Euri-alus, which thing gave unto the Emperor knowledge of the love. For as by custom he used to ride here and there, passing often that way he saw the woman change countenance by Eurialus' coming, which was as next unto him as Maecenas to Octavian,[23] to whom the Emperor, looking aside, said, "dost thou bren° women on° this fashion Eurialus? That woman surely loveth thee." And once in manner as though he had envied his love, when he came before Lucrece's house, he put Eurialus' cap over his eyes. "Thou shalt not see," quoth he," that that° thou loveth; I will myself use that° sight." Eurialus answered, "Sir, what meaneth this? I have nothing to do with her. But take heed what ye do least ye bring suspect° in them that be here about us." Eurialus was mounted upon a high reined chestnut horse,° with a small head, whose short belly and fair hair caused him to show goodly, well breasted, lusty, and courageous so that hear-ing the trumpet he could nowhere rest. He received the fury

---

without A. and B. want.   **lose** A. and B. lease.   **Diana** C. (p. 72) *Hadrianam.*[22]   **eyes** sight.   **bren** burn.   **on** in.   **that** (B. omits).   **that** B. the.   **suspect** suspicion.   **chestnut horse** B. couler [courler]; C. (p. 72) adds: *ardue cervicis* [with his neck held high]. **He received . . . the noise** C. (pp. 72-4) *Micabat auribus et collectum fremens volvebat sub naribus ignem.* [He flickered his ears and, snorting, he exhaled fire from his nostrils].

of the noise,◊ his fair mane hung upon the right side, and the ground resounded, beaten with his foot.[24] And not much unlike him was his master. When he had espied◊ Lucrece who, being alone, as soon as she had seen him could neither temper the flame [of his love] nor herself: so the unhappy Lucrece did burn. In mean houses dwelleth chastity, and only poverty useth good affection,◊ and chastity that haunteth small cottages knoweth not the policies for rich men. Who that aboundeth in prosperity lightly desireth unaccustomed things. Fires, lust,◊ companion to fortune, hath chosen delicate houses and stately mansions.◊[25] Lucrece, that oftentimes◊ beholding Eurialus passing by, might not assuage her ardent desire, busily thinking to whom she might herself discover. For who that secretly brenneth more grievously suffereth. There was among the servants of her husband one Yosias,◊ an Almaine◊ old and faithful to his master, whom he had long served very honestly.◊ Him doth she◊ go unto, trusting more to the nation than to the man.

The Emperor, accompanied with many noble◊ men, went solacing◊ through the town,[26] and even now did he pass by the house of Lucrece whom, when she knew that Eurialus was there, "come hither," quod she, "Yosias, I would speak with thee.[27] Look here out of the window. Where in the world is there any youth like this? Seest thou how upright◊ and fair spread shoulders they have? Behold their bushes◊ and well kept hairs. O what faces! What fair necks! What noble hearts their countenances doth pretend.◊[28] This is another kind of people than

espied spied, saw. **affection** passion. **rightly desireth . . .** **stately mansions** C. (p. 74) *luxu fluit semperque insolita appetit, delicatas eligit domos et penates magnos, dira fortunae comes libido.* [abounds in luxury and always desires new things; and lust, Fortune's dread companion, chooses luxurious and expensive houses]. **Fires, lust** B. Fyers, luste. **oftentimes** B. aften times. **Yosias** A. 3osias; B. Zosias; C. (p. 74) Sosias. **Almaine** German. **very honestly** (C. omits). **she** C. (p. 74) adds: *amans* [loving]. **noble** (C. omits). **solacing** for pleasure and recreation. **upright** C. (p. 74) add: *ut omnes calamistrati sunt.* [that all have curly hair]. **bushes** beards. **pretend** present.

our country doth breed. They seem gods or of heavenly kind. O that fortune had given me a husband of° one of these. If mine eyes had not seen them, I would never have believed thee if thou had told me of them. Yet the fame is that the Almaines excelleth all other people, and surely I believe that the cold giveth to them great whiteness,° the country's so drawing toward the north. But dost thou° know any of them?" "Yea, many," quoth Yosias. "Then," quoth Lucrece, "Eurialus the Franconian, dost thou know him?" "Yea, as mine own self," sayeth Yosias, "but why dost thou ask?" "I shall tell thee," quoth she. "I know it shall not be disclosed, this hope hath thy goodness given me. Among all them that are about the Emperor none pleaseth me like him. In him my mind moved. I wot not with what flames I burn; I can neither forget him, nor yet myself appease, except that° I may make myself acquainted with him. Go therefore, I beseech thee, Yosias. Seek Eurialus; tell him I love him. Nothing else I desire of thee, and yet this shalt thou not do in vain." "What is this?" quoth Yosias. "Shall I either do such outrage or once think it Madame? Shall I betray my master? Shall I now, old, begin to deceive which I have hated in my youth? Rather, most noble lady of this town, cast forth the wicked furore out of thy chaste breast. Follow not thy cruel hope, but quench the fire. He doth not painfully put back love that resisteth the first assaults, but he° that the sweet ill-flattering doth nourish giveth him to the bondage of a right hard and cruel master nor when he would may not forsake the yoke,[29] which, if thy husband should know, alas, under what fashion would he torment thee? No love can long lie hidden. "Hold thy peace," quoth Lucrece, "there is no fear at all: nothing he feareth that feareth not death. I am content to suffer it whatsoever happeneth.[30] What opinion dost thou hold?"° "O unhappy," quod Yosias, "thou shalt shame thy house, and only of all thy kin thou shalt be adulteress. Thinkest, thinkest° thou the deed can be secret? A thousand eyes are

of from.   **whiteness** i.e. fair hair and complexions.   **thou** B. to.
that (B. omits).   **he** B. thee.   **What opinion dost thou hold** (C. omits).   **thinkest** (B. omits).

about thee. Thy mother, if she do according,° shall not suffer
thy outrage to be privy, not thy husband, not thy cousins, not
thy maidens,° yea, and though thy servants would hold their
peace, the beasts would speak it, the dogs the posts and the marble stones. And though thou hide all, thou cannot hide it from
God, that seeth all. Understand that pain is present unto a guilty
thought, and the mind, filled with offence, feareth himself. Faith
is denied in great crimes. Assuage, I beseech thee, the flames of
wicked love.° Fear to mingle strange bodies° in thy husband's
bed." "I know," quoth she, "it is according as thou sayest; but
the rage maketh me follow the worse. My mind knoweth how
I fall headlong;° but furore hath overcome and reigneth, and
over all my thought ruleth love. I am determined to follow the
commandment of love. Overmuch, alas, have I wrestled in vain.
If thou have pity on me, carry my message." Full heavy was
Yosias with this word, and said to her thus: "For these hoary
hairs on my head, by age,° and for the faithful service that I have
done unto thy kin, humbly I beseech thee leave this furore and
help thyself. A great part of health is will to be healed." To
whom saith Lucrece, "all shame hath not forsaken my mind. I
will obey thee, Yosias. In the love that cannot be hid,° only the
eschewing of this ill is by death to prevent the offence." Yosias,
affeared° with this saying, "Moderate," quoth he, "my lady, the
rage of thy unbridled mind. Temper thy thought. Now art
thou worthy life, when thou judgest thyself worthy of death. "I
am determined," quod Lucrece, "to die. Collatinus' wife, the
fault committed, venged° with a sword.[31] I, more honestly, shall

if she do according (C. omits).   **maidens** maids.   **love** C. (p. 76)
adds: *expelle facinus mente casta horridum* [cast such dreadful wickedness
out of your chaste mind].   **bodies** A. makes.   **headlong** C. (p. 78)
adds: *et ruit sciens* [and fully aware it hastens to ruin].   **age** C. (p. 78)
adds: *fessumque curis pectus* [and a heart tired with cares].   **In the
love...hid** C. (p. 78) *amorem, qui regi non vult, vincam.* [love, which does
not want to be controlled, I shall conquer].   **affeared** frightened.
venged was avenged.   **I, more...prevent it** C. (p. 78) *ego honestius
morte preveniam committendum* [I shall more honestly anticipate what is
to be accomplished by death].

prevent it.° I study but the kind° of my death: a cord, sword, fall or poison shall revenge chastity — one of these I shall assay." "I will not suffer thee," quoth Yosias. Quoth Lucrece, "Who that determineth to die cannot be let. Portia,° at the death of Brutus, when weapon was taken from her did eat hot coals."[32] "If the furore be so forward in thy mind," quoth Yosias, "thy life is rather to be succoured than thy fame. Deceitful is fame that to the ill, better, and to the good, worser, is often given. Let us assay this Eurialus and let us intend° to love. The labor shall be mine; and, as I think, I shall bring it to effect." With these words the kindled thought he enflamed° and gave hope to her° doubtful mind,[33] but his mind was not to do as he said. He sought° to defer° the mind of the woman, to assuage the desire, as oftentimes time quencheth flames and sufferance healeth diseases.° Yosias went with false trust° to drive her forth till the Emperor should depart or she should change her mind, lest if he had denied her,° another messenger should have been found, or else the woman should have slain herself. Oftentimes therefore he fained himself to go and come, and that he rejoiced in her love, and sought a convenient time that they might talk together, sometime that° he [Yosias] could not speak with him, some time he sought to be sent out of the town, and till his return deferred her glad days. So, many days he did feed the sick mind, and because he should not lie in all things, once only he brake° unto Eurialus, saying: "O how thou art here beloved!" Yet when he asked what that meant he answered not. But Eurialus, stricken with the secret° dart of Cupid, gave no rest nor sleep to his limbs, the fire so crept in his veins and utterly wasted his marrow.°

kind manner.   **Portia** A. and B. Perria; C. (p. 78) *Portia Cathonis* [Portia, the daughter of Cato].   **intend** decide.   **enflamed** C. (p. 80) adds: *amore* [in love].   **her** A. and B. the.   **sought** thought. **defer** change.   **sufferance healeth diseases** C. (p. 80) *adimit aegritudinem dies* [time carries away sorrow].[34]   **Yosias ... trust** C. (p. 80) *Existimavit Sosias falsis gaudiis puellam producere.* [Sosias thought to entice the girl with false hopes.].   **her** A. it; B. adds: yf.   **that** (B. omits). **brake** spoke(?).   **secret** C. (p. 80) *certo* [sure].   **marrow** A. and B. mary.

Yet knew he not Yosias, nor thought him to be the messenger of Lucrece. So have we all less hope than desire. He, when he saw himself burn, a great while with this wisdom wondered, and under this fashion oftentimes blamed himself. Lo, Eurialus, thou knowest what the rage° of love is: long plaints° and short laughters; few joys and many dreads, always he dieth and is never dead that loveth. What dost thou meddle in vain? At last, quoth he, all° for nought.° O wretch, why strive I against love? May not I do that Julius, that Alexander, that Haniball did? And these were worthy warriors.[35] Look besides upon poets: Virgil drawn up by a rope, hung in the midway to the window,° trusting to have embraced his love. If any man will excuse the poet as a follower of a more dissolute life, what shall we say of philosophers, masters of learning, and rulers of good living. A woman did ride Aristotle like a horse and ruled him with a bridle and spurred him. It is not true that is said commonly: honour and love accord not together.°[36] The Emperor's power is equal with the gods, and who is a greater lover than he? They say that Hercules (that was strongest of all men, and of the race of gods) the disroile° of the lion and his quiver laid apart,° took in hand a° rock and trimmed rings for his fingers, and set in order his red bush,° and with his hand, wherewith he wonted to carry a mace, by tirling° of a spindle he drew a thread.[37]

---

rage C. (p. 80) *imperium* [rule].   **plaints** complaints.   **What dost thou meddle in vain? At last, quoth he, all° for nought.** C. (p. 80) *"Quid tu te his nugis inmisces iterum?" At cum se frustra niti videret:* ["Why are you meddling again in this nonsense?" But when he saw that it was useless to fight it:].   **all** B. and.   **window** C. (p. 80) *turrim* [tower]. **together** C. (p. 82) adds: *nec in una sede morantur* [nor do they stay in the same seat]. In C, the line which follows ("The Emperor's power . . . gods") precedes this sentence.   **disroile** skin.   **apart** aside. **a** (B. omits).   **bush** beard.   **tirling** turning.

It is a natural passion. Birds are brent with° this fire. The
turtle and the dove doth love.° What shall I say of beasts? The
horse moveth battle for love. The fearful hart seeketh to fight,
and by believing, sheweth his furor. The fierce tiger, and the
cruel boar whetting his teeth, doth use it. And the lions of Libya
set up their rough manes when love moveth. The monsters of
the sea do feel this heat.° Nothing is free, nay, nothing unto love
denied. Hate giveth place unto it. It stirred the fierce flames of
youth, and unto very age° it revoketh the dead heat, and striketh
the breasts of maidens with a brenning fire.°[39] Why then do I
strive against the laws of love? Love overcommeth all thing, and
let us give place unto him."[40]

When these things were concluded, he seeketh a bawd to
whom he might take her letters to carry to her.[41] Nisus was
his faithful fellow[42] and understood much in such matters. He
taketh the business in hand, and hireth a woman to whom the
letters were taken, written as followeth:

Eurialus unto Lucrece: "I would send the greeting and health
with my letters if I had any myself, but surely, both of my health
and life the hope hangeth in my hands.° More than myself I
love thee, and I ween° it is not unknown unto thee. My face oft
moisted with tears[43] may show token of my wounded breast and

brent with excited by.   **The turtle . . . doth love** C. (p. 82) *Nam
niger a viridi turtur amatur ave et variis albe iunguntur sepe columbe, si
verborum memini, que ad Pharaonem Siculum scribit Sapho.* [For the black
turtle-dove is loved by the green one, and often the white doves join
with those of varied hues, if I remember the words which Sappho wrote
to Sicilian Phaon.].[38]   **The fearful hart . . . this heat** C. (p. 82)
*timidi cervi prelia poscunt et concepti furoris dant signa mugientes, uruntur
Hircane tigres, vulnificus aper dentes acuit, Peni quatiunt terga leones. Cum
movit amor, ardent insane Ponti bellue* [the fearful stags yearn for battle
and, bellowing, show their conceived fury. The Hyrcanian tigers are
inflamed, the wild boar sharpens his teeth, the lions of Libya strike
their backs. When love moves them, the monsters of the Black Sea
burn insanely.].   **very age** A. weryag; C. (p. 82) *senibusque fessis* [old
age].   **brenning fire** C. (p. 82) *ignoto . . . igne* [unknown fire].
hangeth in my hands C. (pp. 82, 84) *ex te pendet* [depends on you].
ween believe.

the sighs° which in thy presence I have cast forth.[44] Take it well, I beseech thee, that I discover me unto thee; thy beauty hath taken me and the grace of godly heed,° wherein thou passest all other, holdeth me. What love meant unto now I never knew, but thou hast subdued me to the power of thy desire. Long did I strive (I confess) to escape so violent a master, but thy brightness hath overcome mine endeavour. The beams of thine eyes passing the sun hath overcome me. I am taken and am no more mine own. The use of meat and drink thou takest from me.[45] Continually° I thee love, thee I desire, thee I call, thee I await, thee I think on, thee I° trust in, and with thee I delight me. Thine is my mind, and with thee it is whole.[46] Thou only mayest save me; thou only mayest lose° me.[47] The one of these choose; and what thou intendest write it unto me. Be no more hard in thy words in answering me than thou was with thine eyes in binding me. It is no great thing that I ask. To speak conveniently with thee I ask. This only desireth my letters. That that I write, I may say afore thee, this if thou grant me, I live and well happy I live; if not, thou slayest my heart that thee more than me loveth. I recommend me unto thy good grace, and to the trust that I have in thee.[48] And thus farewell the delight and residue° of my life."

These letters sealed, when the woman had received [them], hastily she went unto Lucrece, and finding her alone said unto her thus: "The most noble of the Emperor's court, thy° lover sendeth thee these letters, and prayeth thee instantly to take him unto thy grace." This woman was noted for a bawd, and that knew Lucrece and took it very displeasantly to have a naughty woman sent unto her, and to her she said:° "What madness hath

---

sighs A. and B. sights; C. (p. 84) *suspiria* [sighs].   **thy beauty . . .**
godly heed C. (p. 84) *Cepit me decus tuum vinctumque tenet eximia, qua omnibus prestas venustatis gratia* [Your exceptional beauty has taken and conquered me, with your grace superior to all others].   **from me.**
Continually B. from me contynually.   **I** (B. omits).   **lose** A. lese;
B. lefe.   **residue** succor; C. (p. 84) *subsidium* [succor].   **court, thy**
B. court. Thy.   **said** C. (p. 84) adds: *Que te . . . scelesta in hanc domum audacia duxit?* [What evil audacity brings you to this house?].

moved thee to come to my presence? Art thou so bold to enter the houses of noble men? Darest thou provoke great ladies to violate sacred marriage? Scant° can I hold my hands from thy ear!°[50] Bringest thou letters unto me? Speakest thou unto me? Darest thou look me in my face? If I regarded not more what becometh me than what thou deservest, I should so order thee that thou shouldest after this day never carry more letters of love. Enter out of my sight abominable queen,° and take thy letters with thee. Yea, rather give them me° that I may cast them in the fire." And, snatching the paper from her, tore it in pieces and trod under her feet, spitting at it, cast it in the ashes. "So should thyself be punished, bawd," quoth she, "more worthy the fire than thy life. Pick thee hence shortly lest that my husband, finding thee here give thee that that I remit unto thee. And while thou livest, never come in my sight."

Another would have been afraid, but she well acquainted with the manners of women, thought to herself, "now wouldest thou most when thou showest most the contrary," and said unto her, "forgive me, madame. I thought I had not done amiss and that it should have stood with thy pleasure. If it be otherwise, pardon mine ignorance. If thou wilt not that I return unto thee, I shall obey thy commandment; but take thou heed what a lover thou forsakest," and with these words departed from her. And when she had found Eurialus: "Be of good comfort," quoth she, "thou lover, the woman loveth more thee than she is loved. But now it is was° no time to write unto thee. I found her sad; but when I named thee and gave her thy letters, she made good countenance and kissed the paper a thousand times. Doubt not, thou shalt shortly have an answer," and thus the old woman departing, she was well ware° no more to be found lest she had suffered° for her lying.

Scant scarcely.　　ear C. (p. 84) *capillos* [hair].[49]　　queen C. (p. 86) *venefica* [sorceress].　　me C. (p. 86) adds: *lacerem . . .-que* [that I may tear them to pieces and].　　now it is was at that moment there was. ware aware.　　suffered been punished.

Truly Lucrece, after the woman was departed, sought up the pieces of the letter and set each in their place, and joined so the torn words that she made it legible which, when she had read it a thousand times, a thousand times she kissed it, and at the last wrapped it in a fair napkin and put it among her jewels, and remembering now this word, now that word, continually she soaked in more love,[51] and determined to write to Eurialus, and sent her letter on this fashion endited:◊

Lucrece to Eurialus: "O Eurialus, leave to hope after that thou canst not attain. Leave to bear◊ me with thy letters and messengers. Think not that I am of that sort that sell themselves. I am not she that thou takest me for, nor unto whom thou shouldest send a bawd. Seek for thy lust another. No affection but chastity shall follow. With other do as thee liketh, but of me ask nothing, for be thou sure I am unmeet◊ for thee. Farewell."[52] This letter (though it seemed unto Eurialus very hard, and contrary to the woman's words) yet did show him the ready way how to send his letters; for he doubted not to trust whom she trusted, but the ignorance of the Italian tongue combred◊ him. Therefore with busy study he learned it and because love made him diligent he was in short while cunning, and himself alone endited his letters, which afore he was wont to borrow when he should write anything in Italian.◊ He answered then to Lucrece that she should not be displeased with him because he sent an unhonest woman to her, sithen◊ he as a stranger knew it not, and could use none other messenger. The cause of his sending was his love, desiring no dishonesty. He believed her very honest and chaste, and so much more to be beloved, and that unhonest women and over-liberal of their honour he did not only not love but also greatly hate. For, chastity lost, nothing is in◊ a woman◊ to be praised — for beauty is a delectable pleasure and a frail,[53] and nought to

endited wrote.   **bear** burden.   **unmeet** unsuited.   **combred** restricted.   **Italian** C. (p. 88) *Hetrusco* [Tuscan].   **sithen** since. **in** (B. omits).   **woman** B. adds: not.

be esteemed without honesty — and that she that honesty win-
neth with beauty,◊ passeth in both gifts, and that therefore he
did lemmahonour herhonour her,◊ and only he desired to speak
with her that he might by his words declare his mind, that he
could not by his letters. With such manner of letters he sent her◊
a token, not only rich in value, but excellent in the workmanship.

To these letters Lucrece thus answered: "I have received thy
letters, nor is it not the woman now I blame thee for. That thou
lovest me I esteem not greatly, for thou art neither alone nor the
first whom they say my beauty hath deceived. Many have loved
me and do love me; but thy labour as well as theirs shall be in
vain. I neither can nor will talk with thee and except thou were
a swallow thou canst not find me alone. The houses be high and
the gates be kept.◊ I have taken thy token for that the fashion
pleaseth me, but because I will nothing of thine for nought, and
that it shall not be as a token of love, I send the ring which my
husband gave my mother, that it may be to thee as price of thy
jewels for it is of no less value than thy gift. Farewell."

To these letters Eurialus replied: "Great comfort were thy
letters unto me that thou complainest no more of the woman. But
that thou settest thy love so light grieveth me sore, for though
many do love thee, none of their love is so fervent as mine. But
thou believest it not. For that I may not speak with thee, but if
I might, thou shouldest not weigh it so light. Would to God, as
thou sayest, that I might be a swallow,[54] yea, or a less thing◊ that
thou might not shut thy window against me. But my most grief
is not that thou cannot, but that thou wilt not.◊ Ah, my Lucrece,
what meaneth that thou wilt not? If thou might, wouldst thou
not speak with me that am all thine, and that nought desireth
so much as to please thee? If thou bid me go into the fire, I

beauty C. (p. 88) adds: *eam divinam esse mulierem* [she is a god-like
woman].   **honour her,** C. (p. 88) adds: *qui nil ab ea peteret libidinosum
aut offensurum fame* [who seeks nothing from her that is lustful or that
will harm her reputation].   **her** (B. omits).   **kept** guarded.
a less thing C. (p. 90) *pulverem* [dust].   **not** C. (p. 90) adds: *Nam
quid ego nisi animum respicio?* [For what else do I consider except your
feelings?].

THE TWO LOVERS 135

shall sooner obey than thou shalt command. Send me word, I beseech thee, that if thou might, thy will were good. Give me not death with thy words that mayest give life unto me with thine eyes. If thou wilt not speak with me because thou mayest not, I am content. But change° that word, I pray thee, that sayest my labour shall be in vain. God forbid in thee° such cruelty. Be, I beseech thee, more gentler to thy very lover. If thou continue so, thou shalt slay me — and be thou sure, sooner thou with a word than another with a sword.° I ask,° thou hast none excuse, no man can forbid thee that. Sayest thou lovest me, and I am happy that my token remaineth with thee;[55] howsoever it be, I am glad of it. It shall sometime remember thee of my love; but it was too simple, and that that I send thee now is less, but refuse not thou that thy lover sendeth thee. I shall have out of my country daily better. When they come thou shalt not lack them. Thy ring shall never part from my finger, and instead of thee I shall moist it with continual kisses. Farewell, my health, and in that thou may help me."

At the last after many writings and answers Lucrece sent him such a letter. Lucrece to Eurialus: "I would fain Eurialus do thee pleasure, and as thou desirest, reward thee with my love,° for that asketh thy nobleness and thy conditions deserveth it, that thou shouldest not love in vain — besides thy beauty and goodly face — but it is not for me to love thee. I know myself. If I begin to love I shall neither° keep measure nor rule. Thou canst not long be here, and if I fall unto thee, I cannot lack thee. Thou wouldest not take me with thee and I surely would not long tarry behind thee. Many examples do move to refuse a

change B. chaunce. **thee** B. that. **sword** C. (p. 90) adds: *Desino iam plura poscere* [I shall now cease to ask for more]. **I ask** C. (p. 90) adds: *ut redames tantum postulo* [only that you love me back]. **reward thee with my love** C. (p. 92) *amoris mei participem facere* [make you my lover]. **neither** B. neuer. **Many examples . . . love** C. (p. 92) *Monent me multarum exempla, quae peregrinos amantes deserte sunt, ne tuum amorem sequar* [I am warned by the examples of many women who were deserted by foreign lovers, lest I follow your love].

stranger's love.° Jason that° won the golden fleece by Medea's counsel forsook her. Theseus had been cast to the Minotaur's had not the counsel of Adriana° helped him; yet did he leave her behind him in an island. What became on the unhappy Dido that received the wandering Aeneas? Was not her love° her death?[56] I know what peril it is to receive a stranger's love, nor I will not put me into such hazards.[57] You° men are of more stronger mind, and sooner can quench the fire.[58] woman when she beginneth to love only by death maketh an end. Women rage; they do not love, and except they be answered with love, nothing is more terrible. After the fire be kindled, we neither regard fame° nor life. The only remedy is the obtaining of the lover, for that that we most lack, we most desire. Nor we fear no danger for our appetites. Since I then am married, and unto a noble rich man, [I] am determined too exclude all loves,° and specially thine, which can not be continual least° I be noted as Phyllis° or Sappho.[59] Therefore I desire thee no more to ask my love, and little by little to assuage and quench thine, for it is more easy to men than to women; nor thou, if thou love me, as thou sayest, wouldst not desire that that° should be my destruction. For thy token I send thee a cross of gold, set° with pearls which, though it be little, is of some value. Farewell."

Eurialus to this letter held not his peace, but as he was° with the new writing kindled so took he the pen in hand, and under this form following endited a letter. Eurialus unto Lucrece: "Honour and health be unto my dear heart Lucrece, she that giveth me health with her letters. Though they be meddled° somewhat with gall, yet I trust when thou hast heard mine thou shalt withdraw it. Thy letters are come to my hands sealed, which I have read oftentimes and kissed as oft. But it seemeth to mean another thing than thy mind would. Thou desireth

---

that C. adds: *vigilem interemit draconem et* [killed the watchful dragon and].   **Adriana** Ariadne.   **love** C. adds: *peregrinus* [foreign].
You B. yong.   **fame** reputation.   **loves** B. louers.   **least** B. laste.   **Phyllis** C. (p. 92) adds: *Rodopeia* [Thracian].   **that** B. the.
, set (B. omits).   **was** (B. omits).   **meddled** mixed.

me to leave to love, because it is not meet for thee to follow a stranger's love, bringing examples of such that hath been so deceived (so eloquently) that I must rather wonder of thee° than forget thee. Who would then leave to love when he seeth such wit and learning in his mistress? If thou wouldst have swaged° my love thou shouldest not have showed thine eloquence, for that it° is not to quench the fire, but to make it rather flame. The more I read it, the more I burned, seeing thy beauty and honesty so joined with learning. But it is in vain to desire me to leave to love thee.° Desire the hills to become plain[s], and the rivers to return into the springs. For as well may I leave to love as the sun° his course.[60] If the high mountains° may want snows, or the sea fishes, if the forests may want deer,° then may Eurialus forget thee. Men are not so prone as thou weenest, Lucrece, to quench their desires; for that that thou givest unto our kind,° men do ascribe it unto yours. But I will not undertake that to debate. To that must I answer which toucheth me near. For the deceits of other[s], thou bringest in examples whereby thou wilt not reward me with thy love. But more are to be brought, my Lucrece, whom women hath deceived: Troilus° by Cressida; Deiphus° by Helena; and Circe by her enchantments deceived her lovers°[61] — but it were not according by the deeds of a few to judge all the rest. Shouldest thou for a certain ill man abhor

---

thee C. (p. 94) adds: *et amare tuum ingenium* [and love your cleverness]. **swaged** assuaged.   **it** (B. omits).   **But it is . . . love thee** C. *Verba sunt tamen, quibus rogas, ut amare desistam* [But they are words with which you ask me to stop loving you].   **sun** C. (p. 94) *Phebus* [the god of the sun, Phoebus Apollo].   **mountains** C. (p. 94) adds: *Scythie* [of Scythia].   **deer** C. (p. 94) *feris* [wild beasts].   **kind** B. mynde. **Troilus** C. (p. 96) adds: *sicut nosti Priami filium* [Priam's son, as I know]. **Deiphus** Deiphobus.   **deceived her lovers** C. (p. 96) *vertebat in sues atque aliarum terga ferarum* [transformed her lovers into pigs and other kinds of wild beasts].   **Shouldest thou . . . all men** C. (p. 96) *Nam si sic pergimus et tu propter duos tresve malos aut etiam decem viros omnes accusabis horrebisque* [For if we continue thus, you will accuse and shun all men because of two or three or even ten evil ones].

and accuse all men?$^\lozenge$ Or I, for many ill women, hate all the rest?$^\lozenge$
Nay, rather let us take other examples, as was of Anthony and
Cleopatra, and of other[s] whom the shortness of my letters letteth to rehearse. But it is read$^\lozenge$ that the Greeks, returning from
Troy, have been holden by strangers' loves, nor never have come
to their countries, but tarried with their loves, content rather to
want their friends, their houses, their reigns,$^\lozenge$ and other dear
things of their country, than to forsake their ladies.[62] This I beseech thee, my Lucrece, remember and note those few things
that be against our love.$^\lozenge$ So do I love thee, to love thee always,
and ever to be thine. Nor call me no stranger, I pray thee, for
I am rather of this country than he that is born here, sithens he
is but by chance and I by mine own choice. No country is mine
but where thou art. And though I depart at any time, my return
shall$^\lozenge$ be short; nor I shall not return at all into my country, but
to set order in my businesses, that I may dwell long with thee,
wherefore occasion may be found soon enough.[63] The Emperor
hath much to do in these parties,$^\lozenge$ the charge whereof I will sue
to have, sometime as ambassador, sometime as commissioner,$^\lozenge$
and he must have a lieutenant in Strucia,$^\lozenge$ and that will I obtain.
Doubt not my delight,$^\lozenge$ my heart, and my only trust. If I may
live,$^\lozenge$ yet pity$^\lozenge$ thy lover that melteth like snow afore thee. Soon
consider my travails, and now at last set an end to my torments.
Why punishest thou me so long I wonder of myself. How I have
suffered so many evils, how I have waked so many nights, how
I have forborne my meat and drink so long — behold how lean

Or I . . . all the rest C. (p. 96)*et propter totidem feminas cetere omnes
erunt odio mihi.* [and I shall hate all other women because of the same
number.].   **But it is read** C. (p. 96) *Si tu Ovidium legisti* [If you read
Ovid].   **reigns** kingdoms.   **remember . . . our love** C. (p. 96)
cogites non illa, que nostro sint amori adversa et que pauci fecerunt [do not
think of those which are against our love and which few have done].
shall B. at all.   **parties** parts.   **sometime as commissioner** (B.
omits).   **Strucia** C. (p. 96) *Hetruria* [Tuscany].   **delight** C. (p. 96)
adds: *Lucretia* [Lucrece].   **live** C. (p. 98) adds: *absque corde . . . et te
relinquere possum* [without a heart and I could give you up].   **pity** C.
(p. 98) adds: *tandem* [at last].

I am[64] and how pale.[65] A small thing is it◊ that holdeth the life within my body.[66] If I had slain thy parents or thy children, thou couldest punish me no sorer. If thou so handle me for that I love thee, what shalt thou do to them that have offended thee.[67] Ah, my Lucrece, my lady, my health and my succour, take me into thy grace, and at last write unto me that I am thy beloved; nothing I would else, but that I might say I am thy servant. Pardie,◊ both kings and emperors love their faithful servants, nor the gods disdain not to know them that loveth them. Farewell, my trust and my dread."

Like as a tower cracked within, sounding outward imprevible◊ if a piece of ordinance be shot against it, forthwith it rent in pieces.[68] So was Lucrece overcome with Eurialus' words, for after she had perceived the diligence of the lover, her dissembled love she declared with such letters. Lucrece to Eurialus: "I may no more Eurialus resist thy requests, nor longer withhold my love from thee. I am overcome,◊ unhappy woman, by thy letters,◊ which, if thou observest not according to thy writing,◊ thou◊ shalt be of all perjured traitors, the worst. It is easy to deceive a woman, but so much is it the more shameful, now that I am come into thy love,◊ and, as a woman, can consider but little. Thou that art a man, take charge both of thyself and of me. Thine I am, and thy faith I follow, and thine would I not be, except it were forever. Farewell, the stay and leader of my life."

is it B. it is.   **Pardie** by God (pardieu).   **imprevible** impregnable.
overcome C. (p. 98) adds: *iamque sum tua* [and now I am yours].
letters C. (p. 98) adds: *nimium multis exponenda sum periculis, nisi tua me fides et prudentia iuvet.* [I must be exposed to many dangers, unless your trust and prudence save me.].   **which, if thou . . . writing** C. (p. 98) *Vide, quod serves, que scripsisti. Si me deseris* [Be sure to obey what you have written. If you desert me . . .].   **thou** A. that.   **love** C. (p. 98) adds: *Adhuc res integra est. Si putas me deserendam, dicito, antequam magis amor ardeat. Nec incipiamus quod postmodum incepisse peniteat. Omnium rerum inspiciendus est finis.*[69] [Until now it has been secret. If you think you will have to abandon me, tell me now before love burns any more. And let us not begin what we will later have to repent. An end must be sought in all matters].

After this were many letters written on° both parties, and Eurialus wrote not so vehemently as Lucrece did answer fervently.
And that had both one desire of their meeting, but it seemed hard,
and almost impossible, sithens the eyes of everybody did behold
Lucrece, which never went forth alone, nor wanted° a keeper.
Nor Argus never kept Juno's cow so diligently[70] as Menelaus
caused Lucrece to be kept. This vice is of property to° the Italians, to shut up their wives as their treasure and on my faith (to
my judgement) to little purpose; for the most part of women be
of this sort: that most they desire that most to them is denied,
and when thou wouldest they will not, and when thou wouldest
not, they would.[71] And if they have the bridle at liberty, less they
offend, so that it is [as] easy to keep a woman against her will
as a flock of flies in the heat of the sun, except she be of herself
chaste. In vain doth the husband set keepers over her, for who
shall keep those keepers?[72] She is crafty and at them lightly she
beginneth, and when she taketh a fantasy she is unreasonable
and like an unbridled mule.°[73]

Lucrece hath a half brother;° he carried her letters and was of
counsel in her love. With him she had appointed to shut privily
Eurialus in his house, and he dwelled within° his stepmother,
that was Lucrece's mother, whom Lucrece did oftentimes visit,
and was also of her oftentimes visited, for they dwelt not far
asunder. Now this was the order of it: Eurialus should be shut in
the parlour, and after the mother was gone to the church, Lucrece
should come as it were to speak with her, and not finding her,
should tarry for her return. In the meantime she should be with
Eurialus. This should be within two days, but these two days
were two years to the lovers; for to them that hope well the hours
be long, and too them that trust little, they be as short. But fortune
followed not their desires. The mother mistrusted, and at that

on by.   **wanted** lacked.   **of property to** to a common practice
among.   **and when . . . unbridled mule** C. (p. 100) *Indomitum animal
est mulier nullisque frenis retinendum.* [A woman is an indomitable animal
and can be held by no reigns.].   **half brother** A. and B. brother-in-law;
C. (p. 100) *spurious frater* [illegitimate brother].   **within** with.

day when she went forth, shut her stepson° out, which brought
to Eurialus the heavy news, to whom the displeasure was no
less than to Lucrece, which, when he° saw her craft perceived,°
"let us go," quoth she, "another way to work;[74] yet shall not
my mother let my appetite." One Pandalus was her husband's
cousin, whom she had also made privy of her secrets, for the°
flaming mind might no where rest. She advertised° Eurialus to
speak with him, for he was trusty, and could find well a mean
for their meeting. But Eurialus thought it not sure to trust him,
whom he saw always with him Menelaus, fearing thereby deceit.
In taking deliberation, he was sent by the Emperor to Rome to
determine with the Pope for his Coronation, which was both
unto him and her grievous, but it° must be obeyed; so was his
journey two months long. In the meantime Lucrece kept [to] her
house, shut up her windows, put on sad apparel, and no where
went she forth. Everybody marvelled and knew not the cause,
sithen the widows of the town showed themselves. And they
of the house thought themself in darkness, as though they had
wanted the sun, seeing her often on her bed and never merry,
thought it sickness and sought all remedies that might be; but
she never neither laughed nor came out of her chamber till time
she knew that Eurialus was come to the presence of the Emperor;
for then, as waked out of a° sleep, she laid apart her sad clothes
and dressed with her former gorgeousness, opened her windows
gladly looking for him whom, when the Emperor saw, "Deny°
no more," quoth he,° "Eurialus, that° matter is perceived. Never
man in thy absence might see Lucrece. Now that thou art come,
we may see° the bright morning. What measure is in love?[75] It
can not be cloaked nor hidden with hems."

stepson A. and B. son-in-law; C. (p. 102) *privignum* [stepson].   **he**
B. she.   **perceived** C. adds: *Hac non successit* [It did not work.].
the B. that.   **advertised** encouraged.   **it** C. (p. 102) *Cesaris*
imperium [the emperor's authority].   **a** C. (p. 102) adds: *gravi* [deep].
Deny B. adds: it.   **he** (B. omits).   **that** B. the.   **see** B. adds:
in.

"Ye mock, sir," quoth Eurialus, "and find your laughter at me. I know not what it meaneth. The neighing of your horses[◇] hath peradventure wakened her."[76] And, when he had said, privily he beheld Lucrece and fixed fast his eyes in hers, and that was their first salutation after his return. Shortly after Nisus, Eurialus' trusty friend, diligently pursuing his friend's cause, found a tavern which, behind Menelaus' house had a window towards Lucrece's chamber. He maketh the taverner his friend, and when he had void the place bringeth thither Eurialus, saying: "Out of this window mayest thou speak with Lucrece." Betwixt both houses was a dark canal which no man came to, dividing Lucrece's window from the chamber by the space of three ells. Here sat the lover awaiting if by chance he might see her and he was not deceived, for at[◇] last she came to the window, and looking here and there. "What dost thou," quoth Eurialus, "the nouris[◇] of my life, whether turnest thou thine eyes my dear heart? Hither turn them, I pray thee, look hither, my health, behold thine Eurialus is here, I myself am here."[77] "Art thou there?"[◇] quoth Lucrece. "O my Eurialus, now may I speak with thee, and would god I might embrace thee." "It shall not need no great business," quoth Eurialus, "I shall set to a ladder, open thy chamber: too long have we deferred the enjoining of our love." "Beware of that," quoth she, "my Eurialus, if thou love my life. Here is a window on the right hand, and a very ill neighbour, and the taverner is not to be trusted that for a little money would peradventure betray both thee and me. But let us work. Otherwise it is enough if here we may talk together." "But this[◇] is death to me," saith Eurialus, "without I might in mine arms embrace thee. In this place did they talk long, and at the last reached each to other tokens upon a reed, and Eurialus was no more liberal in his gifts than Lucrece was.[◇] Yosias perceived the craft and said to himself: "In vain do I resist the mind of

horses C. (p. 104) adds: *et prolixe barbe strepitus tue* [and the rustling of your long beard].   **at** B. adds: the.   **nouris** nourishment.
there B. here.   **this** C. (p. 104) adds: *visio* [sight].   **was** (B. omits).

the lovers, and except I provide wisely, my mistress is undone and the house shamed forever; of both these ills◇ it is best to withstand the one. My mistress loveth. If it be secret, it maketh no matter, she is blind for love and seeth not well what she doeth.◇ If chastity can not be kept, it is enough to hide the noise least the whole house be slandered, or least there be any murder◇ done; surely I will go to her and help her. While I might I did withstand that no offence should be done, and because I might not, it is now my part to hide that that needs will be,◇ lest it be known. Love is an universal reigning mischief, nor none there is not infected with this sickness, and he is judged most chaste that is most secret.[78] And thus thinking with himself, Lucrece came out of her chamber, and Yosias meeting her, said thus: "What meaneth it that thou devisest with me no more of thy love? And, nevertheless, Eurialus is beloved of thee,◇ take heed whom thou trustest. The first point of wisdom is not to love at all. The next that at the least it be secret, and thou alone without a messenger canst not do it. In what trust thou mayest put me in, by long time thou hast learned. If thou wilt trust me, tell me, for all my most care is lest this love, if it be known, thou shalt suffer, and thy husband most of all."◇

To this answered Lucrece: "It is as thou sayest, Yosias, and I trust thee much; but me thought I wot not how negligent, and against my desire. Now that thou offerest thyself,◇ I will use thy diligence, and I fear not to be deceived of thee. Thou knowest how I burn, and long I may not endure this flame. Help me that we may be together. Eurialus for love languisheth and I die. Nothing is to us worse than to let our appetites. If we may once meet together, our love shall be more temperate and it

ills B. both of these; elles,.   doeth (B. begins a new paragraph here).
murder C. (p. 106) *parricidium* [parricide].   be C. (p. 106) adds: *parum enim refert, non agere, et sic agere* [for it does little good not to act, and thus to act].   thee C. (p. 106) adds: *et, ut clam ames* [and, so that you may love in secret].   most of all C. (p. 106) *omnium oblocutiones ferat* [will be mocked by everyone].   thyself C. (p. 106) adds: *sponte* [willingly].

shall well be hid. Go then and show° Eurialus the only way to
come to me, if he will. Within these four days, when the villains
bring in wheat, disguise him like a porter, and clothe himself in
sackcloth, and carry the corn° into the garner.° Thou knowest my
chamber hath a back door by the ladder. Tell all unto Eurialus,
and I shall wait for him, and when time is, I shall be alone in my
chamber, and when he is alone let him put open the door and
come into me."

Yosias, though° it were a high matter, fearing a worse, taketh
in hand the business, and finding Eurialus, appointeth with him
the order of everything, which he as light things gladly accepteth,
and maketh him ready to this message, and nought plaineth but
of long abode. O, insensible breast of a lover. O blind thought.
O hardy mind and unfearful heart.° What is so unaccessible that
thou thinkest not open enough? What way so sharp that thee
seemeth not plain? What is so close that is not to be unclosed?
Thou settest light all dangers; thou findest nothing too hard;
vain is the jealousy of husbands against thee. Neither law nor
fear doth hold thee, to no shame art thou subject, to thee° all
labours is but play. O love, subduer of all things! A noble
man dearly beloved with the Emperor, rich, of good age, well
learned and of great wit, thou bringest in that case, that purple
laid apart, he clothes himself° in sack cloth, he dissembleth his
own face° and, of a master, he is° become a servant and he that
deliciously hath been nourished, now dresseth his shoulders for
the burden and letteth himself to hire for a common porter.[79] O
marvellous thing and almost incredible, to see a man, in other
things a grave counsellor, among the company of° boisterous
porters, pressing himself among such rascal people. Who will

show B. adds: to.   **corn** C. (p. 106) adds: *per scalas* [up the stairs].
garner granery.   **though** B. thoughte.   **heart.** C. (p. 108) adds:
Quid est tam nimium, quod tibi non parvum videatur? [Is there nothing so
vast that does not seem small to you?].   **thee** (B. omits).   **himself**
B. him.   **face** C. adds: *fuco* [with rouge].   **he is** B. is he.
of (B. omits).

seek a greater change?◊ This same it is◊ that Ovid meaneth in his transformations,◊ when he telleth how we men◊ became beasts, stones or trees. That same is it that the noble poet Virgil meaneth when he telleth how Circe enchanted her lovers into beasts; for so fareth◊ it by love, so is the mind of man thereby changed,◊ that little he differreth from a beast.[80]

The morning, forsaking the golden bed of Titan,[81] reduced the desired day, and shortly the sun declaring the colour of each thing rejoiced the waiter,◊ Eurialus, that thought him then happy and fortunate. When he saw himself among the vile porters,◊ so goeth he forth into the house of Lucrece, charged himself with wheat and setting it in the garner, descended last of the company and as he was taught. The door of the chamber◊ then◊ was put too; he thrust open and went in, and shutting the door after him, he found Lucrece about silkwork. And, coming toward her, "Good speed," quoth he, "my dear heart and the only help and hope of my life, Lucrece."◊ Though she had appointed this◊ matter, at the first sight was somewhat abashed, and thought it had been rather a spirit than her lover, Eurialus; for she could not well believe that such a man as he would venture such bills.◊ But afterward in kissing and embracing she knew well Eurialus and said: "Art thou here," quoth she, "poor porter, art thou here mine

change A. and B. charge; C. (p. 108) *transformationem* [change].   **it is** B. is it.   **transformations** C. (p. 108) *Metamorphoses* (the title of a work by Ovid).   **we men** B. women.   **fareth** B. fearethe.   **changed** B. chaunced.   **waiter** B. wayfer.   **porters** C. (p. 108) adds: *nulli noscendum* [unrecognizable to anybody].   **chamber** C. (p. 108) adds: *quod in medio scalarum clausum videbatur* [which from halfway down the stairs seemed to be closed].   **then** B. that.   **Lucrece** C. (p. 110) adds: *Nunc te solam offendi, nunc quod semper optavi, semotis arbitris te amplector. Nullus iam paries, nulla distantia meis obstabit osculis.* [Now I find you alone; now, just as I have always hoped, I hold you with no witnesses present. Now no wall, no distance will be an obstacle to my kisses.].   **this** B. his.   **venture such bills** B. adventure suche perrylles.

own Eurialus?" And then she, straining him straighter, looking in his face,[◊] began her words again thus: "Alas," quoth she, "my dear heart, Eurialus, what danger hast thou adventured! What shall I say now? I perceive I am most dear unto thee; I have made proof of thy love, and thou shalt never find me none otherwise unto thee. God send us only good luck in our love! And while the spirit shall rule my limbs,[82] none shall be before thee with Lucrece. No, not my husband, if I call him right — my husband that was given me against my will, whereto my mind never consented. But now I beseech thee, my Eurialus, cast away this sackcloth, and show thee unto me as thou art. Put away this porter's garment and lay away these ropes. Let me see my Eurialus. Then he cast off the filthy apparel and shone all in gold and purple, and began to intend busily to the office of love when Yosias, scraping at the door, said take heed ye lovers. Menelaus, seeking I wot not what, cometh hither; hide all thing privily, for out ye cannot scape.[◊] "Then," quoth Lucrece, "there is by the bed a dark closet where be jewels.[◊] Thou wottest what I wrote unto thee if my husband came in while thou were with me. Go thou thither, there thou mayest be sure in the dark, and neither stir nor spit. Eurialus, being in doubt what he should do, followed the woman's bidding. She set open the door and went to her work. Then[◊] came Menelaus, and one Bertus, a scrivener, with him to seek things that belonged to the common weal, which, when they were not in divers boxes found, "they are peradventure," quoth Menelaus, "in the closet. Go, Lucrece, and fetch a light for to seek here." With this word, Eurialus was sore afraid and began straight to hate Lucrece, and to himself said: "Ah, fool that I am. Who caused me to come hither but mine own lightness. I am taken; I am ashamed. I shall lose the Emperor's

---

And then . . . his face C. (p. 110) *Et rubore per genas fuso, complexa est arctius hominem et media fronte dissaviata.* [And with the red rouge on her cheeks, she embraced him more tightly and kissed his brow ardently.].
scape C. (p. 110) adds: *dolisque virum fallite* [and fool him with tricks].
there is . . . be jewels C. (p. 110) *Latibulum . . . sub strato est* [there is a hiding place under the bed]. **Then** B. There.

favour. What for favour? I would God my life were safe. Now shall I scape alive? I am sure to die, O, vain, and of all fools most foolish. I am fallen into these briars° wilfully. To what purpose is the enjoying° of love if it be bought so dear? The pleasures be short and the dolours° infinite. O, if we would endure these things for heaven! It is a marvellous foolishness of men that forsaketh light labours for long joys and for° love, whose joys be comparable to smoke. We put ourselves into extreme dangers. Lo, myself now shall I be a tale and example to everybody and know not what end shall become of it. If any good saint would help me hence, never again shall such labour deceive. O good Lord, help me hence and pardon my youth. Remember not mine ignorances, but save me to repent me of this fault. She hath not loved me, but, as a deer, hath taken me in the net. My day is come, no man may help me but thou, good Lord. Oft have I heard the deceits of women and I could not eschew it. If I escape now, there shall never no craft of women deceive me. But Lucrece was all ill combred that feared as much his health as her own, and, as women's wit is more ready than man's in sudden perils, had found a remedy. "Come hither," quoth she, "husband, here is a casket in this window wherein I have seen you put divers things of charge. Let us see if the writing be there." And, running as it were to open it, overthrew it into the street and as it had been by chance. "Alas," quoth she, "come hither, husband, lest we lose anything. The casket is fallen out of the window. Go quickly, lest any jewels or writings fall out. Go, go for God's sake, why tarry ye? I will look out that no man take nothing." See the deceit of the woman. Now trust them° hardly; no man is so circumspect that cannot be deceived. He was never kindly deceived whom his wife never assayed to deceive. We are oft more fortunate than wise.

briars A. brees; C. (p. 112) *sentinam* [foul place].   **enjoying** A. and B. enjoining; C. (p. 112) *gaudia* [joy].   **dolours** pains.   **and for** B. auef or.   **them** C. (p. 114) *feminis* [women].

Menelaus and Bertus abashed with this same ran both hastily into the street. The house was high after the Italian° fashion and many steps down. Whereby Eurialus had space to change and put himself by her counsel into another dark corner. They, when they had gathered the writings and the jewels, because they found not that that they sought, went into the closet° where they found it, and so, bidding her farewell, departed, and she barred the door.

"Come forth," quoth she, "Eurialus, come forth, my dear heart, and the sum of my joys. Come the well of my delights and spring of my gladness. All thing is sure. We may talk at liberty and now is the place sure for our embracings. Fortune would have letted our kissings, but God hath favoured our love, and hath not forsaken so faithful lovers.° Why tarriest thou?° Here is thy Lucrece. Why lettest thou to embrace her?"

Eurialus, at the last forsaking high fear,[83] claspeth her with his arms. "I in my life," quoth he, "was I never so feared;° but thou art well worthy for whom such things should be suffered. These kissings and sweet enbracings," quoth he, "no man should have for nought. Nor I (to say truth) have not bought dear enough so great a pleasure. If, after my death, I might live using thy company, a thousand times would I die to buy thy embracings so often. O how happy and how blessed! Is it a vision, or is it in deed? Do I hold thee° in mine arms, or do I dream? Surely it is thyself, and thee I have."

Lucrece was in a light garment that, without plight° or wrinkle,° showed her body as it was: a fair neck, and the light of her° eyes like the bright sun, gladsome countenance and a merry face, her

Italian C. (p. 114) *Hetrusco* [Tuscan].   **closet** C. (p. 114) adds: , *iuxta que latuerat Eurialus*, [, in which Eurialus had been hiding just before,]. **lovers** C. (p. 114) adds: *Veni iam meas in ulnas, nihil est, quod amplius vereare, meum lilium rosarumque cumulus.* [Come now into my arms. There is nothing more to fear, my lily and bed of roses].   **thou** C. (p. 114) adds: *quid times?* [why are you afraid?].   **feared** afraid. **thee** (B. omits).   **plight** pleat.   **wrinkle** C. (p. 116) adds: *nec vel pectus vel clunes mentiebatur* [neither her chest nor her buttocks were disappointing].   **her** (B. omits).

cheeks like lilies meddled° with roses;⁸⁴ sweet and sober was°
her laughing, her breast large, and the two paps seeming apples,
gathered.° in Venus' garden, moved the courage of the toucher°
Eurialus could no longer suffer the spur, but, forgetting all fear
and soberness laid apart, said unto the woman: "Let us now
taste of the fruit of love." He pressed her sore, and she to the
contrary resisted,° showing how she cared for her honesty,° and
that her love desired nothing but only words and kisses. Unto
which Eurialus, smiling, did answer." It is known," quoth he,
"that I am here, or it is not known. If it be known, there is no man
that will not judge the rest;° if it be not known, no more shall this
be: it is the reward of love, and let me die rather than want that."
"O, but is° offence," quoth Lucrece. "It is offence," quoth Eurialus, "not to use pleasure when thou mayest. Should I forsake
such occasion granted and desired so greatly?"⁸⁵ And taking her
garment, the striving woman that would not be overcome, he
overcame.° Yet did he not quench the desire of Venus, but rather
provoked a greater thirst.° But Eurialus, fearing a further danger
after he had a little banqueted, departed, something against her
will and mind, and no man suspected, because he was as one
of the porters. As he went through the street, Eurialus, wondering on himself, said: "O, if the Emperor should now meet with
me and know me! What suspect would this garment bring him

meddled mixed.   **was** B. as.   **her breast large, and the two paps
seeming apples, gathered.° in Venus' garden, moved the courage of
the toucher** C. (p. 116) *papille quasi duo Punica poma ex utroque latere
tumescebant pruritumque palpitantes movebant.* [her breasts were like two
pomegranates, which swelled on both sides and moved with desire.].
gathered A. gatheres.   **resisted** B. rested.   **honesty** C. (p. 116)
adds: *et fame* [and for her reputation].   **rest** C. (p. 116) adds: *et
stultum est, infamiam sine re subire* [and it is stupid to undergo the infamy
without accomplishing the deed].   **is** (B. omits).   **And taking
. . . overcame** C. (p. 116) *Acceptaque mulieris veste pugnantem feminam,
que vincere nolebat, abs negotio vicit* [And having taken off her clothes,
without effort he overcame the struggling woman, who did not want to
overcome him].⁸⁶   **thirst** C. (p. 116) adds: *ut Amoni cognita Thamar
peperit*⁸⁷ [as that known to have happened with Thamar and Ammon].

in? How would he mock me! I should be a tale for everybody, and ever a laughter for him. Never would he leave me, till time that he knew all, and needs tell him I must what this apparel meaneth. But I would say that it were for another woman than this, for peradventure he loveth her, and also it were not meet to declare him my love, for I would never so betray Lucrece that hath both received and saved me and thus. As he thought he saw Nisus, Achates,[88] and Plinius,◊ and goeth afore and was not known of them till he came home. Whereas changing his clothes, under colour of other names, he telleth the chance of the matter, and, as he remembereth the fear and the joy, so did he in telling fear and rejoice; and, in the midst of his fear, "ah, fool that I was," quoth he, "I trusted a woman with my head. So was I not counselled of my father when he taught me to trust the faith of no woman,◊ for that they were cruel, deceitful, changeable, and full of divers passions, and I, ill remembering the lesson,◊ put my life in a woman's hands. What if any man had known me, when I was charged with wheat? What shame; what slander had both I and mine had forever? The Emperor would have refused me and, as light and mad brained, might have esteemed me.◊ What if her husband had found me in the closet? The civil law◊ is cruel to adulterers; but the furor of the husband would have had greater pain. The one◊ had been but short death; the other, death with cruel torments.◊ But set case that he hath favoured my life,◊ at the least he would have bound me, and sent me shamed unto the Emperor. Yea, though I had escaped his hands because he had no weapon and I had a sword◊ by my side, yet had he a man with him, and weapons hung at hand upon the wall, and there

Plinius C. (p. 118) *Palinurum.*   **woman** C. (p. 118) adds: *Ille fem-inam animal esse dicebat indomitum* [He used to say that woman is an indomitable animal].   **lesson** C. adds: *paterne* [of my father]. **me** C. (p. 118) adds: *Potuissem hec contemnere?* [Should I condemn these things?].   **civil law** C. (p. 118) *lex Iulia* [Julian law].[89]   **The one** A. and B. tone.   **torments** C. (p. 118) adds: *quosdam mechos et mugilis intrat.*[90] [and another inserts a fish into the adulterer].   **But set . . . my life** But say that he had granted me my life.   **a sword** B. answered; C. (p. 118) adds: *fidus* [faithful].

was° many servants in the house, the noise should have risen
and the doors shut and I should have been handled according.
Alas, mad that I was, no wisdom, but chance hath delivered me
from this danger sorrow for chance, and it was the ready wit
of her. O trusty woman. O wise lover. O noble and excellent
love, why should I not trust unto thee? Why should I not trust
thy faith? If I had a thousand lives, I° durst trust thee° with
them all. Thou art faithful and wise, and wisely thou can love
and help thy lover. Who could so soon have the way to avoid
them that sought me, as thou had? Then° hast saved my life,
and I vow it unto thee; the life that I live is not mine, but thine,
and it shall not be grievous unto me for thee to lose that by the
I have. Thou hast the right of my life, and commandment on
my death. O fair breast! O pleasant tongue! O sweet eyes! O
fresh wit! O goodly° limbs and well furnished![91] When shall I
see you again? When shall I bite that same coral lip and hear
thee speak within my mouth?° Shall I never handle again those
round breasts? O Achates, it is but little that thou hast seen in any
woman in comparison to this; the more nearer she is, the more
fairer she is.° Lydia, the fair wife of Candalus the king,° was no
fairer. I wonder not if he would show her naked unto Satius°
for to do him the greater pleasure;[92] for, on my faith, if I might,
so would I show thee this lady, for else may I not declare unto
thee her beauty nor thou perceive what joy I had.° But rejoice
with me, I beseech thee, that my pleasure was greater than can
be expressed with words."

was (B. omits).   **I** (B. omits).   **thee** thee.   **Then** B. Thou.
goodly C. (p. 120) *marmarea* [marble].   **hear thee . . . my mouth** C.
(p. 120) *tremulam linguam ori meo inmurmurantem denuo sentiam* [feel again
your trembling tongue murmuring in my mouth].   **is** C. (p. 120) adds:
utinam mecum una fuisses [if only she were with me].   **Lydia . . . the**
king C. (p. 120) *Candaulis regis Lidie formosa uxor* [the beautiful wife of
Candalus, king of Lydia].   **Satius** C. (p. 120) *socio* [to a companion].
what joy I had C. (p. 120) *quam solidum quamque plenum meum fuerit*
gaudium [how solid and how full my joy would be].

Thus talked Eurialus with Achates, and Lucrece with herself said as much; but so much less was her gladness that she might trust none to show it unto, and unto Yosias she durst not for shame tell all.

In the meantime, a knight called Pacorus,° of a noble house, following the Emperor began to love Lucrece and, because he was fair and goodly, thought to be beloved and only reckoned the chastity of the woman to let him. She (as the custom of Italy° is) beheld everybody with a louring° countenance, whether it were by deceit or craft, lest the true love should appear. Pacorus rageth and cannot be in rest till he have felt her mind. The matrons of Siena went oft to visit the chapel of our Lady of Bethleem.° Hither was Lucrece come with two maidens and an old wife. Pacorus followed her with a violet with golden leaves in his hand, in the stalk whereof he had hid a letter of love, written in fine letters.° And have no marvail° thereof, for Cicero sayeth there was showed him the whole history of Troy° so finely written that it might all have been closed in a nut shell. Pacorus offereth the violet to Lucrece, recommending him unto her, and she refuseth it. He desireth her instantly to take it. "Take the flower, madame," quoth the old wife, "what fear you? There is no peril; it is but a small thing, wherein, peradventure, ye may do the gentleman pleasure." She followed her counsel and took the flower, and when she had gone a little way, she took it unto one° of her maidens. And shortly after they met with two scholars, which, I wot not how lightly, obtained the flower of the maid and, opening the stalk, found the pleasant letter. Now after the matrons of Siena had found the lovers° that the Emperor brought,° and after the Court was come thither, these folk were

Pacorus C. (p. 120) adds: *Pannonius* [Hungarian].   **of Italy** C. *nostris dominabus* [for our ladies].   **louring** alluring.   **Bethleem** Bethlehem.   **written in fine letters** C. (p. 122) *subtilibus inscriptam membranis* [written on fine paper].   **marvail** astonishment.   **history of Troy** C. (p. 122) *Iliadem* [the Iliad].   **one** A. and B. tone. **Now after … brought** C. (p. 122) adds: *Solebat hoc hominum genus pergratum esse nostris matronis* [This kind of men used to please our women]. **lovers** the young men they admired.

mocked and deceived and little esteemed, for the clattering of harness delighted more these women than eloquence of learning. Here upon grew great envy,◊ and the long gowns sought always how to let the courtiers.◊ Then, when the craft of the violet was known, straight was Menelaus gone unto, and desired to read the letter. He,◊ being very angry, goeth home, blameth his wife, and filleth all the house with noise. And she to the contrary denieth that there is one fault in her and telling the whole tale bringeth the old wife for witness. The Emperor is gone to, complaint is made, Pacorus is called for, and he confesseth the fault, asketh forgiveness and sweareth never more to vex Lucrece, but right well knew he that Jupiter rather laugheth than taketh angerly◊ the perjuring of lovers;[93] and so the more that he was let, the more he followeth the vain flame.

The winter is come, and the north winds had brought down snows.◊ The town falleth on playing. The wives cast snowballs into the streets, and the young men out of the streets into the◊ windows. Here had Pacorus gotten occasion and had enclosed in wax another letter and putteth it in a snow ball, and casting it unto Lucrece's window. Who will not say that fortune ruleth all thing?◊ One happy hour is more worth to thee than if Mars should recommend thee in his letter to Venus.[94] Some say that fortune hath no power in wise men. I grant it to such wise men that only delight in virtue and, suffering poverty, sickness, and prison◊ can think themself blessed. Which one yet I never saw, nor never think there was. The common life of men needeth

envy C. (p. 122) adds: *et simultas ingens* [and great rivalry].   **and the long . . . courtiers** C. (p. 122) adds: *querebantque techne vias omnes, quibus nocerent sagis* [and they sought every means of trickery, by which they could do harm to the soldiers].   **He** (B. omits).   **angerly** angrily.
The winter . . . snows. C. (p. 124) *Venit hiems exclusisque Nothis solum Boream admittebat. Cadunt ex celo nives.* [Winter came and, driving the South Winds away, brought in the customary North Wind. Snow fell from the sky.].   **the** B. theyr.   **thing** things; C. (p. 124) adds: *quis non favorabilem cupiat eius flatum?* [who does not desire its favourable breeze?].   **prison** C. (p. 124) adds: *in equo Phalarides clusi* [enclosed in the horse of Phalarides].[95]

fortune's favour. She, whom she will she advanceth, and whom she listeth, overthroweth. Who hindered Pacorus, but fortune? Was it not wisely handled in a violet's stalk to hide his letters and now again to send his letter closed in snow? Would any man say it might be craftier, so that if fortune had help he had be judged crafty and excellently wise? But contrary chance brought the ball that fell out of her hand to the fire, so that the snow, once wasted and the wax melted, the letters appeared, which both an old woman that warmed° her and Menelaus, being by, did read, and there began a new noise, which Pacorus did not tarry to excuse, but went his way.[96] This noise° helped Eurialus,° so that it is true that hath been said: it is hard defending that is diversely.° The lovers awaited for the second marriage.° And there was a little straight lane betwixt Lucrece's house and her neighbour's, by the which, setting his feet upon each wall, he had not over hard climbing to Lucrece's window. But this might only be by night. Now must Menelaus go into the country and there must he lie all night, which day was waited for of those two lovers, as it had been a Jubilee.° The good man is gone, and Eurialus, changing his clothes, is come into the lane. There had Menelaus a stable wherein by the teaching of Yosias all the evening he lay hid in the hay. And, lo, where Dromo[98] came, that was a servant of Menelaus, and had rule of his horses, to fill the racks. And hard by Eurialus side did pull out hay, and had taken more and stricken in him with the fork had not Yosias helped, who, when he saw the danger, "Brother," quoth he, "give me this work. I shall give hay to the horses. Thou in the meantime look that our supper be ready. We must be merry while our masters is forth. Our mistress is [a] better fellow. She is merry

warmed warned.   **noise** C. (p. 124) *amor* [love].   **Eurialus** C. (p. 124) adds: *Nam dum vir gressus et actus Pacoris speculatur, insidiis Euriali locum facit* [For while the husband was watching the moves and behaviour of Pacorus, it left room for Eurialus' schemes].   **it is hard . . . assaulted** it is difficult to defend against attacks from all sides.
second marriage a second consummation of their love; C. (p. 126) adds: *post primum concubitum* [after their first marriage].   **Jubilee** C. (p. 126) *saturnaliorum* [the Saturnalia].[97]

and liberal; he is angry, full of noise, covetous and hard. We are never well when he is at home. See, I pray thee, what lank bellies we have. He is hungry himself to starve us for$^\diamond$ hunger. He will not suffer one moist piece of brown bread to be lost, but the fragments of one day he keepeth five days after. And the gobbets of salt fish and salt eels of one supper he keepeth unto another, and marketh the cut cheese, lest any of it should be stolen. The fool that by such wretchedness seeketh$^\diamond$ his riches, for nothing is more foolish than to live poor for to die rich.$^{\diamond 99}$ How much are we better with our mistress that feedeth us not only with veal and kid but with hens and birds and plenty of wine. Go, Dromo, and make the kitchen smoke."$^\diamond$ "Marry," quoth Dromo, "that shall be my charge, and sooner shall I lay the tables than rub the horse. I brought my master into the country today that the devil broke his neck and never spoke he word unto me, but bade me when I brought home my horses to tell my mistress that he would not come home tonight. But, by God, quoth he, I praise thee, Yosias, that at the last hast found fault at my master's conditions. I had forsaken my master if my mistress had not given me my morrow meals as she hath. Let us not sleep tonight, Yosias,$^\diamond$ but let us eat and drink till it be day. My master shall not win so much this month as we shall waste at one supper." Gladly did Eurialus hear this, and marked the manners of servants and thought he was served alike.$^\diamond$ And when Dromo was gone, Eurialus arose and said, "O happy night that through thy help, Yosias, I shall have that hast brought me hither, and wisely taken heed that I was not discovered, and thou shalt not see that I shall be unkind."$^\diamond$ The hour was come, and the glad Eurialus, that had passed two dangers, climbed up that$^\diamond$ wall, and at the window went in where all thing was ready,

for B. to.   **seeketh** B. soketh.   **rich** B. richli.   **and make . . . smoke** C. (p. 126) *cura, ut quam uncta popina sit.* [see to it that our meal is prepared as well as possible].   **Yosias** B. Zosia.   **alike** in a similar way; C. (p. 128) adds: *cum domo abesset* [when he was away from home].   **unkind** C. adds: *Vir bonus es meritoque te amo* [You are a good man and I rightly esteem you].   **that** B. the.

and Lucrece by the fire. She, when she saw her lover, clasped him in her arms. There was embracing and kissing, and with full sail they follow their lusts and wearied Venus, now with Ceres, and now with Bacchus was refreshed.[100] Alas, how long business and how short be the pleasures! Scant had Eurialus one glad hour and° lo where Yosias brought word that Menelaus was come and marred all the play. Eurialus° maketh him ready to depart. Lucrece, when she had hidden the blanket, meeteth her husband, welcoming him home. "Welcome," quoth she, "my husband. By my troth," quoth she, "I weened that thou haddest been lost in husbandry. What hast thou done in the country thus long?° Why tarriest thou not at home. Thou makest me sad with thine absence. I fear lest thou have some other that thou lovest. These husbands be so false to their wives. If thou wilt that I shall not mistrust thee, never sleep out of my company, for I can sleep no night without thee; but let us sup here and go to bed." They were than in the hall where they used to dine, and she sought for to have kept him there till Eurialus had space for to go his way, for it required some leisure. But Menelaus had supped forth and hasted toward his chamber. "Now, on my faith and troth," quoth Lucrece, "thou art unkind. Why diddest thou not rather sup with me, because thou was from hence. I have eaten no meat° today, and there were here men of the country° that brought in marvellous good wine° — as they said — and yet I tasted not of it. But now that thou art come let us go into the cellar, I beseech thee, and taste if the wine be as they say." And so, having the lantern in her one hand, pulling her husband with the other hand, went into the cellar, and so long pierced this vessel and that, and supped with her husband till she thought that°

and (B. omits).   **Eurialus** C. (p. 128) adds: *timens* [frightened].
long C. (p. 130) adds: *Cave, ne quid olfaciam.* [Beware, lest I detect anything.].   **meat** C. (p. 130) adds: *nec bibi* [nor have I had anything to drink].   **of the country** C. (p. 130) *ex Rosalia* [from Rosalia].   **wine** C. (p. 130) *Trebeianum* (a kind of wine drunk on celebratory occasions).
that (B. omits).

Eurialus was gone. And so at the last went with her husband to the evil pleasant° bed.

Eurialus in the still of the night went home. And on the morrow, either for that it were necessary to take heed or for some ill suspect, Menelaus walled up the window. I think, as our citizens be suspectuous° and full of conjectures, so did he fear the commodity of the place and° would eschew the occasion. For, though he knew nought, yet wist he well that she was much desired and daily provoked by great requests, and judged a woman's thought unstable which hath as many minds as trees hath leaves, and that their kind alway is desirous of new things, and seldom love they their husbands whom they have obtained. Therefore, did he follow the common opinion of married men: to avoid mishap, though it come with good luck. So was their meeting let, and their sending of letters also stopped, for the taverner that dwelt behind Lucrece's house (where as Eurialus was wont to speak with her and give her letters°) at Menelaus' persuasion was put out by the aldermen.° And° only remained the beholding of their eyes, and with becks° the lovers saluted each other — and scant might they use this uttermost point of love.[101] Their sorrows were great, and their torments like the death, for they° could neither forget nor use their love. While Eurialus doth study diligently what advice he might take in this matter, he remembered Lucrece's counsel, which she wrote unto him of Menelaus' cousin, Pandalus, and did as these cunning physicians whose manners is in dangerous sickness to give indifferent medicines, and in extreme to use the last medicines, rather than leave the disease incurable. He determined to go unto Pandalus and follow that way that afore he had forsaken. And when he had sent for him, called him into a secret place. "Sit down," quoth he, "my friend, I must tell thee a great thing that requireth such things as be in

pleasant C. (p. 130) *ingratos* [ungrateful].   **suspectuous** suspicious.
and C. (p. 130) adds: *utque parum fidebat uxori* [since he did not trust his wife very much].   **letters** C. (p. 132) adds: *per arundinem* [from his pen].   **aldermen** C. (p. 132) *magistratus* [magistrates].   **And** (B. omits).   **becks** gestures.   **they** B. the.

thee, that is, diligence, faith, and secretness.[102] I would ere now
have showed it thee, but I knew thee not. Now I do know thee,
and because thou art an honest, faithful man, I love thee and
entreat thee. So that I knew nothing else,◊ it is enough that thy
neighbours praise thee, and my fellows too, with whom thou
hast entered friendship; and who and of what sort thou art they
have told me. Of whom I have learned that thou desirest my
friendship, which I promise now unto thee, for thou art as well
worthy mine as I am thine. Now, for because among friends a
thing is done in few words, what I would I will show thee. Thou
knowest how the kind◊ of man is prone unto love. Whether it
be virtue or or vice, it◊ reigneth everywhere, nor no heart there
is of flesh that sometime hath not felt the pricks of love. Thou
knowest that neither the wise Solomon◊ nor the strong Samson
hath escaped from this passion. Furthermore, the nature of a
kindled heart and of a foolish love is this: the more it is let, the
more I burn. With nothing sooner is this disease healed than
with the◊ obtaining of the loved.[103] Many there hath been,◊ both
in our time and in our elder, to whom their let hath been cause
of cruel death, and, again many, after the thing obtained,◊ have
left to rage. Nothing is better when love is crept into the bones[104]
than to give place to the rage. For who so striveth against the
tempest oft times suffereth wrack,◊ and who driveth with the
storm escapeth. This I tell thee for that thou shalt know my love,
and what for my sake thou must do, and then what profit thou
shalt have thereby. I will show thee all, for now I reckon thee
as one part of my heart. I love Lucrece, and truly, Pandalus, it
is not by my fault, but by the governance of fortune, in whose
hands is the whole world that we inhabit. The customs of the

So that . . . else even if I knew no more of you.   **kind** nature.
it (B. omits); C. (p. 132) *ista calamitas* [such a catastrophe].   **Solomon**
C. (p. 132) adds: *sanctissimum David* [most holy David].   **the** (B.
omits).   **been** C. (p. 132) adds: *tum viri tum mulieres* [both men and
women].   **the thing obtained** C. (p. 134) *concubitum et amplexus passim
concessos* [consummation and embracings promiscuously obtained].
wrack destruction.

country° were unknown to me. I thought your women had felt
in their hearts that they showed with their eyes,° and that hath
deceived me. For I thought Lucrece had loved me, because she
beheld me pleasantly and I again began to love her, for I thought
such a lady was not unmeet to be beloved for love. And yet did
I not know thee, nor none of thy kin. I loved and weened to
have been loved. Who is so stony hard (being loved) that doth
not love. But after I saw I was deceived° (lest my love should be
vain)° with all manner of ways I assayed to kindle her with like
and like fire. For I burned and piteously wasted, and shame and
trouble of my mind day and night did marvellously torment me.
And I was so tangled that with no ways I could escape. And at
the last I continued so long that the love of us both was° like;
she is kindled and I burn; and we both° perish, nor we see no
remedy to our lives but only thy help. Her husband keepeth
her in his chamber. The waker dragon did never keep so well
the golden fleece nor Cerberus the entry of hell[105] as Lucrece is
kept. I know your kindred, and also I know that ye are noble
and rich° and among the best of this town beloved.° But who
can withstand destiny? Alas, Pandalus! It was not by my choice,
but by chance,° and thus standeth this matter. It is as yet secret;
but, without it be well guided, it is like — as God forbid — to
breed a great mischief. I peradventure might appease myself,
if I went from hence, which though it were grievous unto me, I
would do for our families, if I thought that should help. But well
I know her rage: either she would follow me or else, if she were
constrained to tarry, would kill herself, which would be unto

country C. (p. 134) adds: *nec huius urbis* [and of this city].   **eyes** C.
(p. 134) adds: *sed inescant homines vestre marite, non amant.* [but your
women lead men on; they do not love them.].   **I saw I was deceived**
C. (p. 134) *fraudes novi meque dolis irretitum* [I recognized the trick and
knew that I was snared by deceptions].   **(lest . . . vain)** (B. omits the
parentheses).   **was** (B. omits).   **she is kindled and I burn; and
we both** (B. omits).   **rich** C. (p. 136) adds: *potentes* [powerful].
beloved C. (p. 136) adds: *utinam nunquam novissem hanc feminam.* [if
only I had never met this woman.].   **chance** C. (p. 136) adds: *amandam*
[that she would be loved].

your house a perpetual dishonour. That I sent for you is for your
cause to withstand these mischiefs; nor there is none other way
but that thou wilt be governor° of our love, that the dissembled
fire may be secret. I recommend, I give and I vow me wholly
unto thee. Be diligent in this furor, lest while it be let it flame the
more. Do so much that we may meet together and so shall the
heat be aslaked,° and made more sufferable. Thou knowest the
ways of the house; thou knowest when the good man is absent;
thou knowest how to bring me in — but Menelaus' brother must
be had out of the way, which waiteth ever diligently for these
matters, and keepeth Lucrece instead of her brother, and marketh
diligently her words, her looks, her countenance, her spittings,
her coughs, her laughs, and each thing he considereth.[106] Him
must I deceive, and it cannot be without thee. Help, therefore, I
beseech thee, and when her husband, Menelaus, is from home,
advertise° me. And his brother that tarryeth, bring them out
of the way that he neither take heed to her, nor set none other
keepers over her,° which, if thou wilt undertake and help me
as my trust is in thee, all is safe. For thou mayest privily while
the other be fast in sleep let me in, and ease our furious love.
What profit shall ensue of this, I think thou understandest by
the discretion. For first thou shalt save the honour of the house,
and hide the love that in no wise can be published without your
shame. Secondly, thou shalt save thy cousin-in-law's life, and
also too Menelaus save a wife, to whom it shall not be so hurtful
that she were mine for one night (no man knowing of it) as if
he should lose her, all the world wondering, when she should
follow me. Divers women have° followed their lovers.° What
if she determined to follow me? What dishonour should it be

governor governor.	**aslaked** satisfied.	**advertise** warn.	**her**
C. (p. 136) adds: *Tibi credet et quod dii faxint hanc fortasse provinciam tibi*
committet [He trusts you and, if the gods grant it, perhaps he will entrust
you with this duty].	**Divers women ... their lovers** C. (p. 138) *Nupta*
senatori Romano secuta est Ippia ludium ad Pharon et Nilum famosque menia
Lagi. [Ippia, married to a Roman senator, followed a gladiator to Faro
and the Nile and the famous walls of Lago.].[107]	**have** (B. omits).

to your kin?◊ What mock among people?◊ What shame as well to all the town as to you?◊ Some peradventure say, 'put her to death◊ rather than she should do thus'; but woe be unto him that fileth◊ him with bloodshedding, and remedieth one fault by a greater. Mischievousness be not to be increased but to be lessed. Of two good things we know the best is to be chosen; and, of a good and of an ill, the good; and, of two ills, the least. Every way is dangerous, but this that I show thee is least perilous, by which thou shalt not only help thine own blood, but also me that am almost out of my wit to see Lucrece suffer as she doth for me who I would rather did hate me than I would entreat thee. But thus it is and at this point, and without thy craft, thy wit, and thy diligence the ship be guided there remaineth no hope of health. Help therefore both her and me and save thy house from shame, and think not that I will be unkind. Thou knowest what I may do with the Emperor. And what thou wilt I will get thee granted. And this I promise thee on my faith: thou shalt be an earl by patent, and all thy posterity shall enjoy that◊ same title. I commit unto thee both Lucrece, we, our love and fame, and◊ the honour of thy kin. I trust unto thy faith;[108] thou art the arbiter,◊ and all these be in thine hands. Take heed now what thou dost, for like as thou mayest save, so mayest thou spill."

Pandalus, when he heard this, smiled, and after a little pause said: "All this have I known," quoth he, "Eurialus, and would God it had not happened. But now, as thou sayest, it is at that point that I must needs do as thou biddest me, except I would shame all our kin and raise a great slander. The woman indeed brenneth and hath no power over herself. And, without I help, she will slay herself with some knife, or break her neck out of some window. Neither careth she for her honour, nor for her life;◊ she hath told me her desire. I have blamed her. I have

---

? B. !.   ? B. !.   B. !.   **put her to death** C. (p. 138) *absumenda potius ferro aut extinguenda venenis est mulier* [the woman should rather be put to the sword or killed by poisoning].   **fileth** B. syleth.
that B. the.   **and** (B. omits).   **arbiter** A. arbite.   **life** B. selfe.

busied me to quench the flame, and all in vain. She careth for nought but for thee. Thou art always in her mind. Thee she wisheth, thee she desireth, and thee only she thinketh upon,[109] often times calling me by thy name. So is the woman changed by love that she seemeth not the same.[110] Alas! What pity and what sorrow. There was none in all the town more chaste or more wiser then Lucrece. It is a marvellous thing if nature have given love such law over the minds of men. This disease must be helped, and with none other cure than thou hast showed. I will go about this business and, when time is, I shall warn thee. Nor I◊ seek no reward of thee. It is not the office of an honest man to ask thank where none is deserved.[111] I do it to avoid the fame of our house, and if thou take any benefit thereby I am not therefore to be rewarded. "Yet, quoth Eurialus, "for all that I thank thee and, as I said, I promise thee to cause thee to be made earl. And refuse not hardly this honour." "I refuse it not," quoth Pandalus, "but I would not it should come by this means. If it come let it come. I will nothing do by covenant. If I might have done it by unknown to thee, that thou might have been with Lucrece, I would gladly have done it. Farewell." "And thou also," quoth Eurialus, "now that thou hast given me comfort, make fain, find, or do by some means, that we may be together." "Thou shalt praise me,"[112] quoth Pandalus, and he departed full glad that he had entered in Eurialus' grace, hoping to be an earl whereof he was more desirous, inasmuch as he showed least — for there be many men, so women like, that when they say most nay they would fainest. He hath gotten by furtherance of love the name of an earl, and his posteriors◊ shall show for their nobleness a gilted bull.◊

Not long after there was a fray◊ in the country among Menelaus' husbandmen, and divers of them that had drank overmuch were slain. Wherefore Menelaus must go forth to set good order in these matters, to whom Lucrece said, "husband thou art heavy

---

I (B. omits).   **posteriors** descendants.   **bull** a patent of nobility; (C. adds a long digression[113]).   **fray** fight.

and weak, and thy horse goeth hard. Borrow therefore some am-
bling horse." And when he asked where he might borrow any.
"Marry," quoth Pandalus, "Eurialus had a° very good one, and
sure he will gladly lend him thee. If thou wilt I shall ask him."
"Do," quoth Menelaus, and Eurialus as soon granted as he was
desired, taking it for a good token, and to himself said, "if thou
leap upon my horse, I shall do the same unto thy wife." Now, the
covenant was that at five of the clock Eurialus should wait in the
street, and should hope well if he heard Pandalus sing. Menelaus
was gone, and the cloudy night had covered the heaven. Lucrece
tarried her time in her chamber, and Eurialus was afore the door
and tarried the token, but he neither heard him sing nor spit. The
hour was past; Achates moved him to depart.° It was hard to depart, and imagined now one cause now another. Pandalus sang
not because Menelaus' brother was left there, that sought each
corner for fear of deceits, and waked all the while. To whom
Pandalus said, "shall we not go to bed this night?° And I am
wondrous sleepy. I wonder of thee that art a young man and,
like an old man to whom dryness[114] taketh away sleep, thou
never dost sleep but before day° when other men do rise. Let us
go to bed. To what purpose do we watch?" "Let us go," quoth
Agamemnon,[115] "if thou wilt; but let us look first to the doors, if
they be well shut for doubt of thieves." And when he was come
to the door, he put to it now one lock, now another, and bolted it.
There was a great bar of iron that scant two could lift wherewith
the door was never shut, which, when Agamemnon could not

a (B. omits).   depart C. (p. 144) adds: *delusumque dicebat* [and told
the lie].   night C. (p. 144) adds: *iam nox medium poli transcendit
axem* [it is now the middle of the night].   day C. (p. 144) adds: *dum
currus volvitur septentrionalis Elices* [when the Great Bear goes around
the chariot].

put to, desired help.◊ "Thou shuttest the door," quoth Pandalus, "as if the house should be besieged. Are we not in a sure city? We are at liberty in this town, and quietness is come to us all. The Florentines, our enemies with whom we have war be far hence. If thou dread enemies, this house cannot help us.◊ I will this night lift no burdens; my shoulders ache and I am sore bruised within. I am not meet for the burden. Therefore lift thou thyself, or let it alone." "Well then," quoth Agamemnon, "it is enough," and went to bed. Then quoth Eurialus: "I will tarry here this hour to see peradventure if anybody do appear." Achates that was with Eurialus was weary of so long tarrying, and privily cursed Eurialus, which had kept him so long from sleep. Yet they tarried not long after, but they saw Lucrece through a crevice, carrying a light in her hand. Toward whom Eurialus went, and said, "Good speed," quoth he, "my dear heart,[116] Lucrece," and she, being affeared, would have gone her way, but then remembering herself: "what man art thou," quoth she, "that callest me?" "I, thine Eurialus, am here," quoth he, "open the door, my delight. I have tarried here half this night." Lucrece at the last knew his voice, but because she feared deceit, she durst not open till she knew some token that it was he. And so with great labour she removed the locks, but because there were many fastenings to the door that a woman's strength could not undo, she opened it but half a foot wide. "Good enough," quoth Eurialus, and stretching himself at last got in and taketh her in his arms. Achates watched without. Lucrece, either for fear or for joy, swooned in Eurialus' arms,

desired help. C. (p. 144) adds: *"Iuva me," inquit, "Pandale, admoveamus ferrum hoc hostio, tum dormitum in utramvis aurem otiose poterimus." Audiebat hos sermones Eurialus et, actum est, tacitus ait, si hoc ferramentum adjungitur. Tum Pandalus: "Quid tu paras, Agamemnon?"* ["Help me, Pandalus," he said. "Let us move this iron bar across the door, then we will be able to sleep in peace." Eurialus heard these words and thought to himself, "If this iron is fastened, all is lost." Then Pandalus said, "What are you doing, Agamemnon?"].   **us** C. (p. 144) adds: *Si fures times, sat clausum est*; [If you are afraid of thieves, it is locked well enough;].

and, her strength failing,° with pale face, seemed already dead, but that her pulse and heat remained. Eurialus, with the sudden chance affeared, wist not what to do. "If I go hence," thought he, "the fault of her death shall be in me to leave a woman in such danger. If I tarry, Agamemnon or some of the house, shall come, and then I am undone. Alas, unhappy love that hast in thee more gall than honey;[117] the bitter wormwood is no more sour than thou art. What dangers hast thou already put me in? With how many deaths hast thou threatened my head? And hast thou left me now to have a woman die in mine arms? Why hast thou not rather slain me? Why hast thou not torn me with lions? Alas, how much had it been that I had died in her lap than she in my bosom?" Love had overcome the man and, regarding not his own health, tarried with the woman, and lifting up her body, all bemoisted with tears kissed her. "Alas, Lucrece," quoth he, "where art thou become? Where be thine ears? Why answerest thou not? Why hearest thou not? Open thine eyes. I beseech thee look upon me. Smile on me as thou art wont. Thy Eurialus is here. He doth embrace thee. Why dost thou thus trouble me? I wonder art thou gone, or dost thou sleep? Where shall I seek thee? If thou wouldst die, why diddest thou not warn me that I might have died with thee? If thou wilt not hear me, my sword shall straight open my side and we shall both die at once. Ah, my life, my darling, my delight,° my only hope, and my whole health, shall I thus lose thee? Open thine eyes. Lift up thy head, thou art not yet dead. I feel thou art warm and thy breath is yet in thee. Why dost thou not speak to me? Dost thou receive me of this sort? Dost thou call me to such pastime? Dost thou give me such a night? Rise, I beseech thee, my dear heart, look on thy Eurialus. I am here." And with that word the flood° of his tears flushed so upon her face° that as with drops of water° the

failing C. (p. 146) adds: *et amisso verbo ac oculis clausis* [and having spoken these words and closed her eyes].   **delight** B. adds: and.
the flood B. he stoude.   **upon her face** C. (p. 148) *super frontem et mulieris tempora* [upon the woman's forehead and temples].   **water** C. (p. 148) adds: *rosarum* [of roses].

woman awaked out of her sleep.° And, seeing her lover, "Alas,"
quoth she, "Eurialus, where have I been? Why diddest thou not
suffer me to die? Happily had I died in thy arms, and would
God I might so die ere thou should depart the town. Thus talking together, they went into the chamber, where they had such
a night as we judge the two lovers Paris and Helena had after
he had taken her away; and it was unto them so pleasant that
they thought Mars and Venus had never none such. "Thou art,"
quoth Lucrece, "my Ganymede, my Hippolytus, my Diomedes."
"Thou art," quoth Eurialus, "my Polyxena, my Emily,° yea, and
Venus herself."[118] And her mouth, and now her eyes, and now
her cheeks he kisseth.° And sometime, casting down the clothes,
he saw such beauty as he never afore saw. "I have found more,"
quoth he, "than, I weened, such a one saw Acteon of Diana
when she bathed her in the fountain.[119] What is more pleasanter
or more fairer than these limbs, now have I bought them with
peril. But what thing should I not have suffered for thee? O fair
neck,° and pleasant breasts! Is it you that I touch? Is it you that
I have? Are ye in my hands? O round limbs! O sweet body!
Have I thee in my arms? Now where doth pleasant in the fresh-
ness of my joy that no displeasure might hereafter hurt it.° Do I
hold thee, or do I dream?° O pleasant kisses! O dear enbracings!
O sweet bitings! No man living is more happy than I, or more
blessed. But alas how swift be these hours? Thou spiteful night!
Why goest thou away? Abide Apollo[121] and tarry under the
earth. Why dost thou so soon put thy horse into the chase?° Let
them repast. Give me this night as thou diddest to Alcmena.[122]

---

awaked out of her sleep C. (p. 148) *quasi de gravi somno surrexit* [awoke
as if out of a deep sleep].   **Emily** Emilia.   **kisseth** C. (p. 148)
commendabat [praised].   **neck** C. (p. 150) *pectus* [breast].   **Now
where . . . hurt it** The immediate pleasure is such that nothing could
ever detract from it; C. (p. 150) *Nunc mori facilius est* [it would be very
easy to die now (meaning that it would be a pleasant time to die, with
the ecstasy still fresh)].   **dream** C. (p. 150) adds: *verane ista voluptas
est an extra mentem positus sic reor? Non somnio, certe vera res agitur.* [is
this pleasure real or am I out of my mind? I am not dreaming, certainly
what is happening is real.].[120]   **chase** B. chayret.

Why doest thou Aurora[123] leave so soon the bed of Titan? If thou were as pleasant unto him as Lucrece is to me, he would not suffer thee to arise so early. Never saw I so short a night, yet have I been in Britain and in Denmark." Thus said Eurialus, and Lucrece said no less, nor suffered not one kiss nor° one word to pass unrecompensed. He strained, and she strained, and when they had done they were not weary, but, as Athens,° rose from the ground stronger, so after battle were they more desirous of war. The night ended when Aurora took from the ocean her dew.° Here he departed, and long after might not return, by the daily watch that was put unto her. But love overcame all thing, and at last they found way for their meeting, which long while they used.

In the mean time the Emperor, that already was reconciled to Eugenius, determined to go to Rome. This did Lucrece perceive, for what is that that love knoweth not? Or who can deceive a lover?[125] And° therefore Lucrece wrote thus unto Eurialus: "If my mind could be wroth° toward thee, I would now be angry with thee, for that thou hast dissembled thy departing;[126] but it loveth thee better than me, and may for no cause be moved against thee. Alas, my heart, why hast thou not told me of the Emperor's departure? He maketh him ready towards his journey and I know well° thou shalt not tarry behind. Alas, what shall become of me? What shall I do, poor woman; where shall I rest? If thou do forsake me, my life lasteth not two days. For these letters therefore moisted with my tears, and for thy right hand, and thy promised faith, if ever I have deserved anything of thee, or if ever thou hast had any delight by me, have pity on thy unhappy lover.[127] My desire is not that thou shouldest tarry but that thou shouldest take me with thee. I will make as I would go in the evening to Bethlem,° and take but one old woman with me. Let two or three of thy servants be there and by force take me away. It is no great pain to take one away that would be gone,

nor B. not. **Athens** C. (p. 150) *Antheus*.[124] **dew** C. (p. 150)
crines [hair]. **And** B. one. **wroth** angry. **well** (B. omits).
Bethlem Bethlehem.

nor think it no shame. For Paris the son of a king did likewise,° and thou shalt do no wrong unto my husband, for he shall in algates° lose me, for if it be not by thy taking, it shall be by death. But I am sure thou wilt not be so cruel to leave me behind to die that ever hath made more of thee than of myself.° Farewell, my only trust."°

To whom Eurialus answered after this fashion: "Hitherto have I hid from thee my Lucrece my departing, because thou shouldest not torment thee overmuch afore the time. I know thy conditions and under what manner thou sorrowest, but the Emperor departeth not so that he shall not return. And when we shall return from Rome, this is in our way to our country; and if so be the Emperor will go any other way, if I live° thou shalt see me return. Let God never suffer me to come into my country, but make me wander like Ulysses,[128] if I come not hither.° Comfort thyself, therefore, my dear heart and be of good cheer. Be not sad, but rather live merrily.° Thou sayest thy taking away should be the greatest pleasure that could be to me. It is truth, and greater delight I could not have than thee always at my desire. But I must rather take heed to thy° honour than to my lust, for the faith that thou bearest unto me bindeth me to give thee such faithful counsel as should be meet for thee. Thou knowest° thou art married into a noble family and hast the name of a right beautiful and chaste lady. And it is not only in Italy but as well in Teutonia,° Panonia,° Bohemia, and all the worthy parties,° so that if I take thee away (beside my shame that for thy sake I set little by) what dishonour shouldest thou do to all thy friends?° What sorrow should thy mother take?° What should be then spoken of thee?°

For Paris . . . likewise C. (p. 152) *Nam et filius Priami coniugem sibi raptu paravit.* [For the son of Priam also carried off his lover.].   **algates** any case.   **myself** B. lyfe.   **Farewell, my only trust** (C. omits). **live** B. leue.   **hither** B. adds: so.   **merrily** A. and B. merely; C. (p. 152) *leta* [merrily].   **thy** B. my.   **knowest** C. (p. 153) adds: *praenobilem esse et* [that you are a noblewoman and].   **Teutonia** Germany.   **Panonia** Hungary.   **all the worthy parties** C. (p. 154) *omnes septentrionis populi tuum nomen agnoscunt* [all people of the North know your name].   ? B. !.   ? B. !.   ? B. !.

What rumour should all the world hear of thee? Lo, Lucrece, that was called more chaste than the wife of Brutus and better than Penelope,[129] followeth an adulterer, not remembering neither her parents, nor country. It is not Lucrece, but Ippia or Medea that followed Jason.[130] Alas, what grief should it be to me to hear such things. Our love is yet secret; there is no man that dispraiseth thee. Thy taking away should mar all. Nor thou were not so praised as thou shouldest then be blamed. But besides our honour, how were it possible that we should use our love? I serve the Emperor. He hath made me rich and of great power, and I cannot depart from him without the loss of my state, so that if I should leave him I could not conveniently entertain thee. If° I should continually follow the court, we have no rest; every day we change places. The Emperor hath tarried nowhere so long as he hath done here,° and that because of war, so that if I should carry thee about with me and have thee in my tent as a follower of the field,° what reprefe° and shame should it be both to thee and me.° For these causes I beseech thee, my Lucrece, put away this mind and remember thy honour, and flatter not rather thy rage than thy self. Another lover peradventure would otherwise counsel thee and desire thee to run thy way that he might abuse thee as long as he might, nothing regarding what should befall of it while he might satisfy his appetite. But he were no true lover that would regard rather his own lust than thy fame. I counsel thee, my Lucrece, for the best. Tarry here, I beseech thee, and doubt not in my return. Whatsoever the Emperor hath to do here,° I will sue to have it committed to° me that I may accompany with thee without danger. Farewell. Live and love me, and think my fire no less than thine own, and most contrary to my mind I depart. Farewell again the delight and food of my life."

With these letters the woman somewhat had appeased herself, and answered that she would follow his counsel. Shortly after,

If B. ye.   **here** C. (p. 154) *Senis* [at Siena].   **a follower of the field** a prostitute who follows an army.   **reprefe** reproof.   **.** B. !.   **here** C. (p. 154) *apud Hetruscos* [among the Tuscans].   **to** B. vnto.

Eurialus went to Rome with the Emperor, where he had not been long but he was sick of an hot ague.° The poor unhappy man, when he was burning in love, began also to burn in sickness, and when love had wasted his strength by dolour° of the disease, little remaineth of his life. And that spirit was rather entertained with physicians than tarried of itself. The Emperor visited him daily, comforting him as his son, and commanded that he should have all cure of medicines that might be; but none was of more effect for his remedy than a letter from Lucrece. Whereby he understood her health, which somewhat minisheth° his sickness, and made him recover his feet, so that he was at the coronation of the Emperor and there was made knight. After this, when the Emperor went to Perusia,° he tarried at Rome,° and from thence went to Siena, although he were but yet weak and very green of his sickness. But he might only behold Lucrece, and not speak to her. Many letters went betwixt them, and again there was practising for° her going away. Three days did Eurialus tarry there, and when he saw no manner of ways to come to her that as then was taken from him, he did advertise his lady of his departing. But never had they such pleasure in their conversation as they had displeasure in their departing. Lucrece was in her window when Eurialus rode through the street, and with their moist eyes the one beheld the other. He wept and she wept, and both were distrained with grievous dolours as they that felt their hearts torn of their places. If any man doth not know the dolour of death, let him consider the departing of two lovers, which hath more heaviness and more painful torment. The soul suffereth in death for that it part from the beloved body. And the body (the soul once departed) suffereth not. But when two minds be joined together, so much is the division more painful,° in so much as the delight of either of them is more sensible. And surely here was not two minds, but surely as weeneth Aristophanes, one soul in two bodies.[131] So departed not one mind from another, but one love and one mind was in two divided; and the heart suffered partition. Part of the mind went and part remained; and all the senses were disperpled° and plained° to depart from their own self. Nor one drop of blood remained in the lovers' faces but only tears and bewailings, and very death appeared° in their visages. Who may write or declare to think the griefs of those minds but he that hath once in his life been likewise mad. Laodomia, when Prothesilaus went to the siege of Troy, swooned,° and when she knew of his death, died.[132] Dido,° after the predestinate departing of Aeneas, slew herself. And Percia° would not live after Brutus' death. But this our earth, was taken up by her maidens and laid in her bed. And when she, Lucrece, after Eurialus was out of her sight, falling to the came to her self, all purple and golden clothes and glad apparel she laid apart, and wore displeasant tawny and never after was heard sing or seen laugh. Nor by no sports, no° joy nor mirth, might ever be recomforted. In which condition, when she had a little while continued, she fell into sickness. And because her heart was absent, the mind would receive no consolation. And at the last betwixt the arms of her much weeping mother (using vain comfortable words) she gave up the wearied ghost,° disdaining the sorrowful life.

Eurialus, after he had passed the sight of those eyes that should never again see him,[133] never spoke to anybody in his journey, but carried only Lucrece in his mind, and thought busily if he might return. And, at last, came unto the Emperor at Perugia,° and went with him to Ferrar,° to Mantua, to Trident,° to Constantia,° and to Basil,° and so into Hungary, and to Bohemia. But, like as he followed the Emperor, so did Lucrece follow him in his sleep and suffered him no night's rest, whom, when he knew

disperpled divided.   **plained** complained.   **appeared** B. pered.
swooned B. snowned.   **Dido** C. adds: *Phenissa* [the Carthaginian].
Percia Portia.   **no** B. nor.   **gave up the wearied ghost** died.
A. Perusia.   **Ferrar** Ferrara.   **Trident** Trent.   **Constantia**
Constance.   **Basil** Basel.

his true lover to be dead, moved by extreme dolour, clothed him in mourning apparel and utterly excluded all comfort. And yet though the Emperor gave him in marriage a right noble and excellent lady, yet he never enjoyed after but in conclusion pitiful° wasted his painful life.°

And yet ... painful life C. (p. 158) *nisi postquam Cesar ex ducali sanguine virginem sibi tum formosam tum castissimam atque prudentem matrimonio iunxit.* [until after the emperor married him to a maiden of noble blood and as beautiful as whe was chaste and virtuous.]; C. (p. 160) adds: *Habes amoris exitum, Mariane mi amantissime, non ficti neque felicis, quem qui legerint, periculum ex aliis faciant, quod sibi ex usu siet, nec amatorium bibere poculum studeant, quod longe plus aloes habet quam mellis.* [This, my dearest Marianus, is the end of a love which is neither false nor happy. Let those who read it learn these dangers from these others, and let them make use if it, that they may not try to drink from the cup of lovers, which is much more bitter than it is sweet]. **pitiful** B. pitifully.

A***[134] to the Reader

By this little book thou mayest perceive my friend
The end of love not fained nor fortunable,◇
By which right plainly thou mayest intend
That love is no pleasure but a pain perdurable,◇
And the end is death which is most lamentable,
Therefore, ere thou be chained with such care
By others' perils, take heed and beware.

First by Eurialus, by whom perceive thou mayest,
The best it is to eschew shortly
To drink of the cup, or of it to taste
That savoured more of gall than of honey.
Also, I could show the histories of many
That if they by time had made resistance
They might have eschewed all such inconvenience.

There was also the noble Troilus,
Which all his life abode in mortal pain,
Delayed by Cressida whose history is piteous,
Till at the last Achilles had him slain.
Yet other there be, which in this careful chain
Of love have continued. All their life days
Death was their end, there was none other ways.

We read also of Pyramis and Thisbe
Which slew themself by their fervent love
Of Hercules and of the fair Joyle
With many other, which I could not attain.
And of Dido, which with herself strove
For love of Aeneas, when she could not attain
Till at the last she had herself slain.◇

---

fortunable lucky.   **perdurable** lasting.   **To the Reader . . .**
slain (B. and C. omit).

Yet could I show you of many other more
If leisure not wanted, but now I let it° pass
Which by their love were constrained also
To mortal death; more pity alas.
Therefore this book in English draw was
For an example thereby to eschew
The pains of love, ere after they it rue.°

---

it A. is.   **Yet could . . . it rue** (C. omits; B. has only the first word,
"Yet," as acatchword at the bottom of the last page).

Textual Notes and Commentary

1. The Latin text continues: "unde tibi et mihi origo est" [where your family and mine are from]. Aeneas is addressing here Mariano Sozzini (c. 1397–1467), his friend and former teacher, and the person at whose request the tale of Eurialus and Lucrece was supposedly written. In its original version, Aeneas' story is enclosed in a letter addressed to Sozzini, and the personal addresses here and elsewhere in the text (all of which are omitted in the English translation) are in a sense a continuation of this letter (on the letter to Sozzini, see the Introduction. Although Aeneas was not born in Siena itself (his birthplace is Corsignano, a small town nearby; after he became Pius II, he renamed it Pienza, in his own honour), both of his parents came from noble Sienese families.

2. In 1432, Sigismund of Austria passed through Siena on his way to Rome, where he would be crowned Holy Roman Emperor by Pope Eugenius IV on 31 May of the following year. It was customary in the fifteenth century for the leading citizens of a town to welcome foreign dignitaries with a formal reception. For early Renaissance triumphal entries see Giovanni Carandente, *I trionfi del primo Rinascimento*. (Torino: Edizioni R.A.I., 1963).

3. Tophore, in modern Italian, "Tufi", is a gate located in the south-central wall of the city.

4. Paris, son of King Priam of Troy, was chosen by the god Hermes to judge which of three goddesses — Hera, Athena and Aphrodite — was the most beautiful. In exchange for the title, Hera promised him power over Asia; Athena, victory in battle; and Aphrodite, the most beautiful mortal woman. Paris chose Aphrodite, and the goddess told him that his prize was Helen, wife of King Menelaus of Sparta. Paris traveled to Sparta, and while Menelaus was away, he sailed off with his wife. The abduction of Helen marks the beginning of the long and bloody war between the Trojans and the Greeks known as the Trojan War, and ultimately the destruction of the kingdom of Troy. In some versions of the story, The Judgement of Paris takes place in a dream.

5. Ovid, *Amores*, III.6.667–68. Ovid is describing the reaction of Rhea Silvia, a vestal virgin and the mother of Romulus and Remus, when

the river god, Anio, reminds her of her violation at the hands of Mars. Ashamed of the crime, she casts her eyes down.

6. Virgil, *Aeneid*, XII.65–69. This very striking metaphor is taken from Virgil's description of Lavinia, the daughter of King Latinus of the Latins and bride-to-be of the Trojan Aeneas. In the passage from which this allusion is taken, the Latin soldier Turnus, the man to whom Lavinia had originally been betrothed, has just announced his decision to fight Aeneas and the Trojans so that he might win back Lavinia's hand in marriage, and thus the Kingdom of the Latins, from the foreigner, Aeneas. Lavinia's blushing has been interpreted in various ways. According to Servius (fourth century A.D.), it is a sign of how ashamed she is for having caused the Trojans so much anxiety. However, in the eyes of many modern critics, it is a sign of her secret love for Turnus.

7. The physical description of Lucrece is very similar to Petrarch's description of the ideal female beauty. There are, nevertheless, many details in Aeneas' portrait which make her significantly more realistic than Petrarch's. Moreover, the allusion to Ovid's *Amores*, III.I.V.23, adds a distinctly seductive dimension to her image. The line concludes Ovid's detailed description of the naked body of a young woman, Corinna, who feigns resistance to the poet's advances.

8. Quintus Hortalus Hortensius (114–150 B.C.) was a prominent orator and contemporary of Cicero. His orations were especially known for their florid and theatrical Asiatic style. His daughter, Hortensia, was also famous for her eloquence; see Valerius Maximus, *Factorum et dictorum memorabilium libri novem*, VIII.iii.3.

9. Cornelia was the daughter of Scipio Africanus, the wife of Tiberius Sempronius Gracchus, and the mother of political leaders Tiberius (162?–133 B.C.) and Gaius Gracchus (153?–121 B.C.), both tribunes of the Roman Republic. A highly educated woman, she was celebrated for her literary acomplishments, especially her lettters which were seen as models of elegant style and which Cicero himself is said to have praised.

10. On Menelaus, Helen and Paris, see above, n. 4. Andromache, daughter of the King of Thebes, was the wife of Hector, Paris' older brother.

11. The identity of this woman is unknown.

12. Ovid, *Metamorphoses*, XI.1–2; 17–18.

13. Mennon, son of Titan and Aurora, and mythical king of Ethiopia, was famous for his horses.

14. Cf. Ovid, *De remedio amoris*, I.135–36; 139–140, 144: "Ergo ubi visus eris nostra medicabilis arte, / Fac monitis fugias otia premia meis. / . . . Otia si tollas, periere Cupidinis arcus / Contemptaeque iacent

et sine luce faces / . . . Res age, tutus eris . . . ." [When therefore I shall find you amenable to my skill, obey my cousels and first of all shun leisure. Take away leisure and Cupid's bow is broken, and his torch lies extinguished and despised . . . . Be busy and you will be safe.] (Ovid, *The Art of Love and Other Poems*, vol. 2, J.H. Mozley, trans. [London: Harvard University Press, 1979], pp. 187, 189). Idleness was seen as a leading cause of love-sickness. See D. Beecher and M. Ciavolella, eds. *Jacques Ferrand, A Treatise on Love Sickness* (Syracuse: Syracuse University Press, 1991), pp. 115, 247.

15. The translator is attempting to sustain parallel descriptions of Lucrece and Eurialus.

16. Seneca, *Hippolytus*, 387–89. The Seres were a people of eastern Asia who were famous for their silks.

17. Ovid was the first to tell the tale of Pyramis and Thisbe, a young man and woman from Babylon who, against their parents' wishes, fell in love. One night, while Pyramis was waiting for Thisbe to arrive for a secret rendezvous, he saw a lion with a piece of her clothing hanging from its mouth. Thinking his lover had been eaten by the beast, Pyramis took his own life. The lion had not, in fact, killed Thisbe; he had only taken a piece of her clothing that it had found lying on the ground in the woods. When the girl arrived at the appointed spot and found Pyramis dead, she killed herself in despair. See Ovid, *Metamorphoses*, IV.

18. The concept of love entering through the eyes was a topos of courtly love; see Marsilio Ficino, *Commentary on Plato's Symposium on Love*, trans. Jayne Sears (Dallas: Spring Publications, 1985), especially Orat. VII.

19. Virgil, *Aeneid*, IV.1–5. The passage is taken from the book in which Virgil recounts the romance between Dido, Queen of Carthage, and Aeneas, the hero of the *Aeneid*, who had been shipwrecked on the shores of Libya. In these lines, the poet describes Dido's feelings of passion for Aeneas.

20. Virgil, *Aeneid*, II.773. The lines are taken from the tale of the fall of Troy which Aeneas recounts to Dido. Here he is describing the image of his wife, Creusa, which stands before him as he flees the burning city. Creusa was ultimately left behind.

21. Much of the passage up to this point is drawn directly from Ovid, *Metamorphoses*, VII.10–73, in which Medea, daughter of King Aeetes of the Colchians, is describing her sudden and overwhelming feelings of passion for Jason of Argos, an enemy of her father whom Aeetes has just sent on a dangerous mission to fetch the Golden Fleece.

22. Ariadne, the daughter of the King of Minos, fell in love with Theseus, a handsome young Athenian who was one of the youths chosen to be sacrificed to a monster known as the Minotaur, half-bull and half-man, who lived in the labyrinth in her father's palace. Ariadne helps Theseus escape the labyrinth by giving him a golden thread to unravel as he is led away from the entrance. He retraces his steps, is freed by Ariadne, and together they flee Minos. Theseus then leaves Ariadne behind on the island of Naxos and continues home to Athens.

23. Maecenas, a Roman aristocrat and patron of the arts, was the trusted friend, counsellor and diplomatic agent of Octavian, or Augustus.

24. Virgil, *Georgics*, III.79–88. The poet is describing the kind of horse that is good for mating. Throughout the story, images of horses, both implicit and explicit, have a distinctly sexual connotation.

25. Seneca, *Hippolytus*, 204–14. Phaedra, wife of Theseus, falls in love with her stepson, Hippolytus. In these lines, Phaedra's nurse is lamenting the lustful feelings of her mistress. See also Virgil, *Eclogues*, II.29.

26. Virgil, *Aeneid*, I.497; IV.136. Both of these references are to Dido: in Book I, when she sees Aeneas for the first time; and in Book IV, when she arrives for the hunting expedition during which they will consummate their love.

27. Terence, *Andria*, I.i.2. The line is from the very first speech in the play. Simo, father of Pamphilus, is about to explain to his servant, Sosia, the fake marriage he is planning that afternoon for his son.

28. Virgil, *Aeneid*, IV.11. These are the words with which Dido describes Aeneas to her sister, Anna.

29. Seneca, *Hippolytus*, 127–34. This speech is largely drawn from that of Phaedra's nurse as she continues to scold her mistress for her love of Hippolytus.

30. Seneca, *Hippolytus*, 138–272. The conversation that follows (until "The labour shall be mine") is taken almost word for word from that between Phaedra and her nurse.

31. This is a reference to Lucretia, the wife of an influential Roman aristocrat of the *cognomen* Collatinus in the time of the Etruscan kings. She was raped by Sextus Tarquinius, son of Tarquin the Proud, and took her own life out of shame for her stained virtue. On the significance of Lucretia in Aeneas' tale, see the Introduction.

32. Portia was the wife of Marcus Brutus, one of the assassins of Julius Caesar. According to some historians, after her husband died she committed suicide by eating hot coals.

33. Virgil, *Aeneid*, IV.54–55. Virgil is describing Dido after her conversation with her sister, Anna, who has encouraged her to pursue Aeneas.

34. Time was seen as a natural cure to lovesickness in many cases.

35. Julius Caesar, Alexander the Great, and Hanibal were all famous and successful military generals of ancient history. All of them were also involved in love affairs.

36. Ovid, *Metamorphoses*, II.846–47. Ovid's statement is in reference to Jove who, in accordance to this statement, sets aside his thunderbolt and sceptre and transforms himself into a bull so he can seduce Europa.

37. Seneca, *Hippolytus*, 317–24. The Chorus is describing Hercules smitten with love for Omphale, Queen of Lydia.

38. Ovid, *Heroides*, XV.37–38.

39. Seneca, *Hippolytus*, 335–37; 290–93. These lines are part of the Chorus' long description of Cupid and the evils and sufferings he brings (274–356). The translator suggests that the manes of lions stand up by way of mating display.

40. Virgil, *Eclogues*, X.69. Here the poet sings of his friend's unhappy love for the mistress who has deserted him.

41. Cf. Ovid, *Ars amatoria* I.455–56: "Ergo eat et blandis peraretur littera verbis, / Exploretque animos, primaque temptet iter" [Therefore let a letter speed, traced with persuasive words, and explore her feelings, and be the first to try the path.] (Mozley, p. 45). The *Ars amatoria* is a satirical poem in three books describing the art of love. The first two books are addressed to men, and explain respectively how they can meet and win a woman, and how they can keep her; the third, addressed to women, describes how they can please men.

42. Nisus is a Trojan warrior and the faithful companion of Euryalus in the *Aeneid*.

43. Cf. Ovid, *Ars amatoria*, I.659–60: "Et lacrime prosunt; lacrimis adamanta movebis: / Fac madidas videat, si potes, illa genas" [Tears too are useful; with tears you can move iron; let her see if possible your moistened cheeks] (Mozley, p. 59).

44. Ovid, *Metamorphoses*, IX.535–49. The passages here and below are taken from Byblis' confession of love for her brother. Ovid identifies her as an example of why girls should not love unlawfully.

45. Cf. Ovid, *Ars amatoria*, I.733: "Arguat et macies animam" [Let leanness also prove your feelings] (Mozley, p. 63).

46. Terence, *Eunuchus*, I.ii.113–15. Phaedria, a young love-crazed man, is pleading with his courtesan mistress, Thais, to keep him foremost in her mind even when she is with another man.

47. Ovid, *Metamorphoses*, IX.535–49. See above, n. 44.

48. Terence, *Eunuchus*, V.ii.47. Here, Phaedria's brother, Chaerea, is pleading with Thais to have mercy on him for what he did to her half-sister, Pamphila. Madly in love with Pamphila, Chaerea sneaked into Thais' house disguised as her new eunuch; and, when left alone with Pamphila, he raped her.

49. Ovid, *Heroides*, XII.155–56. Medea is describing her reaction when she sees the wedding of Jason to Creon's daughter.

50. Terence, *Eunuchus*, V.ii.20–21.

51. Virgil, *Aeneid*, I.749. The passage describes Dido as she listens to Aeneas telling of his adventures.

52. Cf. Ovid, *Ars amatoria*, I.481ff: "Quae voluit legisse, volet rescribere lectis: / Per numeros venient ista gradusque sonos. / Fortisan et primo veniet tibi littera tristis, / Quaeque roget, ne se sollicitare velis. / Quod rogat illa, timet; quod non rogat optat, ut instes; / Insequere, et voti postmodo compos eris" [She who has consented to read will consent to answer what she has read; that will come by its own stages and degrees. Perhaps even an angry letter will first come to you, asking you to be pleased not to vex her. What she asks, she fears; what she does not ask, she desires — that will continue; press on, then, and soon you will have gained your wish] (Mozley, p. 47). *Ibid.*, III.476ff: "Nec tamen e duro quod petit ille nega. / Fac timeat speretque simul, quotiensque remittes, / Spesque magis veniat certa minorque metus" [But neither promise yourself too easily to him who entreats you, nor yet deny what he asks too stubbornly. Cause him to hope and fear together; and as often as you reply, see that hope becomes surer and fear diminishes] (Mozley, p. 153).

53. Ovid, *Ars amatoria*, II.113. The passage is taken from the book on how to keep a lover, once she has been won. Here Ovid is advising his reader to cultivate his mind as well as his body, since beauty fades with age.

54. Ovid, *Amores*, XV.9–10. Here the poet wishes he could be the ring which he has just given to his lover so that he could touch her body. On the image of the swallow, see Ovid, *Ars amatoria* II.146–50. On the conception of love as a power that transforms men and women into animals, see Ovid, *Metamorphoses*.

55. See above, n. 54, Ovid, *Amores*.

56. See above, n. 22, for the tale of Ariadne and Theseus. Medea and Dido were also abandoned by their lovers, Medea when Jason returned to Argos; and Dido when Aeneas left to found Rome.

57. Cf. Ovid, *Ars amatoria*, III.31ff: "Saepe viri fallunt: tenerae non saepe puellae, / Paucaque, si quaeras, crimina fraudis habent. / Phasida iam matrem fallax dimisit Jason: / Venit in Aesonios altera nupta

sinus. / Quantum in te, Theseu, volucres Ariadna marinas / Pavit, in ignoto sola relicta loco! / Quaere, novem cur una viae dicantur, et audi / Depositis silvas Phyllida flesse comis. / Et famam pietatis habet, tamen hospes et ensem / Praebuit et causam moris, Elissa tuae." [Often do men deceive, tender mainds not often; should you inquire they are rarely charged with deceit. Perfidious Jason sent away the Phasian (Medea), already a mother; another bride came to the bosom of Aeson's son. So far as concerned thee, O Theseus, Ariadne fell a prey to the sea-birds, left desolate in an unknown spot! Ask why one way is called Nine Ways, and hear how the woods shed their leaves and wailed for Phyllis. Famed too is he for piety, yet thy guest, Elissa (Dido), gave thee both a sword and the cause of thy destruction" (Mozley, p. 121).

58. Cf. Ovid, *Ars amatoria*, I.281–82: "Paucior in nobis nec tam furiosa libido: / Legitimum finem flamma virilis habet" [In us (men) desire is weaker and not so frantic: the manly flame knows a lawful bound] (Mozley, p. 33); *Ars amatoria*, I.341–42: "Omnia feminea sunt ista libidine mota; / Acrior est nostra, plusque furoris habet" [All those crimes were prompted by women's lust; keener it is than ours, and has more of madness] (Mozley, p. 37).

59. Phyllis stabbed herself after her lover, Deophoon, deserted her. Sappho threw herself off a cliff when her love for Phaon, a young fisherman, failed. See Ovid, *Heroides*, II and XV for letters from these women to their lovers; see also above, n. 57.

60. Ovid, *Metamorphoses*, VII.199–204. The passage describes Medea casting a spell on Jason's father in order to restore his youth. Medea was universally said to be a witch, and she often used her magical powers to help Jason.

61. Troilus, another of Priam's sons, fell in love with Cressida, and she with him. When Cressida's father arranged for her to be handed over to the Greeks in exchange for a Trojan prisoner, the two lovers swore they would be faithful to one another. Upon her arrival in the Greek camp, Cressida almost immediately became the object of the attentions of a Greek soldier, and soon forgot all about her promise to Troilus. Deiphobus, Troilus' brother, supposedly married Helen after Paris died; according to Virgil (*Aeneid*, VI.494ff), he was betrayed by her to the Greeks, and ultimately killed by her husband, Menelaus. Circe was a seductress and sorceress who lived on the island of Aeaea. She lured men into her house and transformed them magically into animals.

62. See Ovid, *Heroides*, I, the letter which Penelope, wife of Odysseus, the hero of the *Odyssey*, writes to her husband.

63. Cf. Ovid, *Ars amatoria*, I.433: "Promittas facito: quid enim promittere laedit?" [See that you promise: what harm is there in promises?] (Mozley, p. 43); *Ars amatoria*, I.631–62: "Nec timide promitte: trahunt promissa puellas: / Pollicito testes quoslibet adde deos." [Nor be timid in your promises; by promises women are betrayed; call as witnesses what gods you please.] (Mozley, p. 57).

64. Cf. Ovid, *Ars amatoria*, I.735ff: "Attenuant iuvenum vigilitate corpora noctes / Curaque et in magno qui fit amore dolor. / Ut voto potiare tuo, miserabilis esto, / Ut qui te videat, dicere possit 'amas'." [Nights of vigil make thin the bodies of lovers, and anxiety and distress that a great passion brings that you may gain your desire to be pitiable, so that whoso sees you may say, "You are in love."] (Mozley, p. 63).

65. Cf. Ovid, *Ars amatoria*, I.729: "Palleat omnis amans: hic est color aptus amanti." [But let every lover be pale; this is the lover's hue.] (Mozley, p. 63).

66. Eurialus here is describing the classic symptoms of love sickness. See Beecher and Ciavolella, 269ff.

67. Terence, *Andria*, I.i.116. Simo has just recounted how he learned of his son Pamphilus' love for Glicerium when he saw him stop her from throwing herself on her sister's burning funeral pyre. Sosias approves of the fact that Simo did not scold his son for such an act.

68. Although this metaphor is similar to the kinds of images which Virgil uses in the *Aeneid*, it seems to be entirely original.

69. Seneca, *Epistolae*, XX.ii.119.

70. Argus was a monster of many eyes (sometimes said to have three or four, but up to as many as one hundred). Hera, the wife of Zeus, set him to guard Io, one of her priestesses at Argos. When Hera learned of her husband's passion for the woman, she turned Io into a heifer. Cf. Ovid, *Ars amatoria*, III.611–12, 615ff: Qua vafer eludi possit ratione maritus, / Quaque vigil custos, praeteriturus eram. / Te quoque servari, modo quam vindicta redemit, / Quis ferat? ut fallas, ad mea sacra veni / Tot licet observent (adsit modo certa voluntas), / Quot fuerant Argo lumina, verba dabis." [How a crafty husband or a vigilant guardian may be deceived I was about to pass by; . . . but that you too should be watched, whom the rod has lately redeemed, who could endure? Attend my rites that you may learn to decive. Though as many keep watch as Argus had eyes (so your purpose be but firm), you will deceive them." (Mozley, pp. 161, 163).

71. Terence, *Eunuchus*, IV.vii.43. Thraso, a soldier, and his servant, Gnatho, are talking about Phaedria's mistress, Thais. Gnatho assures his master that Thais will repent of how she has treated him.

72. Juvenal, *Satires*, VI.347. The satire consists of a series of criticisms of women.

73. Misogynistic comments such as these appear throughout the story. On misogyny in the text, see the Introduction

74. Terence, *Andria*, IV.i.46. Here Pamphilus' servant, Davus, is assuring his master and friend, Charinus, that all hope is not lost for them to be united with the women they love. Davus' first plan failed miserably.

75. Virgil, *Eclogue*, II.68. Corydon is in love with Alexis, the favourite of his master. Here he is lamenting his unrequited love.

76. Cf. Ovid, *Ars amatoria*, I.741–42: "Ei mihi, non tutum est, quod ames, laudare sodali; / Cum tibi laudanti credidit, ipse subit." [Alas, it is not safe to praise to a friend the object of your love; so soon he believes your praises, he slips into your place.] (Mozley, p. 63).

77. Virgil, *Aeneid*, IX.427. Here Nisus offers himself to the enemy in place of Euryalus, his companion, who has just been captured.

78. Yosias here specifically diagnoses the love sickness of Lucrece and recognizes the danger of the affliction.

79. This debasement for love is a feature of courtly romance as well. See, for example, Lancelot in *Le chevalier et la charette*.

80. On Circe, see above, n. 61. See Virgil, *Aeneid*, VII.10–24; 189–91; 280–83. The image of Circe is often found in cases of lovesickness; see Beecher and Ciavolella, eds., *Ferrand*, pp. 240, 343, 345, 346.

81. The phrase appears several times in Virgil's works, always with negative connotations (*Aeneid*, IX.460, the morning after the death of Nisus and Euryalus; *Ibid.*, IV.585, the day that Aeneas leaves Carthage and Dido takes her life; *Georgics*, I.447, where such a sky is said to forbode hail). Titan is the god of the sun.

82. Virgil, *Aeneid*, IV.336. Aeneas, confronted by Dido about his plans to slip away secretly from Carthage, assures her that he will never forget her.

83. Virgil, *Aeneid*, II.76. Virgil is describing the Greek soldier who convinces the Trojans to bring into their walls the giant horse left outside by the Greeks. The Trojan horse — as it is now known — was full of Greek soldiers who, once safely within the gates of Troy, broke out of their hiding place and laid waste to the city.

84. See above, n. 6.

85. Terence, *Eunuchus*, III.5.57–58. Here Chaerea is recounting to a friend his successful encounter with Pamphila, and defending his actions.

86. Ovid, *Amores*, I.v.15 (see above, n. 7). Cf. Ovid, *Ars amatoria*, I.664ff: "Illa licet no det, non data sume tamen. / Pugnabit primo fartassis, et 'improbe' dicet: Pugnando vici se tamen illa volet." [Though she give them not, yet take the kisses she does not give. Perhaps she will

struggle at first and cry "You villain!" yet she will wish to be beaten in the struggle." (Mozley, p. 59).

87. II Sam. 13:1–20. The reference is to the story of Amnon, son of David, who fell in love with his sister, Tamar, and forced her to have sexual relations with him.

88. Achates is the armour bearer of Aeneas in Virgil's *Aeneid* (I.120; 174).

89. The *Lex Julia de adulteriis coercendis* was a law established by Augustus which imposed severe penalties against adulterers.

90. Juvenal, *Satires*, X.314–177.

91. Terence, *Eunuchus*, II.iii.27. Chaerea is describing Pamphila to his brother's servant, Parmeno.

92. Candaulus, ruler of Sardis, believed that his wife was the most beautiful woman in the world. He wanted the favourite of his bodyguard, Gyges, to witness her extraordinary beauty and ordered him to hide in her bedchamber when she undressed. Candaulus' wife saw Gyges, and in order to prevent him from seeing what he should not see in the future, demanded that Gyges either kill her husband or take his own life. Gyges killed Candaulus, and himself became ruler of Sardis. The story is told by Herodotus (*Historiae*, I.8–9).

93. Ovid, *Ars amatoria*, I.633. Ovid recommends to men that they should be very liberal with the promises they make to the women they are seeking to win, and should not worry about honouring them (631–34). See also above, n. 63.

94. Juvenal, *Satires*, XVI.4–5. Juvenal uses this line in the context of describing the rewards of successful military ventures.

95. Phalaris was the tyrant of Agrigentum. He had a brazen bull (not a horse) made for him, in which he roasted those he had condemned. In antiquity, Phalaris came to mean cruelty.

96. The juxtaposition of the episode of Pacorus with the tale of Lucrece and Eurialus is a powerful statement of how fortune has control over the outcome of human actions.

97. Dromo is the name of a servant in Terence's *Andria* and *Heauton-timerumenos*.

98. Juvenal, *Satires*, XIV.126–37. Juvenal is describing avarice in the larger context of learning from bad examples. This passage, beginning at "See I pray thee . . . ", is quoted almost word for word from Juvenal.

99. The Saturnalia was a feast honouring Saturn which began on December 17 in ancient Rome.

100. Ceres is the goddess of agriculture; Bacchus is the god of wine.

101. Terence, *Eunuchus*, IV.ii.12. Here Phaedria is lamenting his separation from his beloved Thais.

102. Terence, *Andria*, I.i.16. Simo is asking Sosia to assist him in his scheme of planning his son's fake marriage.

103. As found in Avicenna and other medieval physicians, this is a classic remedy for lovesickness: sexual intercourse with the object of desire.

104. Ovid, *Heroides*, IV.70. The phrase is taken from Phaedra's letter to Hippolytus, and more specifically, from the description of her initial feelings of love for her stepson.

105. Cerberus is the hound who guards the entrance to the Underworld. He is usually described as having three heads.

106. Terence, *Heautontimerumenos*, II.iii.131–32. Syrus, the servant of Clitipho, is warning him not to let on that Bacchis is his mistress. Clitipho's father, Chremes, like Agamemnon in Aeneas' story, has a sharp eye and will notice every move his son makes around the woman.

107. Juvenal, *Satires*, VI.82–83. Juvenal describes how Eppia, or Ippia, ran off with a handsome gladiator, forgetful of her country, her husband and her sister (82–114). Faro is an Egyptian island connected to the mainland by an isthmus. Lago was a king of Egypt.

108. Terence, *Heautontimerumenos*, II.iii.110. Here Clitipho is entrusting himself to the schemes of his servant, Syrus.

109. Terence, *Eunuchus*, I.ii.113–14. See above, n. 46.

110. Terence, *Eunuchus*, II.i.19–20. Here Parmeno, Phaedria's servant, is describing how his master has been transformed by love.

111. Terence, *Andria*, II.i.30–31. Pamphilus is assuring Charinus that he is not interested in Simo's daughter, Philumena, the woman whom he is supposed to marry and with whom Charinus is in love.

112. Terence, *Heautontimerumenos*, II.3.133. Clitipho here is assuring his servant, Syrus, that he will carry through very well the role he has been assigned in Syrus' plot.

113. C. (pp. 140, 142) adds: *In nobilitate multi sunt gradus, mi Mariane, et sane, si cuiuslibet originem queras, sicut mea sententia fert, aut nullas nobilitates invenies aut admodum paucas, que sceleratum non habuerint ortum. Cum enim hos dici nobiles videamus, qui divitiis habundant, divitie vero raro virtutis sint comites, quis non videt, ortum esse nobilitatis degenerem? Hunc usure ditarunt, illum spolia, proditiones alium. Hic veneficiis ditatus est, ille adulationibus. Huic adulteria lucrum prebent, nonnullis mendacia prosunt, quidam faciunt ex coniuge questum, quidam ex natis, plerosque homicidia iuvant. Rarus est, qui iuste divitias congreget. Nemo fastum amplum facit, nisi qui omnes metit herbas. Congregant homines divitias multas nec, unde veniant, sed quam multe veniant, querunt. Omnibus hic versus placet: unde habeas querit nemo, sed oportet habere. Postquam vero plena est archa, tunc nobilitas poscitur, que sic quesita nihil aliud est*

quam premium iniquitatis. Maiores mei nobiles habiti sunt. Sed nolo mihi blandiri, non puto meliores fuisse proavos meos aliis, quos sola excusat antiquitas, quia non sunt in memoria eorum vitia. Mea sententia nemo est nobilis, nisi virtutis amator. Non miror aureas vestes, equos, canes, ordinem famulorum, lautas mensas, marmoreas edes, villas, predia, piscinas, iuris dictiones, silvas. Nam hec omnia stultus assequi potest, quem si quis nobilem dixerit, ipse fiet stultus. Pandalus noster lenocinio nobilitatus est.
[There are many grades of nobility, my dear Marianus, and indeed, if you seek its origin, in my opinion, you would find no noble titles, or very few, which did not originate in crime. For we know that, although those who possess great riches are called nobles, while they may be companions of wealth, they are rarely friends of virtue. Who does not know that degeneracy is the source of nobility? Some are enriched by usury, some by thievery, and others by treachery. This one is enriched by poisonings, that one by flatteries. Adultery supplies riches to this one, lies profit not a few, some profit from their spouses, some from their children, and murder benefits even more. He who justly gains riches is rare. No one is more arrogant than one who harvests all of the crops. Men gather many riches; they do not ask where it comes from, but rather how much there is. This verse is pleasing to all: no one asks where you got it, but it is permitted to have it. Indeed, even after the chest is full, nobility demands more; what is thus sought is nothing else but the reward for iniquity. My ancestors were considered nobles. But I do not wish to flatter myself; I do not think my forefathers were better than any others, whom only antiquity excuses because their crimes are forgotten. In my opinion, no one is noble except the lover of virtue. I am not impressed by golden clothing, horses, dogs, the ranks of servants, sumptious tables, marble buildings, villas, estates, fishponds, offices, woods. For a fool can attain all these; even if someone called him a noble, he would still be a fool. Our Pandalus was ennobled by pandering.]

114. Dryness was regarded as a condition of old age.
115. Agamemnon was the brother of Menelaus, King of Sparta and husband of Helen. He was the King of Myceneae and the commander of the Greeks in the Trojan War.
116. Terence, *Heautontimerumenos*, II.iv.26. Clinia, the son of Menedemus, is greeting his beloved, Antiphilam, after a long separation.
117. Juvenal, *Satires*, VI.181. Juvenal argues that a wife, no matter how dignified or beautiful, is not worth it if she is always trying to measure herself against her husband.
118. Ganymede was a beautiful Trojan prince, whom Zeus carried off to be his cup-bearer. For Hippolytus, see above, n. 25. Diomedes was

one of the most important Greek warriors in the Trojan war. He killed Polyxena, daughter of King Priam of Troy. He retuned home to discover that his wife had been unfaithful to him. Emily was the sister of Ippolita, Queen of the Amazons.

119. Acteon was a skilled hunter who one day happened upon the goddess of the hunt, Diana, bathing in the woods. Diana turned him into a stag and he was killed by his own hounds. See Ovid, *Metamorphoses*, III.138ff.

120. Apollo was the god of (among other things) the sun.

121. Alcmena was visited one night by Zeus, who appeared to her in the shape of her husband, Amphitryon. Shortly after, she gave birth to twins: Hercules, the son of Zeus, and Iphicles, the son of Amphitryon.

122. Aurora was the goddess of morning.

123. Juvenal, *Satires*, IV.35.

124. Antheus, or Anteus, was the giant son of Poseidon and Gaia (Earth), who required all who passed his dwelling to wrestle with him. It is said that each time he fell to the ground, and thus touched his mother Earth, he grew stronger than before. Antheus was finally defeated and killed by Hercules.

125. Virgil, *Aeneid*, IV.296.

126. Ovid, *Heroides*, VII.35. The passage is from a letter which Helen writes to Paris.

127. Virgil, *Aeneid*, IV.314–18. The passage is taken from the scene in which Dido confronts Aeneas who is about to leave Carthage without telling her of his departure.

128. Ulysses, or Odysseus, was King of Ithaca and one of the greatest Greek warriors in the Trojan war. In the *Odyssey*, Homer tells of his adventures as he returns home to his wife, Penelope.

129. Portia was the wife of Brutus (see above, n. 32). Penelope was the wife of Ulysses who, despite the offers of many suitors, remained faithful to her husband during his long absence.

130. On Ippia, see above, n. 107. On Medea, see above, n. 56.

131. It is actually Aristotle, not Aristophanes, who noted this. See *Eudemian Ethics*, VII.6, on friendship.

132. Prothesilaus was the first of the Greeks to disembark on the shores of Troy. According to an oracle, the first Greek on Trojan soil would be killed, and Prothesilaus, aware of the prediction, deliberately sacrificed himself. His wife, Laodamia, was so grief-striken by his death that the gods allowed her to see him again for three hours. When their time together was over, Laodamia took her own life in despair. See Ovid, *Heroides*, XIII, for the letter she writes to him before she has heard of his tragic death.

133. Ovid, *Heroides*, II.99. The line is taken from the letter which Phyllis writes to her lover, Deophoon. Here she realizes that Deophoon has departed without any intention of coming back to her.

134. The "***" represent undecipherable letters.

The Barnabe Riche Series

This volume of the Barnabe Riche Series was produced using the TEX typesetting system, with Adobe Palatino PostScript fonts and in-house critical edition macros.

AGMV
MARQUIS
Québec, Canada
1999